THE
LAWYER

USA TODAY BESTSELLING AUTHOR
MARNI MANN

To my Kimmi.
For holding me up, holding me together, and always holding my hand.
They don't make besties like you.

PLAYLIST

"Is There Somewhere"—Halsey
"Sun In Our Eyes" (Don Diablo Remix)—MØ, Diplo
"Bad Boy"—Tungevaag, Raaban, featuring Luana Kiara
"Promises"—Calvin Harris, Sam Smith, featuring Jessie Reyez
"In My Mind"—Dynoro, Gigi D'Agostino
"Bad at Love"—Halsey
"One Kiss"—Calvin Harris, Dua Lipa
"Mad Love"—Sean Paul, David Guetta, featuring Becky G
"Trampoline"—SHAED

ONE

DOMINICK

Los Angeles is fucking lit tonight. That was the only thought in my head as I stood twenty-seven stories up on the roof deck of the city's newest and hottest high-rise hotel, overlooking our famous skyline. Jenner, my middle brother, was the attorney who had represented the closing, and everyone who was anyone had come out this evening to celebrate the grand opening.

Not only was this a huge win for Jenner, but for The Dalton Group as well—the law firm my parents had started over twenty years ago, where my brothers and I were now partners. We represented some of the largest-earning corporations and individuals in the world. In my case, concentrating solely on entertainment law, I was surrounded by many of my clients, this event like a mini version of the goddamn Oscars.

"Jenner has come a long way," Brett Young, my best friend, said. He was next to me on the balcony, nodding toward my brother, who was schmoozing with the CEO of a massive online retailer. "I remember when we were in law school, that motherfucker still had zits all over his forehead. Now, instead

1

of carrying textbooks, he's got multimillion-dollar contracts in his hands, closing transactions like this one every day, from here to fucking Dubai."

Brett pointed at Ford, my youngest brother. "And the baby in the family? Man, I definitely didn't anticipate him being the first one in our group to father a child." He smirked. "Certainly not before me or you." His eyes caught mine. "I think you wake up every morning, hoping like hell that some woman doesn't come banging on your door, asking for a paternity test."

I laughed in agreement. "Isn't that the fucking truth?"

Before Brett had met James Ryne, one of the highest-paid actresses in Hollywood, he had lived the same lifestyle as me. Bachelor brothers was what we used to call ourselves. But now, they were engaged, and he was more whipped than a sub.

He clinked his glass against mine, and we downed what liquor was left. Immediately, a waitress appeared to hand us refills.

He held his scotch over the side of the railing, balancing the liquor in the air.

I did the same, sighing as I gazed at all the twinkling lights below. "It's been a hell of a run for us so far, and we're only getting started."

When Brett and his buddies had opened The Agency—a firm of agents representing actors, athletes, and musicians—I had just passed the bar, and we would refer clients to one another. Now, all these years later, we sat in many of the same meetings, negotiating deals for the top earners in the business.

"You've got that right, my friend. Wait until I tell you about this new actress I just scouted and how much money she's going to earn us ..." His voice faded as he grabbed his phone and read the screen. "Fuck."

"What's wrong?"

Still staring at his cell, he said, "You know our client

Naomi, who I cast for that reality TV show that's filming in two weeks? Her manager just texted and said she's in the hospital with two herniated discs in her neck and another three in her back." He slowly glanced up at me. "Ski accident in Vail this morning."

"Jesus, is she all right?"

"She's going in for surgery tomorrow. She'll be bedridden for the next nine to twelve weeks, which means she'll miss all of filming."

"That shit is painful. I hope she pulls through." I took a drink. "I also know what that means for you—you have to find someone to replace her."

He typed a reply, calling over a waitress the moment he put his phone away. "Another round for both of us and two tequila shots." As she walked toward the bar, he said to me, "Getting drunk is the only solution to this."

"Tell me exactly what you're looking for. Maybe I can help."

"If you remember, the show is about well-off, young girls, living the LA life. Private jets, VIP club treatment, walk-in closets that have as many Birkins as my fiancée. The studio will provide all of that. I just need the right face."

I quickly glanced around the roof, taking an inventory of the different looks and talent up here. "What kind of face?"

He twirled the glass in his hand, the scotch swirling like a tornado. "Early twenties, gorgeous. She needs to have perfect tits and a body to fucking die for. Personality-wise, I need someone who can put the cast members in their place—not a villain, but someone with spark."

Not finding what I was looking for, I mentally ran through my roster of actresses who focused only on reality television. Daisy Roy was the most talented one I had. Even though she was a villain off camera, she was the girl next door on-screen.

3

She was good-looking, but she didn't possess the heat he was after.

I shook my head. "I can't think of anyone."

"I was afraid of that."

The waitress returned, setting the four glasses on the balcony's wide brick edge.

We went straight for the tequila, downing the shots before we moved on to the scotch.

Brett held the fresh drink against his chest, tugging at the strands of his hair. "We start filming in two weeks. I need someone—yesterday."

I grabbed his shoulder, shaking it to loosen him up. "Don't stress, brother. When I get to the office tomorrow, I'll dig through my clients and see who I can find."

The words had barely left my mouth when I turned toward the thick crowd and linked eyes with the most beautiful girl. Goddamn it, she was more stunning than any woman I had ever seen. Long, dark hair with pouty, thick lips and a light-blue stare that was so intense that I could see the color from all the way over here.

But the connection didn't stop with her looks.

I could almost feel her in my hands, as though her body were lying beneath mine, slowly caressing her smooth, naked skin, warming the areas that my mouth was soon going to devour.

Fuck me.

"Do you know who that is?" I asked Brett.

"Who?"

I broke our connection to look at my best friend. "I can't point—she's watching—but the girl at three o'clock in a tight emerald-colored dress with endless fucking curves. There's a tall blonde next to her, who doesn't compete at all."

4

"I've never seen either of them before, but you're right; the brunette is hot as hell."

With my eyes on her again, I brought the glass up to my mouth, not feeling the burn as I swallowed.

Because there was only one fire in my body.

One that sparked an aching need to be inside her.

"Whoever she is"—I licked the wet booze off my lips—"I'm tasting her before this night is over."

"Is that right?"

A smile grew across my face as I started at her heels and worked my way higher. "Hell yes." When I reached the top of her head, I glanced at Brett. "You do remember what it's like to have a one-night stand, don't you?"

He laughed. "It's been an eternity, but I'll leave those nights to you, bro. James is more than enough for me."

"I won't hold that against you," I bantered.

The space between us got busier, filling with people, causing my view of her to disappear. My brothers happened to be part of that congestion and were making their way over to us.

I clasped Jenner's arm the moment he was within range, pulling him in for a hug. "You've outdone yourself, my man. A hell of a hotel your team has built here, and this party is off the charts. Whoever put together the guest list deserves a fucking raise. Some of the women here tonight—*mmm-mmm*."

As I looked over his shoulder, there was sexiness every-where. Outfits that revealed bare, toned backs, lean arms, legs for fucking centuries.

And then there was the girl in the green dress, the queen of them all.

Through the smallest opening, a crack between two men, her eyes met mine again.

"Speaking of women ..." Jenner said, pulling back to reach

inside his sports coat. He placed something in my hand and then Ford's, skipping right over Brett. "No reason to bring one home when I got you a room downstairs."

A key card was now tucked under my fingers, the room number written on its paper sleeve.

I put it in my pocket, punching Jenner's shoulder with just a little strength. "Always looking out for us single men."

"I've got your back," he replied, including Ford. "Always."

The four of us raised our glasses, carefully tapping them together, before we went our separate ways, kicking off several hours of small talk with the industry professionals in attendance tonight. I gave out my card to a few up-and-coming musicians, their popularity rising enough to where they were ready for representation, and to some influencers whose following was gaining them endorsements, contracts they couldn't negotiate on their own.

Many more drinks later, I was coming out of the restroom when I spotted her.

The girl in the emerald dress.

She was standing at the mouth of the hallway that led to the ladies' and men's rooms, her back against the wall, her arm wrapped across her narrow waist as she spoke on her phone.

I assumed she'd come in here to get away from the noise, to have some privacy since there was none to be had on the rooftop.

Her focus elsewhere gave me the opportunity to appreciate the view, and I took my time to observe every goddamn inch of her.

Hair I wanted to twist around my wrist and pull.

Lips I wanted sucking on my crown.

Legs I wanted to spread wide.

An ass I wanted pulsing around my cock.

6

Perfection came in many forms. Hers was unique and breathtaking.

I walked until I was in front of her, and her eyes instantly locked with mine, widening the longer she looked at me.

"It's you ... the guy from across the bar."

Her whispered admission made me grin.

"I have to go," she said into the phone. "I'll get it all done, I promise."

She slipped her cell inside her purse, and I reached for her hand the second it was free.

"Dominick."

Her gentle fingers fell into my grip. Ones that would soon be wrapped around the base of my dick while she sucked my crown down her throat. "I'm Kendall."

"I want to tell you something, Kendall."

Her cheeks reddened, and her breathing sped up, her chest rising faster with each inhale.

"Since the moment I saw you, there's only been one thought in my head."

She pushed herself further against the wall, her knee bending so she could place her heel there as well. "And that is?"

"That I would do anything to taste you."

Her lips stayed parted, like my tip was already between them, her voice getting lost in her breathing.

"Do you know what happens when I want something?" The top of her head came to the center of my chest, and I placed my palm on the wall just above her. There was plenty of room for her to leave, but it was a tight-enough cage that positioned her right where I wanted her. "I do everything in my power to make it mine." I leaned in close, my lips hovering inches away from hers. Her eyes told me she was preparing for me to kiss her, but after a few exhales, I moved my mouth to her ear. "You're all I can think about."

7

"I"—the syllable sounded like a gasp—"don't know what to say."

My finger ran across her cheek and down her collarbone, goose bumps meeting me. "Say I can have you." I pointed toward an escape route. "Or walk away. You have ten seconds to decide."

While my hand circled the back of her neck, the key in my pocket was like a thirty-pound weight, conjuring up all the surfaces in that room that I could potentially fuck her on.

"Nine," I breathed the number against her mouth. "Eight, seven." I counted in my head until I reached, "Five."

She shifted her weight, her foot dropping to the ground, her gaze changing every time I voiced a lower number.

"Four, three."

Her chest stilled, telling me she was holding air in her lungs.

"Two."

"Dominick ..." My name came out like a moan.

"One."

TWO

DOMINICK

Since she'd still made no effort to move, I cupped Kendall's face and pressed my lips to hers, my tongue immediately finding its way in. She tasted as sweet as she looked, the flavor of a margarita, her skin the scent of an island breeze.

The heat from her body scorched my hand as I rubbed down her silky dress, her back arching away from the wall the deeper I traveled. When my fingers climbed, the tip of her tit flirted with me, her nipple taunting me.

I growled, "If you don't start walking to the elevator, I'm going to carry you there."

She licked me off her pouty, thick lips. "Where are we going?"

"To the nineteenth floor."

"You're staying at the hotel?"

I nodded.

"And you're going to carry me ... in front of all these people?"

I hadn't realized we were sharing the hallway with anyone.

Nor did I care.

"Do you want to test me, Kendall?"

Her smile told me she already was.

With the back of her dress fully open, I shimmied my fingers under the tight fabric, moving around to the front. "Fuck," I moaned when I reached her wet, bare cunt. "No panties."

"I've been waiting for you."

I circled the top of her clit, soaking her into my skin. "Is that so?"

I flicked the same spot, and her neck elongated, pressing her head into the wall.

"I ..." She was too lost in sensations to answer.

Every one of my movements was to make her feel even better, but I made sure no one could watch, using my body to block her from any viewers.

I pulled my hand out, licking off her wetness. "You taste"—I put my whole finger in my mouth, making sure I didn't lose a drop—"fucking unbelievable."

The second my hand was free, I grabbed hers and led her toward the elevator. Once we were inside, I hit the button for the nineteenth floor and walked her to the back wall. I held her neck, aiming her face up at mine, and devoured her lips, the sound of her breathing making me want to tear off her dress.

"You feel so fucking good," I whispered.

I hauled her body against mine, my cock so hard that it was fucking throbbing, my tip threatening to rip through my pants if I didn't get them off soon.

"I need more of you," I hissed, tasting the desire on her tongue.

The elevator chimed, signaling our arrival.

Knowing she couldn't move as fast as me, not in the heels she had on, I bent down and folded her over my shoulder, lifting her into the air and carrying her out the open doors.

"Dominick," she squealed, the sound of her surprise causing me to smile as I rushed us down the hallway toward the room. "You're crazy."

She hadn't experienced crazy.

That wouldn't happen until my cock was inside her.

It took me no time to get us inside the room and flip on the lights, setting Kendall back on her feet.

I surrounded her ass, squeezing her cheeks, imagining my dick between them. "Take off this dress before I shred it."

"If you thought I was wet before ..." Her body quivered as she paused. "That was nothing compared to what I am now."

"Show me."

She reached behind her neck, loosening the strap that was tied there and then lowering the zipper on her hip, the emerald material soon cascading down her legs.

There was no bra covering her full, round, palm-sized natural tits.

No panties at the bottom of her flat stomach, just a pussy that was more gorgeous than any art hanging in my house. Legs that were toned and muscular with a gap between her thighs that was wider than my tongue.

"Fuck me," I groaned as I took her in once more. "You ..." I met her eyes, shaking my head, words failing me. "You're beautiful, Kendall."

I couldn't keep my hands off her for long, brushing my thumb across her nipple while I licked the other one.

She unhooked my belt and unbuttoned my pants, fisting my cock as soon as she freed it from my boxer briefs. "Holy fuck ... I wasn't expecting this. At all."

"I'm glad you like it." She pumped my shaft several times, and I added, "Yes. That's it." I bit the end of her nipple, moaning, "Harder."

With her other hand, she began taking off my shirt,

popping the buttons through their holes, pulling my arms through the sleeves.

"You want to know what's beautiful?" Her hand stilled around my dick, but her grip tightened as she added, "This." She then traced each ripple between my abs. "And this."

"It's all yours tonight, Kendall."

I dropped my pants and boxers and slipped out of my shoes. Bending down, I reached inside my wallet, where I always kept a few condoms. Once I got one out, I backed her up to the large wooden table in the dining room of the suite.

Her hand surrounded me, stroking my dick several times. "How much longer do I have to wait to have this?"

Now, that made me chuckle. "You dirty fucking girl."

I lifted her onto the top of the table and spread her legs around me, tearing off the corner of the foil and rolling the rubber over my cock.

"Get over here," I barked, pulling her ass to the edge of the wood.

Her tits bounced from the movement, earning each of them a quick lick.

Once my teeth grazed her skin, her head tilted back, and a long-drawn-out groan came from her lips that ended in, "Dominick."

I was teasing her pussy with my tip, spreading her wetness over me. It took every bit of restraint I had not to plunge all the way in. This was the phase where things needed to go slow even if my desire for her caused me to want to move fast.

"*Mmm*," she sighed when my crown slid in.

Her pussy was sucking me in farther, goading me, testing every bit of patience I had.

"Goddamn it." I was now in several inches deeper. "You're so fucking tight."

Her legs bent, feet curling around the lip of the table, her breathing louder than it had been before.

Slamming into her wasn't the way to keep her turned on. Not when you were my size. She needed to crave the build, the torment of anticipation, her pussy clenching my cock the moment I finally thrust all the way in.

And that was exactly what happened.

"*Yesss!*" she screamed once I was fully buried.

I wrapped my arms across her back, my face in her neck, holding her while her pussy pulsed. "You feel fucking amazing."

Tighter and wetter than I'd ever felt.

I rammed my mouth over those savory lips, giving her my tongue to suck on while I reared my hips back and drove into her.

She felt like a narrow, sopping tunnel of pleasure, barely big enough to fit me, and when I reached the end, I arched upward to brush my tip back and forth over her G-spot before I pulled out and did it again.

Her nails nipped my skin, her teeth grinding together as she screamed, "Dominick! Fuck!" Her legs circled over my ass, feet locked.

"You like my cock?"

"Oh God, yes." Her nails moved to my shoulders, stabbing even harder as I picked up speed. "Don't stop."

She was handling the pounding I was giving her.

But I needed more.

I needed to watch her fuck me, to take control, to free up my hands so they could roam across her body.

Sinking into her, I lifted her into the air and straddled her legs around my waist. My intention was to bring her to the bed, but I made a stop at the closest wall, pushing her back against it to pump into her pussy.

She rocked against me with each drive. "Fuck!" she yelled. "Yes!"

Her nails never left but moved spots, this time to the back of my shoulders. Mine dug into her ass, dipping until I found that forbidden hole, circling around it.

"*Ahhh*," she exhaled.

"You want more?"

Her moan was my answer.

But my cock wasn't going there. Anal wasn't for one-night stands; there was far too much prep involved, and I didn't have the patience for that now.

Not when I needed her this badly.

But that didn't stop me from playing, rimming that little hole.

"Oh fuck," she howled.

Oh fuck was right. I would bet anything that her ass was even tighter than her cunt.

And even though I wouldn't see this girl past tomorrow morning, my mind couldn't stop fantasizing about what that tightness would feel like around my cock.

Goddamn it.

I carried her to the bed and placed her down, giving her a few hard plunges before I flipped her onto her knees. I moved her into doggy style and got in behind her, wrapping her long hair around my fist.

"Dominick," she panted. "*Yesss!*"

From back here, I could reach an even deeper spot, especially if I bowed and twisted on the way in. But before I did that, I made sure she could handle this position. Once I knew it wasn't too much for her, I showed no mercy. No restraint. She got every fucking inch of me, all my power, every bit of friction I could provide, hitting her G-spot with each stroke.

And to add to it, I rubbed her clit.

14

"Oh my God!"

Every sound that came from her caused my balls to clench, my orgasm on the verge of exploding.

She felt too good.

Too tight.

I was too fucking close to coming.

I turned her over, moving her legs around my lap while I pressed my back to the headboard. "Ride me," I demanded.

As she started to gain momentum, her tits bobbed in my face. They were too beautiful not to suck, so I surrounded her nipple, gently gnawing on the end while my finger went deeper into her ass. She was tightening in both spots, her clit hardening, her wetness thickening.

I knew even before she moaned, "I'm going to come."

I switched to her other tit, biting down just enough to give her the slightest wave of pain. As she shifted forward and back, moving faster with each pass, I made sure her clit got the same amount of attention.

"Dominick ..."

Her head fell back, hands gripping my thighs as she worked herself over me, her body shuddering with each pump.

The sight was fucking gorgeous.

"Hell yes," I barked, watching her unravel. "You're even wetter now."

And sexier.

Her ass even narrower.

"Dominick," she cried, telling me she'd hit the peak.

Even though I knew her body was extremely sensitive right now, I wouldn't lighten up, driving into her relentlessly, resuming the flicking across her clit and the fingering in her ass.

There was one thing I wanted from her, one thing I needed to feel, and that was, "You're going to come again, Kendall."

"Fuck."

It took several dips before she found a new rhythm, but once she started, she didn't stop.

My teeth clenched from the friction. The contracting. The quick, hard grinds.

"That's it," I breathed, fighting the build while my mouth was full of her tit. "Ride that fucking cock."

She went up and down like she was on a goddamn horse, her pussy promising to suck every bit of cum out of me. She didn't let up. She didn't slow. She just gave me unrelenting plunges in and out of her perfect cunt.

"Keep that up, and you're going to make me blow my load."

Her movements told me that was what she wanted.

So did her words, "Come in me," when she moaned them in my ear.

She circled that delicious ass like she was dancing over my dick. I hissed from the surge plowing through me, the pressure in my balls.

"Fuck me," I barked louder. "Make me fucking come."

It was as though I had flipped a switch inside her, her body moving with more intensity, her cunt milking me from every angle. She was taunting my cum, challenging it with her pussy, dragging every feeling, urge, tingle until I erupted.

"*Fuuuck*, Kendall."

This stunning girl was forcing my orgasm out, and her screams told me she was having another one of her own.

"Fuck yes," I growled as our bodies shuddered simultaneously, our sounds matching, as though they were fighting for airtime.

"*Ahhh*, Dominick."

I wrapped her in my arms as she pounded her body over mine, her pussy trembling, her body shaking, drawing out my build until she completely emptied me, each shot filling the condom.

"Dammit, Kendall," I whispered now that we'd both stilled, tasting the sweat on her mouth. "You really know how to ride a cock."

Her laugh was light and honest. "You gave me a hell of a cock to ride." She released a gritty sigh. "They're not all built like yours."

That earned her a smile.

She was certainly one of the most interesting women I'd been with. Quick with the words, exquisite to look at, a body that deserved to be fucking worshipped.

I rubbed my thumb across her bottom lip, cupping her cheek, my fingers in the back of her hair. "How does a shower sound?"

"Heavenly."

I gazed at her mouth, picturing it around my cock, the feeling of her throat as it closed in around my shaft, sucking the tip like her pussy had just done. "Just so you know, there's not going to be any sleep." I pulled her lip down, looking at the size of her teeth, thinking of what she could do with them. "At least, not for a while."

"You mean ..." Her voice cut off as she glanced at my cock, seeing that I was already getting hard again. Her eyes were feral when they met mine. "Oh fuck."

THREE

KENDALL

S hit, what time is it?

    I pushed myself up from the bed, out of the cocoon of blanket and pillows I had buried myself in, and immediately covered my eyes from the sunlight seeping in from the blinds.

Ouch.

My hangover was front and center. I'd had far too much tequila last night, those skinny margaritas going down like water. If I'd only woken a half hour earlier, I could appreciate the deliciously perfect naked man lying beside me, reveling in every moment we'd shared together last night. Details I could still recall from the soreness in my body. But as I searched for the clock, one on Dominick's side, it glowed a number that told me I was going to be extremely late for my meeting.

I climbed out of bed, hopping around the room with the balance of a newborn puppy, and tried to find my dress and shoes and purse—everything I'd worn to the hotel party. Each item had fallen in a different place on the floor the minute he carried me in here. Collecting my things in my arms, I brought them all into the bathroom. I slipped on my dress and tied my hair back with an elastic from my clutch, ensuring yesterday's makeup wasn't running down my cheeks before I rushed back to the bedroom.

Dominick was still asleep on his stomach. His arms stretched above his head, dark hair and tanned skin covering them, hints of a morning shadow on the unhidden parts of his cheek.

And then there was his ass.

Two yummy, hard hills that caused a rise in the blanket.

My God.

That man was all muscle and masculinity and sex.

Before last night, I had been positive unicorns like him only existed because of Photoshop.

But proof was directly in front of me.

And because I was an idiot, I didn't have his last name, phone number, or any set plans to see him again.

But after what had gone down in this room—the way he made my body feel, the connection that exploded between us—I needed all of his information.

I just didn't have time to wake him up and have that conversation.

I found a small pad of paper and pen on the dining table. As I jotted down my name and number and an apology for having to leave so fast, my skin flushed as I remembered what he had done to me on this wood.

I left the note on top of his pants and bolted down the hallway and into the elevator, ordering a ride-share that met me in front of the lobby only a minute after I arrived. Even at this early hour, the traffic was brutal, the driver having to navigate a few alternate routes just to avoid some of the heavier congestion.

At the sight of my apartment, I threw the backseat door open and stripped off my dress the moment I got inside. I adjusted my hair into a higher knot and clipped the fallen pieces to the top of my head, and then I stepped beneath the warm spray of the shower. I covered my loofah with my beach-scented body wash and scrubbed Dominick from my skin.

One-night stand. That certainly wasn't a term I was familiar with.

I knew the word *boyfriend.*

Relationship.

Commitment, sacrifice, compromise.

But what had happened last evening—the lack of a last name, the horny minx I had turned into, wildly passionate sex with a total stranger, someone who had learned my body better than any man I'd ever dated—was a language I'd never spoken before.

Now, every time I moved, each inch tugging at the soreness inside, was a reminder.

I could only hope Dominick would keep the message I'd left for him, and we could do all of that again—maybe with food and more conversation next time.

I got out of the shower, wrapping a towel over my wet body, and grabbed the first dress I found hanging in my closet. It happened to be a black maxi that I paired with a cute set of flats and chunky earrings. Returning to the bath-room, I untwisted my hair, the natural waves falling across my shoulders and back, tamed enough that I didn't have to pull it into a pony. I quickly added some mascara, lip gloss, and more blush to my already-flushed cheeks, and I was ready to go.

I had left my purse and keys on my bed and clasped both in my hands before I took off for the parking garage. Once I was inside my car with the music blasting, I hadn't driven more than two blocks and had to slow down for traffic. In Boston, where I'd spent my entire life up until six weeks ago, I hadn't owned a car and relied on public transportation, a quick and efficient method that got me everywhere I needed to go.

Los Angeles wasn't that kind of city.

Miles could take an eternity.

This morning was no different.

I was ten minutes late and still hadn't picked up coffee—a requirement set by my sister when she was scheduled to be anywhere before noon. As her personal assistant, I knew better than to show up empty-handed, and I also knew there was no negotiation to her rules.

I parked a few blocks away from Starbucks, not wanting to waste any more time to look for a better spot, and I hauled ass inside. The line was at least twenty people deep, and it wrapped around the whole back of the shop.

She's going to kill me.

The second I got in place, my phone began to vibrate from inside my purse. If I pulled it out, I imagined there would be multiple texts, missed calls, voice mails, all from my sister, asking where I was.

She was high-maintenance, demanding, and extremely argumentative, a snarky attitude that just wouldn't let you win, so there was no reason to even try. Growing up with her had been an adventure, but having to work with her every day, in this proximity, was an entirely new level of intensity.

I still had no idea how she'd convinced me to leave my favorite city and the job that I loved so much to move here and be her bitch.

Eighteen months younger than her, I had come out of the womb, knowing how to tolerate her behavior. But apparently, I was the only one who could.

Because her last five assistants had quit.

After the final one had abandoned her, she'd begged me to come work for her.

I didn't know what point had eventually sold me, but I was six weeks in.

"*Ugggh*," the guy in front of me groaned. "This line is barely moving." He checked his home screen again, looking at the time or his messages—something he'd done less than a minute ago.

"Right?" I agreed. "I need a magic wand and a miracle. I'm"—I glanced at my watch—"fifteen minutes late to an extremely important meeting."

He turned toward me, his bangs dangling so low in his eyes that I wanted to sweep them behind his ear. "Is it with anyone worth bragging about?" His tie was black and sharp, his eyelids rimmed with a smoky liner that looked far better than the makeup I had on.

"What do you mean?"

He assessed me like he was a wholesale buyer and I was walking down a runway. "How long have you lived here?"

"Not even two months."

"I can tell." He held out his hand. "Charlie, but I prefer Charlize because I'm fabulous like that."

I smiled, loving him already. "Kendall."

"So, Kendall, is your meeting with someone fancy?"

I shrugged. "My sister and some of her team."

"If she's anyone we've all heard of, I'm going to teach you something very important that you need to use to your advantage while you work in this town."

"She's Daisy Roy, a reality TV star."

"Daisy Roy," he repeated. "You mean, the chick who's in the show *Single Girls of LA* and whose face is on that billboard?" He pointed out the window, where there was a giant photograph of Daisy smiling with a beer clasped in her hand—now the newest spokeswoman for that beverage company.

I nodded. "Yep, the one and only."

"*Giiirl*, watch this." He moved to the side of the line, so he'd have a full view of everyone standing in it, and said, "Hey, guys, we have a 911 over here." He waited until most of the people looked in his direction before he continued, "This here is Daisy Roy's sister, and she was sent to get Daisy some coffee, stat, for an audition she has in five. Do you think we can do her a solid and let her cut?"

"Only if you can get me a date with your smoking-hot sister," a guy replied.

"If you buy my coffee, I'll happily let you squeeze in," a woman said from the front.

"You're a lifesaver," I replied to her, and then I looked at Charlize. "Dinner, drinks, whatever—it's all on me."

"Don't think I'm not taking you up on that." He urged me toward my new position and added, "I'll find you on Instagram."

"Search Daisy's account, she only follows a few people and I'm one of them," I said to him before I reached the counter. I gave the barista my order and pointed to the lady behind me. "I'll also pay for whatever she's having."

As I took out my credit card, I saw my phone lighting up with more texts, and I scrolled through my messages while I waited for the drinks.

Daisy: Why didn't you tell me you were running late?
Daisy: Where are you?
Daisy: Are you REALLY doing this to me? Is THIS what I pay you for?
Daisy: I can't believe you're not here yet ...
Daisy: ANSWER ME. WHERE ARE YOU?
Daisy: Twenty minutes. Are you fucking kidding me?
Daisy: You're officially dead to me. Or fired. I can't tell which one would give me more satisfaction right now. There's literally

*smoke coming out of my ears. WHY THE HELL AREN'T
YOU HERE?*

A new notification came in, this one from Instagram, a Charlize Frank requesting to follow my private account. I glanced toward the back of the line, and he was grinning at me, waving.

I hit Accept just as one of the baristas yelled, "Kendall!"

Knowing it was best not to respond to my sister—a text at this point would only make her angrier—I grabbed the two coffees and hurried toward the door, thanking everyone I passed in line. When I reached Charlize, I told him I'd be in touch and headed down the sidewalk toward The Agency, the large high-rise at the end.

This was the second time I would be meeting her agent— her manager and lawyer would also be in attendance today—to discuss some of the contracts she'd recently been offered. I just hated that I was running so behind, making myself look like an unprofessional degenerate in front of her team.

Late, like one-night stand, was another word that wasn't part of my vocabulary.

"I'm here for Daisy Roy's meeting," I said to the receptionist, winded by the time I reached her desk.

"Tenth floor." She pointed at the elevators to my right. "When you get off, take a left, and the conference room is the last door at the end. You'll find them all inside."

"Thank you."

I slid into an elevator just as the doors were closing and tried to prepare myself for the lashing I was about to get.

FOUR

DOMINICK

"I'm so sorry I'm late," I heard as the conference room door flew open.

A blur of black fabric and long hair moved across the open space until the woman landed in the seat next to Daisy.

Not just any woman.

One with lean legs and an incredible ass, a face that was more exquisite than any I had ever seen.

And all of it belonged to the girl who had left my bed this morning.

The same girl Daisy had been complaining about since this meeting had started. Daisy had only referred to her as her sister, so I hadn't made the connection.

Until now.

Fuck me.

Daisy hadn't been at the hotel opening, and Kendall hadn't mentioned they were sisters.

They also looked nothing alike, giving me no reason to align the two. Daisy had more of an innocent appearance with flat hair and big, round eyes. Kendall had more of an exotic appeal with unruly hair that was almost black, a petite nose, and lips that would have stolen the show if it wasn't for those stunning light-blue, almond-shaped eyes.

Goddamn it.

I'd fucked a lot of women in this town. Clients and their family I steered clear of.

As Kendall sat beside my top reality star, an expression so apologetic on her face, I suddenly felt as sorry as she did.

"Excuse my terribly rude sister," Daisy barked. "She moved here from Boston and apparently doesn't know how to tell time."

"I'm sorry," Kendall repeated. "I'm still learning LA traffic, and it's a madhouse out there."

"Whatever." Daisy rolled her eyes. "Kendall, I think you know everyone here, except for Dominick Dalton"—she pointed at me—"my attorney."

Kendall was just getting settled in her chair, taking a drink of her coffee, when our stares met.

As the realization hit her, her body froze, eyes widening, cheeks turning an even deeper shade of red than they had in the hallway of the restroom.

I liked that color on her.

I'd like it even more if it came in lace lingerie that framed her tits with a string up her ass.

"Kendall ..."

She swallowed, taking a long, deep breath, trying to hide the shock that was surely echoing through her body—a feeling that produced the sexiest fucking look on her face. "Dominick, it's nice to meet you."

She wasn't giving away our secret.

That pleased me.

"You as well," I replied.

I wondered if her pussy was wet. If she'd let me spread her legs across the table, the way I had less than twelve hours ago, if we were left alone in here. If her nipples were becoming hard and erect as she gazed at me.

Like my fucking cock.

"Can we get to work now?" Daisy demanded. "I have a photo shoot after this that no one is going to make me late for." She glared at her sister.

"I'm sorry," Kendall whispered to her.

In the eight years I'd been practicing entertainment law, I'd seen many different shades of people. Most in the depths of their career, that level of income in line with what it took to afford me. Half of the people who sat across from me were friendly and humble; the next percentage were cocky assholes.

Then, there were clients like Daisy Roy.

In front of the camera, she was sunshine. Brands loved her airy brightness; her smile alone could sell millions of products. But once the camera turned off and the lights dimmed, there was nothing shiny about her.

She was all bitch.

Fortunately, our meetings were infrequent.

I read her contracts, I gave her legal advice, I negotiated deals on her behalf.

And I sent her my bill with an extra fifteen percent tacked on that made her attitude a little easier to tolerate.

Greg, Daisy's agent, opened the folder that rested in front of him and slid it toward Daisy. "Here are the offers I have for you."

Since Greg had emailed me the contracts a few days ago, I'd done my due diligence and scanned them prior to this meeting. That gave me the knowledge to answer any questions Daisy would have. Now that filming had wrapped on another season of *Single Girls of LA*—the series that had

27

skyrocketed her fame—several other shows were interested in her.

"Before you read any of the offers," Greg started, "I'd just like to say, the more screen time you have, the higher your earning potential becomes. So, look at these with an open mind, and going forward, we have to make sure you're maintaining the image we've worked so hard to achieve."

Daisy's eyelids narrowed. "What are you trying to say, Greg? That I haven't been doing a good job at maintaining my reputation?" She fanned all the pages in front of her. "Do you see how many are here? Clearly, there are plenty of people who want me."

"I'm just telling you, you have to be careful. That's the only message I'm trying to send. I say the same thing to all my clients," he responded.

"Save your lectures. Or better yet, use them on my sister. She's the one who can't seem to follow the rules."

In a different situation, I was sure Kendall could handle herself.

But with me in the room, my patience being tested, I wasn't going to take any more shit that was directly or indirectly aimed at her.

"Daisy, Greg's not attacking you. He's seen plenty of careers go up in flames, and he's only trying to look out for your best interest." I nodded toward the stack in her hands. "He's secured multiple deals that are extremely substantial, and he wouldn't have done that if he didn't see your potential."

Daisy laughed, a sound that told me I was wasting her time —and mine—and she began reviewing the first sheet. "No. Definitely not this one. It's too physical, and I can't stand sweating. Next." She tossed the paper and picked up another one, instantly degrading Greg for presenting it to her.

While she moved on to the third one, I gazed at Kendall,

her eyes never leaving her sister, like she was waiting for an upcoming demand.

Because I couldn't fucking help myself, I asked, "What did you do before becoming Daisy's assistant?"

She inhaled a large breath, slowly turning toward me. "I was an artist."

"Artist?" Daisy snickered. "Let's not get carried away. You were a graphic designer."

"Yes, that's true," Kendall replied with no challenge in her voice, "but I did art on the side, mostly volunteer stuff."

"To ninety-year-olds at nursing homes, whose hands were too arthritic to even hold a paintbrush," Daisy chimed in again. "This offer is a snore-fest." Instead of setting the paper off to the side, she shredded it.

"And you gave all of that up to come here?" I asked Kendall.

She held her coffee against her lips, even after she finished swallowing, telling me the question made her uncomfortable. "I still do some art. Not in the same capacity, but I manage Daisy's social media, and I create and edit all the videos for her accounts and digitally master the photos."

I suddenly had an urge to check Daisy's accounts to see what kind of work Kendall was capable of—something I would do after this meeting.

That thought surprised me.

Beyond their bodies, I normally had no interest in the women I slept with, no desire to contact them when I woke the morning after. But when my housekeeper took my pants in for dry cleaning this week, she would find Kendall's note in the pocket, and she would place it on the island in my closet.

I wasn't sure why I had taken it home with me.

That was the truth that haunted me as I watched Daisy tear up another sheet.

"Is this a joke?" she snarled. "I don't know how to bake, and I'm lactose intolerant. Why would you think I'd be interested in this?"

While Kendall focused on her sister, I stared at her, analyzing every inch of her gorgeous fucking face.

Last night, she had been stunning.

But in the morning light, she was even more beautiful.

Sexy in a subtle, charming way. Riveting. And she had a heart—I could see that from over here. I could sense it in every answer she gave.

On that rooftop bar, she'd made me pause. She was doing the same thing now.

I leaned over the table, and the buttons on the sleeves of my suit made a sound as they scraped over the wood, causing Kendall to look at me.

"Have you ever considered getting into television?" I asked her.

She immediately shook her head, those seductive, dark curls falling across her cheeks. "No way. I don't have the face or the personality."

It was my turn to laugh. "I would have to disagree."

"I know you're not suggesting what I think you are," Daisy said to me as a warning. Then, she shifted her gaze to Greg. "This one"—she threw a contract at him as though it were a Frisbee—"is disgusting. Would you eat a live cockroach for a quarter of a million dollars?"

There was no doubt in my mind that Kendall had a future in TV. I could feel it in my fucking bones. I could see it as she stared back at me—the look that would appease America, the body every man would fucking crave to be inside of, the voice that wouldn't get on anyone's nerves.

It all just depended on whether or not she wanted it.

"What if I told you I could land you a role on an up-and-coming reality show? Would you take it?"

"Wait," Daisy snapped. "Isn't this meeting about me?"

"Your agent worked hard in finding the shows that are outlined in front of you," I responded to her. "This offer is only for your sister."

Daisy ground her teeth together while Kendall's jaw dropped.

"Dominick ... you aren't serious?" Kendall said softly.

"I don't kid."

Those big, breathtakingly blue eyes were opened so wide that they were the size of half-dollars.

"I ..." Kendall shook her head. "I don't know what to say."

I'd heard her speak those words before.

And I knew what they'd led to last time.

"Say yes, Kendall."

"Absolutely not," Daisy interrupted. Now addressing her sister, she said, "You're my assistant. That's why I brought you out here. I'm not sharing a manager and an agent and an attorney and a TV screen with you."

"No one said anything about sharing, Daisy." I leaned back in my chair, folding my arms across my chest. "This building is full of managers and agents who are more than qualified to represent your sister. You have your team. She will have hers."

Daisy glared at Greg. "How the hell does my attorney have a TV gig to offer my sister, and you can't find me a decent show to even consider?" She huffed. "This is bullshit."

"I don't want to upset her more than I already have," Kendall said, her eyes only on me. "Let's just focus on Daisy and finding her the best offer we can."

Daisy thrived when she was surrounded by people like Kendall. Girls who backed down because it wasn't worth the fight, who were kind and easier to manipulate, who would sacrifice their happiness for her.

I had zero skin in this game. I wouldn't make a penny if Kendall took the job. But my best friend needed a star, and there was one sitting in front of me right now.

"Kendall, look at me." It took several moments before her stare found mine. "Tell me what *you* want."

FIVE

KENDALL

Coincidences.

There were times that were so ironic, so mind-blowing, that I had to pinch myself. That was what I'd done when I laid eyes on Dominick, sitting across the table from me in a deliciously handsome, dark suit, a silver striped tie, and the scent of shower and lust wafting over from him.

Really, what were the chances that the man I hadn't been able to stop thinking about was my sister's lawyer?

And now, he was staring at me, waiting for an answer to a question that was completely insane.

Me ... acting ... on a reality TV show?

No.

But the grin on his lips, the promise in his eyes, told me he believed in me. That he wanted this for me, that he was going to make it happen.

I just had to say yes.

I set down my coffee that I'd been holding against my mouth, clearing the thickness from my throat, and glanced at my lap. If I looked at my sister, I knew what her expression would show—her opinion was more than clear. But I needed a moment that wasn't influenced by her to breathe, to get my thoughts straight.

When I finally glanced up again, the confidence in Dominick's eyes hadn't wavered one bit.

"Yes."

My sister gasped, her hand flying across the open space between us to grab my arm, but it didn't pull my focus away from Dominick, and I watched him stand from his chair and make his way over.

He gripped the top of my seat, sliding it away from the table. "Come with me."

My heart pounded so loudly that I was sure he could hear it. "Now?"

"Yes, Kendall. Now."

I didn't feel my feet as he led me out of the conference room, each step happening without my control, bringing me deeper into this crazy dream.

"I can't believe this is happening," I whispered, the door to each office whizzing past me as I fought to keep up with his long strides.

"Believe it."

The scruff on his cheeks early this morning had been shaved off. The fingers that had been inside of me last night were now on my lower back. The tingles he had filled me with had returned, this time in my chest.

"Why are you doing this? I mean, helping me get this job?"

His smile made me want to melt into the carpet.

"I know a star when I see one, Kendall."

I was positive I'd stopped breathing, the air getting especially hot as we began to slow, the last door at the end of the hallway our obvious destination.

When we stopped in front of it, Dominick knocked.

"Come in," was spoken from the other side.

Dominick's hand left me as he said, "Give me two minutes. I need to speak to Brett, and then I'll come back out and get you."

I nodded, words so far from my brain that I couldn't form any if I tried.

He disappeared inside the office, closing the door behind him, and I leaned against the wall beside me, needing its stability to take some of my weight.

What the hell am I doing?

I knew nothing about acting or television, aside from what I'd learned in the six weeks I'd been working for Daisy. And my sister, who considered every girl in the world as her competition, was going to kill me for leaving her meeting and agreeing to Dominick's offer.

I was positive the death threats were already coming through my phone, as it had been vibrating from my clutch since the moment we'd walked out of the conference room.

I unzipped the small bag to look.

> *Daisy: We need to talk.*
> *Daisy: RIGHT NOW.*
> *Daisy: You're my assistant, not a TV star.*
> *Daisy: I can't believe you're even considering this.*
> *Daisy: Get back in here.*
> *Daisy: KENDALL, what the FUCK?!*

The bubbles underneath her last message told me she wasn't done screaming, that there were more texts on the way.

I couldn't read another one.

I zipped up my purse and thanked the clouds above that I had my own apartment and I wasn't crashing at her place. After

35

everything that had happened today, she wasn't going to make things pretty for me.

Is this worth it?

Am I nuts to even entertain this idea?

No one could assist Daisy like me. She needed my help, and I didn't know how this opportunity would affect that. I wouldn't be in LA if it wasn't for her, and now, less than two months later, I was already debating on taking a different job.

What am I getting myself into?

"Are you ready?" Dominick said once he opened the door, startling me. I slipped inside the small crack as he continued, "Kendall, I want you to meet Brett Young."

I didn't need the introduction. His fiancée was one of the most famous actresses in Hollywood, making Brett Young a household name. Pictures of them were on the pages of every magazine and online article. There were Instagram fan pages dedicated just to them.

But professionally, Brett was one of the top agents in the world and one of the owners of The Agency, a company Daisy mentioned at least once a day since her agent worked for him. Having Brett represent her was Daisy's ultimate goal.

And now, I was standing in front of his desk.

What the ever-loving fuck?

"Brett, this is Kendall Roy," Dominick said, finishing the introduction.

Brett stood from behind his desk, extending his hand, and I shook his firm grip.

"It's a real pleasure," I heard myself say.

"Likewise."

He sat down, motioning for us to do the same, and Dominick and I filled the two vacant chairs.

"My friend Dominick has an impeccable eye for talent," Brett began. "In fact, together, we've closed some of the largest entertainment deals in the world." As he paused, a wave of chills ran up my arms and across my chest, each hammer of my heart causing my throat to shudder. "When he tells me he's got someone for one of my shows, I take his word for it." He glanced at Dominick and then back to me. "I see why he chose you."

You do?

That thought didn't leave my head.

Instead, it simmered and boiled.

"Tell me, Kendall, are you interested in hearing about the offer?"

"I ... think so." I cleared my throat. "This is just so unexpected. I mean, I never imagined any of this, so please excuse everything I'm saying. I'm afraid I'm not making any sense."

He laughed, crossing his hands over the dark wooden top. "Filming begins in two weeks. It features a group of six girls, highlighting their lives in LA. Similar to the show your sister is on but more upscale. Think flying in a private jet to Bali, dining at only top-rated restaurants, being chauffeured around town in a Rolls-Royce."

I didn't know this life. My sister earned a shit-ton, but that wasn't me. I'd purchased a seven-year-old used car and would be paying off my student loans and credit card debt until I died. The efficiency I rented was far from phenomenal.

"Don't worry," he added. "The show will assume the cost of everything and pay you a hefty salary." He pushed a stack of papers in my direction. "The preliminary buzz has been so strong that they're anticipating to break all streaming and cable ratings records in their category. Advertising fees have doubled in the last month alone. In other words, I expect a second season."

This was heavy.

But it was nothing compared to the feeling that hit me

when I glanced down and saw the salary listed on the first page of the contract.

I clasped my hands together to stop them from shaking. I'd be able to pay off my student loans and credit card debt along with my car and prepay an entire year—or four—of rent, and I'd still have a massive amount to stow away in the bank.

"That salary is only a starting point," Dominick said. "Brett and I will get you more."

"More?"

"We're good for about a twenty percent increase," Brett admitted.

I couldn't believe what I was hearing.

Seeing.

Reading on the sheet in front of me.

"As for the role, the studio is looking for someone with spark. Not the fire starter, not anyone shy or reserved. I need a woman who's quick-witted and charming." His eyes narrowed. "I get the feeling that's you, Kendall."

"It is," Dominick agreed. "Straight down to her core."

I searched their faces, needing to hear the answer even though they were showing it to me. "You're sure I'm right for this?" My hands gripped the armrests even harder, the wood beneath them probably soaked from my palms.

"There's no doubt in my mind," Dominick replied. His voice lowered, a sound I'd heard plenty of times last night when his body was on top of mine. "America is going to be enamored with you."

I shifted my gaze to Brett, swallowing, as he said, "This will only be the beginning. You're going to get endorsement deals, other TV show offers, paid appearances. The list is honestly endless."

"And you think I can handle this with no training? No time

spent in front of the camera? No knowledge of this business at all, aside from what I've done for Daisy?"

Thoughts were circling so fast in my brain, I couldn't keep up.

"Yes," they said simultaneously.

I shook my head, trying to process. "Can I have a second to think about it?"

Brett lifted the contract from the table and handed it to Dominick. "Your lawyer needs to review the terms, and we have some negotiating to do. That will take about forty-eight hours. Will that be enough time?"

I nodded.

"You need to know, you're not alone in this, Kendall," Dominick told me. "Brett will be your agent now and going forward."

"Unless you would prefer someone else," Brett responded. "We'll also supply you with a manager—Valerie, a colleague of mine, she'd be a perfect addition to your team. And legally, Dominick has you covered for anything you need."

When I quickly peeked at Dominick, his eyes were making that promise.

"Before you leave, I want you to stop by my assistant's desk. She'll need a copy of your license and contact information, so we can email you the contract and get you into our system."

I had to keep reminding myself that I wasn't a fly on the wall. That I was really here, that Brett was going to represent me, not Daisy.

"Do you have any questions for me?" Brett asked.

I had a million, but I didn't even know where to start. But there was something nagging at me, something that probably wasn't defined in the contract, so asking was the only way I'd know.

"Will filming be all day, seven days a week?" I took a

breath. "I'm trying to figure out if there's any way I can still help my sister—I know she needs me—and continue volunteering a few days a week." I looked at Dominick. "I found a super-cute retirement home by my apartment, and the little ladies love my watercolor class."

Dominick turned to glance at Brett and said, "What did I tell you?"

Brett nodded. "You're right. She's fucking perfect."

Charlize: Good thing you budged. I could have birthed a man-baby for how long I stood in that line. Hope your meeting went fabulously and you weren't too late. Awesome to meet you today, girlfriend.

Charlize's private message through Instagram was the first thing I saw when I got in my car and opened my purse. I needed a few minutes to cool down before I called my parents to tell them the good news and attempted to drive home. My phone was the perfect distraction. But even as I scanned his words again, the aftershock of my meeting with Brett and Dominick wasn't just sending waves through me; it was churning a tsunami.

Me: I was sooo late, but something buck wild and completely unexpected happened while I was in there. I was offered a TV role, and now, I need to decide if I'm going to accept it. Who would have thought? Because I seriously wouldn't have.

I hit Send and continued to stare at the screen, wondering why I was confessing this to a total stranger. But I had no one's house to drive to right now, no one to talk to about this. Aside from my sister, I had no friends in LA, and Daisy wanted to disassemble my body at the moment and drop my limbs in the Pacific. My friends back in Boston would think I'd lost my mind—and maybe I had—but something told me Charlize would understand in a way they wouldn't, and he'd give me some sound advice.

Charlize: WHAT? Oh, hell yes. Not that I'm surprised. You're gorg, and you're in LA. It was only a matter of time before you got scooped up. When are we celebrating? And it'd better be with something stronger than a latte.
Me: Tonight?
Charlize: Yes, girl. Yesss!

SIX

DOMINICK

"You know she's scared shitless, don't you?" Brett said the second Kendall walked out of his office. "The whole time she was in here, she looked like a goddamn deer caught in headlights."

"She's humble." I leaned back in the chair, using my palms as a pillow, fanning my arms to each side. "And her sister wants to fucking kill her, so there's that too." I smiled as I thought of the glimmer in Kendall's eyes when I'd offered her the show. The way her lips had turned upward, her brows rising, the heat that had moved into her cheeks. "Man, she's going to be perfect."

He lifted his coffee and moved back in his chair, kicking his feet onto the top of his desk. "You know, when I first met James, I didn't tell her I was an agent. I didn't hide the fact; I just didn't mention it. Jesus, I couldn't keep my goddamn hands off her that night." He shook his head, grinning. "Once we parted that next morning, we texted a few times, and then the opportunity to be her agent fell right in my fucking lap." A serious expression took over his face. "Except there was one problem. I'd already slept with her."

My arms dropped, my foot bouncing in the air after I crossed my legs. "Why are you telling me this?"

"When I sat at that conference table, the chance of being James's agent dangling right in front of me, I had the same goddamn look on my face as you did when Kendall was sitting next to you."

"What are you trying to say?"

"Brother, it takes one to know one, and I saw that shit coming from a mile away." He took a drink of his coffee. "Kendall was the girl in the green dress, the one I assume you took to your hotel room last night?"

When we were on this side of the industry, we all played by the same rules. Brett was the first in our group to break one, and it had worked out for him, but most didn't, and he was trying to warn me.

I sighed. "I didn't know she was Daisy's sister until our meeting this morning."

His feet dropped to the floor, and he leaned his arms over his desk. "It's too late to tell you not to do it, but I can tell you, this could end badly if it continues."

"Continues? You know me better than that." I laughed. "Hit it, quit it—or in this case, work for it. But nothing more besides business will ever happen between Kendall and me—I assure you of that."

His hand went to his face, like he was going to cough, but a long, deep chuckle came out instead. "Fool, who do you think you're talking to? Do you really think I fucking believe that?"

"Why wouldn't you?"

His eyes narrowed. "I saw the way you were looking at her. You were doing everything in your power not to throw her across my desk."

He wasn't wrong.

I couldn't stop thinking about that fucking body. I could practically feel her under my fingertips, taste her skin on my tongue.

But things had changed.

She was soon going to be a client, and that was something I wouldn't mess with.

"Not going to happen, man." I shook my head to emphasize the point. "Trust me."

He tapped his fist on the wood. "What do you want to put on it?"

"Your plane."

He laughed again. "It's a bet I'm not going to lose, so why don't you tell me what I'll get if I win?"

"Name your prize—one of my cars, a trip to fucking Fiji, a hundred grand, whatever you want."

He stretched his hand in my direction. "You've got yourself a deal." Once we shook, he added, "Now, get your ass out of here and go read her contract. We've got a new fucking client to sign."

———

"Was your day as crazy as mine?" my brother Jenner asked from the other side of the small table where we sat on the far side of the bar.

I lifted my dirty martini up to my lips, skipping the sip for a large gulp. "You have no fucking idea." I returned the glass to its place in front of me, wrapping my hand around the thin stem. "I was in a meeting with Daisy Roy. Her sister, who happens to be her assistant, walked in late, and I offered her a reality show on the spot."

"How did Daisy react to that?"

Even my brother, who had nothing to do with the entertainment side of our firm, knew of her reputation.

"Exactly the way you'd expect." I huffed. "Did I mention, her sister is the girl I brought to the hotel room last night?"

"You dirty fucking dog, you."

"Man, she's fucking perfect. An incredibly sick body, a face that needs no makeup. Kind, charismatic"—I paused to groan —"and she can ride some mean cock."

"Perfect for the show"—his eyes narrowed—"or for you?"

"Jesus, you and Brett are fucking relentless. For the show, dickhead."

"All right, I'll semi-accept that. Are we sure Daisy hasn't gutted her yet, turning this into a true crime special?"

I laughed, finishing the rest of my drink, and the waitress immediately swung by to ask if we wanted another round.

"Keep 'em coming," I told her.

The moment she left our table, a flash of movement from several feet away caught my attention. It was a girl, tossing her hair over her shoulder, the long, thick waves stirring a night full of memories in my head. The same locks I had wrapped around my wrist and pulled down her back, exposing her neck. With Kendall's profile now facing me, my gaze lowered, remembering those pouty, thick lips I had gently gnawed.

"No shit," I uttered mostly to myself as I noticed the guy sitting next to her.

His glossy lipstick and painted nails were signs that told me they weren't on a date.

I looked at my brother. "I can assure you, she's very much alive." I pointed toward her table. "That happens to be her right there."

"Damn, you weren't kidding. That girl's a fucking knock-out." He winked. "It's too bad you got to her first."

Ignoring his smart-ass comment, I took in the angles of her

neck, the way her top showed her amazing tits, her beautiful, long legs that had locked around my waist, keeping me deep inside her pussy.

"Mark my words ... she's going to be a fucking star."

I hadn't even closed my mouth yet when Kendall glanced across the bar, her stare slowly skimming the space between us until it finally landed on me.

Dominick, she mouthed, the surprise clear in her eyes.

She looked at her friend and said something to him, and now, both were gazing at me.

I mouthed, *Come here*, and waved her over.

Only about twelve hours had passed since I'd brought her into Brett's office, and the studio was still mulling over the new salary we had counteroffered them, so I didn't know what I would say to her. I just knew I needed her closer. To see that mouth puckered around a straw, to picture my cock sliding into it. To see if her nipples hardened when she got near me, if her skin flushed, if a thin layer of sweat would rise, the same way it had when she milked my dick last night.

As she walked over, skintight leather pants revealed the curves of her hips, the outline of her thighs, the thick gap between them. The tank top she had on was small and snug, each step telling me she didn't have on a bra.

My dick was already hard, screaming to be inside her.

"Hi," she said as she reached me. "This is my friend Charlize." She looked at Charlize and added, "This is my lawyer, Dominick, and ..."

"Jenner," my brother said, introducing himself, shaking their hands.

"Nice to meet you," I said to Charlize as he lightly clasped my hand. Once he released me, I called over the waitress and said, "A round of shots—make them strong—and refills for whatever they're having." I pointed at Kendall and Charlize, so she would know who I was referring to.

"Skinny margaritas for both of us," Kendall told the waitress. She then looked at me. "Thank you. You really didn't have to do that, but we certainly appreciate it."

"What do you mean? We have something to celebrate tonight."

Her smile reached her eyes. "I'm still in total shock. I thought it would wear off or that the tequila would tame it a little." She shook her head. "But it hasn't. At all."

Covered in a deep red shine, her mouth was even more enticing than it had been when I was kissing her. Her teeth glowing behind her lips, white and sharp, made me wonder what part of me she would bite if I slipped my cock in her ass.

"How are things with Daisy?"

"Good Lord," Charlize moaned. "We need more cocktails for that conversation."

I saw how Charlize's admission affected Kendall, her excitement instantly dampening as she said, "I haven't spoken to her. I know her better than anyone, and talking about this now will get us nowhere. She needs time to cool off."

"But girlfriend has been texting her nonstop," Charlize said. "And calling."

"Is there anything I can do?"

The offer seemed valid. Both sisters were now clients. I was the reason Daisy was upset. If I hadn't brought Kendall into Brett's office, she would probably be in front of her computer, digitally smoothing the cellulite off Daisy's ass from her photo shoot today.

"No," she replied. "But it's so nice of you to offer, thank you."

"For the record, she's not the right fit for the show. I don't want her fighting with you over something that isn't even a possibility. If she's just plain old jealous of you, well, there's nothing I can do to change that."

But I understood it. Women could be catty bitches, and Kendall had it all over Daisy in every fucking category.

She glanced down, tucking her hair behind her ear, her breathing speeding up. When her eyes locked with mine again, I saw the stress and worry. "I'm going to talk to her tomorrow. Hopefully, it goes smoothly."

"My offer stands. If you need me to talk to her at any point, just let me know."

Brett's plane was fresh in my mind, but I couldn't stop looking at her, thinking about her body, dreaming about being inside of it.

My tongue wanted to lick every fucking inch of her skin.

"It's reassuring to know I have someone like you backing me," she said. "I mean, none of this would even be possible if it wasn't for you."

I finished my scotch, setting the empty on the table, wishing the glass were full of ice so I could cool my ass down. "You're the talent, Kendall. I just happened to run into you at the right time."

And taste you.

And feel the tightness of your cunt.

My thoughts were interrupted as the waitress appeared with our next round, dispersing the drinks across our group.

Once the shot was in my hand, I held it high in the air, the others doing the same.

"To the future," I said. "And to Kendall ..." I paused, my stare dipping to those glossy, fat lips that I wanted screaming my goddamn name. "On the path to making millions."

"Millions!" she gasped.

I swallowed the fiery cinnamon-flavored liquor. "I told you, this is only the beginning. Brett and I are going to make you so much fucking money."

She put her hand on her chest, like she was trying to slow her heart rate. "I honestly can't even wrap my head around that."

The movement sent me a wave of her scent, the tropical breeze I only smelled whenever I was vacationing on an island.

Or when I was near her.

Fuck me.

"It's going to happen, Kendall." I ran my hand down her arm, and goose bumps instantly followed my fingers, the sight causing a grin to spread across me. "You just have to say yes."

SEVEN

KENDALL

I couldn't remember the last time I had been so tipsy and had this much fun when I didn't have a to-do list five pages long in my hand, each item running nonstop loops through my brain. But as I shook my ass in the center of the dance floor—Charlize getting his groove on beside me, Dominick dancing in front of me—my mind was focused on only one thing.

My lawyer.

Charlize had found himself a hottie to boogie with, and Jenner was at a different table, talking to some women, leaving Dominick and me alone. Therefore, there was only one thing to do, and that was dance.

The DJ was spinning beats that were blasting through the speakers, the bass banging through each of my muscles. Whenever I twirled, causing my stare to break from Dominick's, I missed his eyes. I yearned for their intensity, for the heat of his palms that landed on a new part of me every time I faced him again.

There was something so deliciously enticing about that man.

The attraction had nothing to do with the skinny margaritas or the shots I'd taken. It was the look in his eyes that had me craving more of him, the feel of our bodies grinding together, like we were sticks starting a flame.

But he was my attorney.

And I was paying him a massive wage to negotiate a contract on my behalf. One that, twenty-four hours ago, would have seemed as possible as a rocket hitting me from outer space. The trajectory of my life was changing, and every time I tried to thank him, my words seemed too small. Far too simple. Not nearly heavy enough to express my gratitude, but that appreciation was all I had.

That was, unless I used my mouth in a different way, kissing him like I had last night.

Is that even appropriate?

I didn't know, so I just kept dancing.

Teasing.

Feeling his body pressed to mine, both of us moving to the rhythm of each song.

When my ass ground into the front of him, his grip moved to my stomach, pushing me harder against him. When I bent forward, his hands rose along my sides, stopping just below my breasts. And when I finally faced him again, his scorching gaze was on my nipples.

He made the air in the room turn thick, now impossibly difficult to take a deep breath.

Especially when he growled, "You're so fucking hot."

I wasn't just igniting a blaze between us; I was playing with fire.

I felt that in my chest.

I saw it in his eyes.

"That fucking ass ..." he hissed in my neck. "Keep rubbing

it against me, Kendall, and you're going to get my cock inside it."

Oh God.

I shuddered as my hands landed on his chest. I knew how defined it was—I remembered from last night. But the hardness of his muscles, the etching around his pecs, still made the tingles erupt.

He had a body unlike anything I'd ever felt before.

When it was covered in a suit, the first few inches of his stark white shirt unbuttoned to show the whisper of hairs on his chest, the scent of lust and spice flirting with my nose, he was completely irresistible.

To the point where I was overheating.

I needed air to calm myself down.

"Be right back," I told him, and I hurried toward the front and out the door, slipping into the alley between the buildings.

I leaned against the brick exterior, surveying my surroundings since this was a place I'd never been to before. Several people were gathered along the sidewalk, waiting in line to be let in, their conversations a dull murmur.

But here, I was alone, the cool evening hitting my skin, hoping that it would let me focus on something other than Dominick.

To help with that, I took out my phone. There were messages from Daisy that I hadn't read, ones that had come in since I'd last checked. She was getting angrier because I hadn't responded, my attempt at letting her settle only antagonizing her more.

I had to reply and somehow make this better. To let her know I wasn't abandoning her, that at the very least, I would always be here to manage her social media.

I just didn't know what to say.

THE LAWYER

I pulled up her schedule, seeing what time she was free tomorrow, and then I began to type.

> *Me: I'm not ignoring you. I was trying to let you cool off. You know I can't stand arguing, and that's all it would have led to if I'd replied. I'm sorry. I want to talk about this, so how about I swing by tomorrow at two?*
> *Daisy: Oh, the queen finally speaks. Negative seconds of fame, and you've already turned into a diva. So, that's the time that works best for you? I'm glad I can accommodate your busy schedule.*
> *Me: Actually, based on what you have going on tomorrow, that's the time that works best for you. See you then.*
> *Daisy: You'd better come ready to work. I have a growing list of things that you need to take care of since you completely bailed on me today.*

My fingers hovered over the screen, tempting a reply. But I wouldn't win this, so it wasn't even worth the effort. Some people had the ability to see all angles. My sister wasn't one even if I pleaded with her.

"Tell me you didn't come out here because of Daisy?" I heard from the mouth of the alley, causing me to look up, instantly meeting Dominick's eyes. "I know that's who you're texting. The same expression comes over your face every time her name is mentioned."

I put my phone away, taking a long, deep breath. "She's not the reason."

"Then, what is?"

I swallowed, lifting my shoulders off the wall to push my whole back against it. "I just needed a minute."

As he made his way over to me, his stare traveled to my chest, lowering again before gradually moving higher. "From me?" He stopped a few inches away. "From how badly you were turning me on?"

I couldn't think when I was around him.

I couldn't speak.

I couldn't do anything aside from feel how aroused I was.

"Do you know how fucking hard you made me on that dance floor?"

"I felt that ... yes." My exhale came out as a moan. "I didn't mean to."

His laugh sounded more like a roar. "You knew exactly what you were doing to me." He lifted his arm, his hand now pressed above my head.

"Dominick ..." I tried to inhale and couldn't. "You're my lawyer."

Is that even relevant?

Another question that went unanswered, my brain unable to process anything.

"Is that a problem?"

"I don't know. I don't think so."

His arm caged me in even tighter. "I assure you, it won't make a difference when my dick is inside you," he said against the outer edge of my ear, "when I'm making you come so hard that all you can do is scream."

My face tilted to the side, giving his lips more room, and I felt them lower to my collarbone.

"Let me see if our professional relationship really makes a difference to you."

I had no idea what that meant until he reached into the front of my pants, and I gasped from his touch. His hand dipped further until he was touching the most intimate part of me. I couldn't stop from moaning, the sensation of him far too strong to keep in.

"*Mmm,*" he breathed. "Just what I wanted." His mouth

rubbed across my cheek, like a cat weaving through legs. "Nice and fucking wet." When he lifted his hand out, there was a shimmer on his skin. He ran the slickness under his nose, taking in my scent. "Fuck me, you smell good."

The tingles had returned and were now exploding through my body, my back arching off the wall, as I was unable to stand still.

"Open your mouth, Kendall."

His demand vibrated through me.

It was as though I were a puppet and he held the strings, my body caving to his order.

The moment my lips parted, his finger was between them.

The one that had just rubbed my clit.

The one covered in me.

"Suck it."

I surrounded his skin.

"Like it's my cock."

I added pressure, swirling my tongue around the tip and down the sides.

He pressed his mouth to my ear. "Is that what you're going to do to my dick?" The grittiness in his voice caused my hips to almost buck.

I held his wrist, taking more of him in.

"You're going to deep-throat me?"

I didn't want to stop to answer, so I nodded, flicking my tongue around his nail and over his knuckle.

"My car is parked a block away." His other hand was suddenly on my butt, squeezing me through my leather pants. "Get your ass moving."

Me: I've been kidnapped by Dominick. The good kind of kidnapped, not the kind where you need to call 9 1 1. Ha-ha.
Charlize: Honey, you guys were practically fucking on the dance floor. If you hadn't gone home with him, I would have wondered if he was more into me. Have a blast, darling.
Me: Drinks again REALLY soon.
Charlize: Don't you worry, this is only the beginning for us.

EIGHT

DOMINICK

I pulled into my garage and turned off the car, the purring of the engine coming to an immediate halt. If I hadn't needed to shift, my fingers would have been inside Kendall's pussy the entire drive. She looked fucking gorgeous against my red leather seat. Those beautiful, long legs were crossed, but soon, they were going to be wrapped around me, her tits bouncing like when we'd gone over a bump.

"Get over here," I said when she attempted to get out.

I just needed a quick taste.

As she leaned in, I stuck out my tongue, and her lips immediately surrounded me, sucking it into her mouth. I gripped the back of her head, holding her against me as we kissed, her tropical scent even stronger now that we were this close.

I grabbed her nipple, brushing my thumb across it, adding more pressure as I rolled the tip between my fingers, listening to her moan louder with each pass.

"You should feel how wet I am now," she whispered, our mouths barely separated.

The way her body responded to me was such a fucking turn-on.

"You're teasing me again, Kendall." The thought of sinking into that snug, warm pussy made me bark, "Get out of the car."

I met her by the trunk and held the small of her back as I led her inside and down the hallway into the main living space.

"My God, Dominick," she said the moment I turned on the lights. "Your house is absolutely stunning."

As she tilted her head back, looking at the beams that spanned across the tall ceiling, I kissed up to her ear and across the other side of her neck.

"Your lips," she groaned, fisting my hair from the roots, "are lethal."

I traced the tops of her tits. "So is your pussy." I lifted her into the air and set her ass on the island in the kitchen, spreading her legs wide enough to fit in between. "I'd offer you a margarita, but I'd have to pause what I'm about to do to you, and I don't think I can."

I pulled her tank top over her head, exposing those perfect tits, and drew one of her nipples into my mouth. "*Mmm.*" I tugged on the hardness. "I could suck on these all night."

I licked the edge, circling the rim, flicking the tip back and forth before gently scraping my teeth across it.

"Oh fuck." She pulled my hair even harder, her ass moving against the counter as though she were on top of me.

I massaged her thighs and over to her hips. "Someone needs my cock."

"Now, you're teasing me."

I moved to her other tit, instantly biting down on the base of her nipple, flicking the front with the end of my tongue.

"Oh God, I can't take it." I felt the moan rock through her body. "Dominick, I need you."

She tore at my belt and ripped at my shirt, pulling most of

the clothing from my body. Buttons popped off as she yanked at them, the plastic pinging as it hit the floor, followed by the sound of my shirt and pants as they dropped. I slid out of my shoes and socks, my boxer briefs the only thing left.

"This body ..." She felt across my chest and abs. "I can't get over it."

"It's a good thing you showed up to the bar tonight."

"Why?"

"Because you wouldn't have gotten it if you hadn't been there."

I peeled the leather down her legs, stopping at her heels, appreciating their spikes before I removed them, and she sat, naked before me.

I leaned back to admire her. "Fuck me." I shook my head as I took her all in.

"Wow." She laughed. "You're really something else, Dominick Dalton."

I slowly gazed up to meet her eyes. "Why do you say that?"

"Because you had no intention of calling me, did you?" As I went to answer, she added, "Don't tell me yet." She reached under the band of my boxers, circling my crown with her palm. "I want this first." She pumped me several times, base to peak.

"Greedy fucking girl," I breathed in her ear.

"I just can't get enough of you." She leaned down, surrounding my tip with her lips. "Doesn't look like you're complaining about it."

I hissed as she sucked the crown, stroking the bottom of my shaft, palming my balls.

"Goddamn it."

I pushed her head lower to take more of me in. But she stayed at the top, pumping the rest with her fist, sucking away like a fucking vacuum. Every few dips, she went a little further, taking her time, hitting me at every angle.

Her relentlessness caused me to roar, "Fuck, Kendall."

While she bobbed, I moved her legs apart and reached between them, wetness instantly hitting my fingers. Her breathing increased as I touched her, every exhale vibrating against my cock, the soft moans in her throat doing the same.

She moved her hips closer to me, as though that would hurry my movements.

But she knew this game.

We were on my pace now.

I swept my thumb across her clit, giving her a quick taste, and then traced up and down her thighs, her skin burning as I neared her pussy.

I repositioned her onto her side to give me more access, and the more time I spent on her legs, the more that tight, sopping pussy taunted me.

Her hips jerked forward the moment I grazed her clit again. She needed the pressure, and to urge me on, she sucked even harder. My head leaned back as I enjoyed the suction, every lick and twist of her wrist.

She'd earned herself two fingers, and they dived right into her.

She dripped down my skin as I slid in, and I pulled out to give her more friction, making her miss the fullness before I plunged in again. I arched my hand, hitting her G-spot, rubbing across that sensitive, small area.

She pulled her mouth away and shouted, "Dominick," before she lowered as far as she could go, pumping the remainder with her hand.

"That's it." I gave her a third finger, lost in fucking pleasure. "Suck me."

Her speed increased, her moaning turned louder, my balls clenching, threatening to peak at any second.

I wanted to come in her mouth. There was no fucking

question about that. I wanted to bust between those lips, filling her tongue with my cum, watching her swallow the load down her goddamn throat.

But in this moment, my need to be in her pussy was stronger.

I pulled my dick out, my fingers leaving her next, and I lifted her off the counter. "You're coming with me."

Her legs circled my waist, her arms resting on my shoulders as I carried her to my bedroom. I set her on the edge of the mattress while I got a condom from my nightstand.

Before I put it on, I aimed my tip at her lips. "Lick it again." She went to surround my crown, and I stopped her. "Just lick it."

A smile came across her mouth, her tongue then slowly sticking out to graze across me, past the mushroom bulge and down the center vein.

I fucking throbbed.

Pulsed.

Raged from the torment.

She made eye contact as she got near my balls, and I couldn't take another second.

I tore open the condom, rolling it over me, and climbed on the bed.

I didn't continue the tease.

I didn't take it slow.

I thrust straight inside her before rearing my hips back to go in for another dip.

"Yes!" she yelled, digging her nails into me.

The same word repeated in my head over and over as her pussy squeezed me, her tightness rewarding me for waiting so long, her wetness the best fucking present.

I balanced on my knees, holding her legs apart, driving into her repeatedly. I twisted my hips when I was all the way in, staying plunged, listening to her moan in pleasure.

"Kendall ... fuck."

Her slickness soaked me while she closed in around my cock, her pussy narrowing more with each thrust. When this position started feeling far too good, I moved her onto her side, getting in behind her, and wrapped my arm around her navel, touching her clit at the same time.

She quivered the moment I brushed across her. "Oh God. Yes."

"You like that?"

I slowed my strokes, the speed emphasizing every inch of me. Once I was all the way in, I lifted her hips up and moved mine down, giving her new angles and a different sensation.

"Dominick ..." Her nails stabbed the outside of my thigh. "Whatever you do, don't fucking stop."

I knew why.

I could feel it.

I could fucking hear it.

Concentrating on her clit, I took her earlobe into my mouth, holding it with my teeth as I deepened my acceleration. She was screaming after every plunge, breathing like she was desperate for air.

And just when I sensed she was nearing that edge, I went even faster.

"Dominick!" She dragged out each syllable, turning my name into a moan, her stomach exploding in shudders. Her back arched, her clit hardened, her wetness thickened as I fucked her through each wave of pleasure.

"*Ahhh*," she released. "*Yesss.*"

She was pulsing around my cock, the feeling nagging at my own orgasm.

I slowed until she stopped convulsing, giving her a second

to find herself, and then I rolled her on top of me. With my back flat on the mattress, she straddled my waist.

"Now, you're going to come again."

She sighed, searching for her breath. "I don't know if I can."

I swiped her clit. "Don't ever say those words to me."

She bucked against my hand when I flicked the same spot.

"Kendall, you're going to come." I circled her with my thumb. "And then you're going to come again after I carry you into the shower."

Her palms pressed against my chest, and she lifted her hips, rising to my tip and gradually dropping to my base. I could tell she was still extremely sensitive, but that didn't change how she was making me feel. Fisting her tits, my thumbs running over her nipples, I ground my head into the pillow.

Her cunt was being naughty.

"Goddamn it, Kendall." I hissed out a lungful of air. "You're so fucking tight."

She wasn't pumping me with a heavy rush; she was drawing out the sensations, deliberately teasing me, testing my orgasm. If she kept up this pressure, twisting her hips after each bounce to give my cock that extra grind, she was going to get what she wanted.

My fingers bit into her thighs, rocking her body forward and back before I found her clit, resuming the flicking.

"*Ohhh*," she groaned, her eyes closing.

Each brush across that spot seemed to encourage her more, building her strength and momentum. I was feeding her, and she was responding in speed.

"Kendall ..." I used her wetness to coat my fingers. "Fuck ..." I was getting lost. Far too gone to come back. "That's it."

She fucked with passion. Intensity. A purpose, like making me come was the only thing she wanted in this world. She swung her body, focusing on the pressure of each movement, and she reached behind her ass to tickle my balls.

Her pussy slapped against my lower stomach each time she buried my dick, her dives demanding my orgasm. The ricochets caused her tits to bounce. Following every jab came a moan from her throat that tugged at the spasms inside me.

The combination was doing me in.

"Your cock"—she gasped, dancing across my lap, like we were still at the bar—"is so fucking perfect."

I had seconds left.

"Come." I grazed her clit. "Right now, Kendall."

Her eyes connected with mine, and I leaned up on my elbow and reached behind her. I gathered some of the wetness from her cunt, making sure my fingers were slick, and I stuck one in her ass.

No warning.

Just a place I needed to feel as I came.

"Dominick!" She ground against me even faster, using more power in her thrusts. "*Yesss.*"

Her hips tilted as my balls clenched, an intense surge moving through me.

"Kendall!" I lost control as her cunt milked me. "Oh, fuck yes."

She was moaning just as loud, her nails stabbing me, her body shaking with tremors.

As I shot into the rubber, she was tightening around my finger, bucking, taking my cock on a wild fucking ride that sucked every drop of cum out of me.

When she finally stilled, I pulled my finger out and held her hips steady.

"You ..." I shook my head, pressing my forehead against her tit, her nipple teasing my nose. "You're something else." I looked up to see her smile. "I can't help it. You're addictive."

So was her pussy.

Intoxicating in a way I'd never felt.

And my cock hadn't even dipped into her ass yet. I couldn't imagine what that would feel like.

Fuck.

I held her cheeks, aiming her stare at mine, the most gorgeous face before me.

Her whole life was on the verge of changing, and I was positive she had no idea what she was in for. Constant attention was soon on its way—paparazzi recognizing her wherever she went, endorsements coming in, invitations to exclusive events, and paid appearances.

Nights, where there was nothing on her schedule, like this evening, were going to be rare.

Brett was wrong.

Kendall Roy couldn't be my forever.

I had no fucking interest in living that kind of lifestyle. I thrived off privacy. In front of the camera and on every celebrity gossip site was the last place I wanted to be.

But tonight, she was mine, and everything was perfect.

NINE

KENDALL

As I stood at Daisy's front door, I debated on whether I should use my key and personal code to walk in, the same way I always entered her home. But something about that just didn't feel right today, so I rang the doorbell. Her house was quite large, but it certainly didn't take minutes to walk to the door, which was the amount of time I'd been waiting.

She was doing this on purpose.

I wasn't even surprised.

When she eventually arrived, she stood in the entryway with her hand high on the doorframe, blocking me from entering and staring at me as though she were about to perform facial surgery.

I extended my arm in her direction, holding the cup of Starbucks. "Skinny, extra hot, a small squirt of nonfat whip, and half a pump of vanilla. Just like you like it."

She rolled her eyes, taking the coffee from me, and turned her back toward me to head for the living room.

I followed her inside, shutting the door behind me, and took a seat across from her on the large sectional. "Daisy ..."

"No." She shook her head. "Don't you *Daisy* me. You straight-up ignored me for over twelve hours after the meeting at The Agency. You didn't answer a single one of my texts or phone calls. What kind of sister-slash-assistant are you?"

My head dropped, and I stared at the top of the coffee table, where there was a pile of hardcovers about cities in Europe—places Daisy had never even been to, nor did she care about them. "You're right. I deserved that. But my intention wasn't to hurt you or make you feel ignored. I just wanted you to have some time to cool off—that's all." I glanced back up at her. "Time away from me, so both of our emotions could settle."

"Do you think my emotions were going to settle once I found out what show you're going to be on?" She grinned, but it wasn't out of happiness. "That I had to hear it from my team and not you?"

"I haven't signed the contract yet."

She leaned on the pillow next to her, throwing her legs over the end of the couch. "Please. You're on the verge. You're probably just demanding more money, and that's what is holding up the signing." Her lids narrowed. "So, let's spell this all out, shall we? You landed Brett fucking Young, my unicorn agent; Valerie Spears, the leading manager at his agency; and Dominick Dalton, *my* attorney." Her voice was getting louder by the second. "If you wanted to be me, then why didn't you say that when you moved out here? We could have skipped the whole assistant part, and I could have just handed you my life." She sighed in disgust. "Seriously, Kendall, what the fuck?"

I stared at my sister. Someone who had competed with me since I was a child.

Except it had never been a competition—at least, not in my eyes.

We were on completely different paths.

Daisy, the popular cheerleader, the center of attention, who had dated only athletes—and there had been handfuls of them. She had so many friends that she barely knew most of their names, and instead of going to college, she'd moved to LA and immediately begun auditioning for roles.

I had been the artsy kid, a paintbrush or colored pencil always somewhere in my hair, with only a handful of close friends before earning a bachelor of arts in graphic design from Northeastern. There hadn't been many relationships in my past, but the ones I'd had lasted for years—distance usually the cause of our breakup—and it would take me months and months before I could even consider moving on.

Our last name, childhood home, and our family were the only similarities.

I did me.

Daisy did her.

But that wasn't the way she saw it.

"We both know that isn't what this is about," I started, taking a long, deep breath. "I have no desire to have your life or steal anything from you. I was offered a job, and I'm considering it." I set down my coffee, the idea of drinking something warm and caffeinated making my stomach churn. "Why don't you tell me what's really bothering you?"

Her gaze was practically penetrating me. "This is about you, Kendall. You came here to make my world easier, and one of the first things you did was try to outshine me. That meeting was about me. That team—Brett, Valerie—they were supposed to eventually be mine. The TV audience I've gained is in love with me, and now, once again, I'm going to be compared to you." She crossed her arms over her chest. "This was the one thing I never had to share with you, and now, here we are. Shocker."

I hugged my arms around one of the many throw pillows. "What are you talking about?"

"You're the one everyone was always proud of, the one who crushed every goal that had been set for you, the one everyone cheered for. No one gave a shit about me. No one showed up for me. No one had any high hopes for me. It was you, you, and fucking you." She pushed herself to the edge of the couch. "But I came out here, and I made a name for myself. Suddenly, people started taking me seriously." Her lips were moving so fast that I could barely keep up. "I finally got the attention and credit owed to me, and now, this happens."

Memories from our younger years were swirling through my head—snapshots of holidays, trips, contests at school, events. How could she think this?

"That's not true, Daisy."

"No?" She glared at me. "You should see things from my side. It looks much different than your distorted reality."

"I'm not trying to take anything away from you. I'm an equal. I'm not superior in any way."

"Tell that to the bloggers when they're posting our pictures side by side, when the tabloids get wind that you'll be joining a competing show. You're going to be the hot, new, young blood, and they're going to forget about me."

She lifted a magazine from the end table and tossed it next to my coffee for me to see—a cover that had Beyoncé on it. "Do you see Solange in that photo? Do you ever see her?" Before I could respond, she added, "I didn't think so. It's always Paris, never Nicky Hilton. Kim, never Khloé Kardashian. Kate Middleton because no one gives a shit about Pippa. One sister continuously shines brighter, Kendall, and I'm telling you right now, I haven't worked this hard to have you sparkle like a fucking diamond."

I couldn't believe what I was hearing.

I couldn't believe she wasn't able to see the love and support she had received when she was growing up, the words of encouragement, the praise, the accomplishments. That she was blind and deaf to all of it because she was so focused on my light.

"I'm sorry you feel that way." I held the pillow so tightly against me that it was making it hard for me to breathe.

"Then, do something about it. Turn down the role."

I sighed, the hurt eating at my chest. "You know, it's really sad that you think this is about winning. That we can't be in the same space and build each other up."

"It doesn't work that way. Not in Hollywood." She laughed like Cruella. "Hell, not in life."

I set the pillow aside, crossing my hands between my legs. "Why did you have me come out here? If you wanted things separate, then why bring me into your world?"

"You were barely making your rent, sharing an apartment with three roommates, with not even enough money to buy yourself a skinny margarita after a twelve-hour workday. My financial advisor said I needed to be more charitable, so instead of donating to the food bank, I contributed to you."

God, she was such a bitch.

She couldn't even admit she needed my help. It would pain her to say those words.

But she wanted me to tell her I wasn't going to take the job, that I would stay on as her assistant.

As if that request were even fair.

My sister couldn't see past her ego—that was what this conversation was really about.

"What happens if I take the role?"

Her teeth ground together, her jaw flexing as she stared at me. "You wouldn't dare."

"Answer the question, sister."

My entire body shook as I waited.

She gazed at me for what felt like minutes and finally

replied, "There would be no reason for me to ever talk to you again."

My sister. My blood. Someone I'd shared my entire life with was willing to give it all up over something this ridiculous.

In the past, I would have caved. I would have avoided the controversy and done exactly what she wanted because I always backed down to her.

She would never change.

I didn't care what Thanksgiving was going to look like when we were sitting around my parents' table or Christmas when we were cozied up in front of their fire—traditions we made happen every year.

I had to get to the point where I wouldn't tolerate her behavior anymore even if that meant upsetting my parents, altering our family dynamic forever.

She looked at her nails, assessing them like she would ever allow a chip. "You know, all you're doing is delaying how much work you need to finish before you go home. I have six videos you need to edit, the pool shots from yesterday still need retouching, and you need to take some photos of me using a new mascara I'm endorsing. The fact that you're stalling makes me want to dock your pay. For real, Kendall, what the fuck?"

I'd reached the point.

I was done with this bullshit.

And I was done listening to it.

I pushed myself up from the couch. "No."

Her eyes followed me around the coffee table. "No to what?"

"To everything." I stood by the oversize chair, remembering how she'd sent it back last week because the fabric wasn't white enough. "No to your attitude, to your insane demands. To you asking me to turn down the job offer." I shoved my hands into the pockets of my jeans to stop them from trembling. "Just know that *you* did this, Daisy. Not me."

I swore there was smoke leaving her mouth with every breath that she took.

"Your little tirade back there was to make me feel bad for you. To make me cower, like I always do when it comes to you. Well, no more. I'm done."

Anger shot across her face. "You're that fucking greedy for stardom?" She shook her head. "Wow. I thought I knew you better than that."

"This has nothing to do with that, and we both know it."

She relaxed into the couch, like she was Tony goddamn Soprano. "Oh, sister, don't even think of dropping my name to help you gain popularity. You're all alone out here now, and I promise I won't do a thing to help you."

"I don't need your help." I took several steps back. "In fact, that's the last thing I need."

I left my coffee for her to throw away and headed toward the front door.

"You're fired!" she yelled as I reached the kitchen. "And don't expect to be paid for any of the half-assed work you've done this week. The last check you got from me is the only money you'll ever see from my checkbook."

I glanced over my shoulder, laughing loudly, making sure our eyes were locked when I said, "Trust me, I don't need it."

TEN

DOMINICK

There was absolutely no reason I needed to haul Kendall and her manager, Valerie, into my office to discuss the details of her contract. Everything I had to tell them could have taken place over the phone. But the thought of seeing that fucking body again—those lips puckered around the straw of an iced coffee, those beautiful hips and ass wrapped in a tight dress—was far too tempting.

At least with her manager here, I couldn't swipe away the paperwork on my desk and fuck her on top of it. But it was all I'd been thinking about since the moment she had sat down.

Damn it, this was a tease.

I just wanted a whiff of her pussy.

A quick lick across her clit.

To feel her cunt clench around my cock.

Kendall Roy was worse than an addiction because this need, this fucking ache, couldn't be cured. The two nights I'd had her wasn't enough. And no matter where I tried to put my brain, it always went back to her.

Like now, as I visually fucked her in that navy dress.

I shook my head and glanced down at the contract, knowing it was time to get down to business.

"The requirements of this one are simple as far as reality television standards are concerned. You're required to be present during set filming times, which could be up to fifty or sixty hours a week. The location will be determined by the studio forty-eight hours prior." I pointed at the next section of paragraphs in case she wanted to follow along with her copy. "The studio will provide transportation to the locations, and they're very specific about punctuality. There's a clause that allows them to fine you if you're over fifteen minutes late."

"I'm punctual," Kendall said, the embarrassment on her face coming in red and hot. "That was a one-time thing; it's not my norm."

"No judgment here." There was also no reason for her to defend herself, but instead of telling her that, I said, "If the scene you're shooting is sponsored by a brand—whether it's clothing, beverages, sunglasses, whatever—you're required to use or wear the products for the duration of filming. There will be times when the studio will provide you with social media materials about the show or sponsored products, and it's mandatory you post that content within a certain period."

"All very standard, as Dominick said," Valerie added. "You'll soon be hired for personal endorsements, and the same rules will apply." She smiled at Kendall. "Do you have any concerns so far?"

Kendall gathered all her hair together and rested it over the side of her shoulder, running her fingers through it. "It all seems pretty straightforward. Attend filming, be on time, post when they need me to."

"Easy enough, right?" Valerie pushed.

My eyes didn't leave Kendall.

I wanted to pull those silky, long locks and feel them tickle my chest as she kissed her way down my body toward my cock.

I cleared my throat, my focus returning to the paperwork. "During the next three months of filming, they're going to put you up in an apartment. You're not required to sleep there, but your things need to be moved in, and it must appear as though it's your primary residence. During the hours of nine a.m. to ten p.m., the cameras will be recording. The footage can be used at their discretion—you have no say in their editing. Therefore, they can take dialogue out of context, or they can manipulate the sequence of conversations, presenting things in ways that weren't originally intended." I glanced up. "And you can't sue them for that."

Kendall was now gripping her purse, pulling it closer against her body. "I need to be extremely careful with what I say. At all times. Jeez."

"Even when you're under the influence," Valerie told her. "Which will be a majority of the scenes."

Kendall's gaze deepened. "What if someone comes to the apartment, say a friend who's not associated with the show? Will their visit appear on camera?"

"Yes." I released a long exhale. That was the reason why I would never be stepping foot in that apartment once filming began. "But they must sign a waiver before they enter. If they don't sign it, you can't allow them in."

"They're not giving me a lot of privacy ... are they?" Her voice softened.

"Legally, they can't show you naked or wearing anything less than a towel or bathing suit. However, they will show footage of you in bed—alone or not—during the set filming hours."

She glanced at her manager and then back to me. "Can we negotiate these terms?"

"No." I closed the folder that contained the contract and moved it to the side of my desk. "Once you have some clout, a solid and loyal following, I can ask for anything on your behalf. Until then, it's their rules."

Valerie rested her fingers on Kendall's arm, the one that was wrapped around her stomach. "I know this feels like a lot, and it's overwhelming to hear all of these rules at once, especially given that you're still feeling a bit raw from your argument with Daisy—"

"What argument with Daisy?" I asked.

Both women looked at me before Valerie said, "But once you start filming, these obstacles will feel like second nature. You'll be in the thick of it, you'll find a groove, and it will all feel very natural to you."

My teeth ground together as I stared at Kendall. "What happened with Daisy?" I repeated.

"We talked."

"And?"

Her legs crossed in the opposite direction they had been resting in, and she adjusted her dress to accommodate the new position. "She doesn't want me doing this. She thinks we'll be compared and that the viewers will like me more and she'll lose everything." When our eyes locked, I immediately saw pain. "If I sign the contract, she wants nothing to do with me."

Jealousy was a disgusting trait on a woman.

"How do you feel about that?"

She took several deep breaths. "I don't think she's right. The viewers have put her on a pedestal, and they bow down to everything she says and does. They're obsessed with her. Me coming onto the scene isn't going to change that, certainly not when I'm just trying to share the screen with her, not trying to one-up her." She paused, the hurt even more present. "There's room for both of us—I believe that in my heart. Losing my sister isn't what I wanted."

Valerie's hand went to Kendall's shoulder, getting lost in her nest of hair. "We talked about this in great detail this morning." Valerie's stare moved to me. "We don't think it would have mattered if Kendall hadn't taken the job or not; Daisy would have punished her about something else, and the cycle would have continued to repeat. Daisy needs to work on herself. This outburst has nothing to do with Kendall or her decision."

"I hope you know that's true," I said to Kendall.

"I do." Her throat bobbed as she swallowed. "It just doesn't feel good."

"This might make you feel a little better ..." I reached inside the folder, grabbed the page that showed the breakdown of her salary, and held it out to her. "We got you the twenty percent raise."

Several deep exhales later, she gazed up from the paper and said, "You guys are good."

There wasn't excitement in her voice, and I knew that was due to Daisy. Her sister was ruining this moment for her, and something inside me wanted to fix it, but I couldn't speak as freely with Valerie in the room.

I looked at Valerie and said, "Can I have a minute alone with Kendall?"

She stood from her seat. "Of course. I'll be right outside."

I waited until the door shut before I said, "Are you all right?"

She shrugged. "Sorta."

"Are you having second thoughts?"

I watched her think about my question, the different waves of emotions crossing her face.

Each one made her more gorgeous.

"No, like Valerie said, it wouldn't matter what I did; Daisy would find fault in it. I honestly believe I can't make that girl happy. If I didn't touch up her photos enough, she thought I was trying to make her look fat. If I didn't post for her frequently enough, she thought I was trying to sabotage her social media presence. If I didn't drive fast enough, she thought I was purposely trying to make her late." The look that passed through her face told me she'd spent some time thinking about this. And she was drained—from all of it. "I just have to live my own life and not spend it trying to please my sister."

"You know, I've seen my fair share of women like Daisy, and you're right about everything. The only sensible option is to focus on you. Whether it's showing the world how much of a sweetheart you are or raising awareness on volunteering and art therapy, you're going to find your voice, and you're going to make a difference in your own way."

Her eyes finally softened, and it wasn't out of sadness. "That's all I want."

"We're going to make it happen."

She released a small breath, the ends of her lips lifting. "We?"

"Listen ..." I leaned onto my desk, crossing my hands over the top. "I want to let you in on something you're probably not aware of, something that's not listed in your contract. The production assistants are paid to dig up dirt. They release it to the media in hopes that it will build buzz and momentum prior to the show being aired. The more drama they reveal, the higher the ratings and viewers and ad dollars. It's all part of their marketing."

Her grin grew, reaching as high as her eyes, a sight I was elated to see.

"So, you're saying you're not going to fuck me on the wall of my apartment?"

I laughed.

She only cursed when my dick was inside her, and each occasion made me growl.

This time was no exception.

"Once you start filming, you're going to be so busy that you're not going to have time to think about my cock."

Her eyelids narrowed. "Is that your way of ending things between us, or do you really believe my schedule is going to be an issue for us?" When she shifted her legs again, her dress rode up to her mid-thigh, and she made no effort to lower it. "Because I'm the kind of girl who can work sixty hours a week and find the hours to volunteer and run five miles a day and have drinks with girlfriends and stop by the studio to paint. I know how to juggle, whether it be jobs or balls—I've got both covered."

She was quick with her mouth.

Another reason she was fucking perfect for this show.

But it was a mouth that also sucked cock like I'd never felt before, and that was what was on my mind right now.

Damn it.

I lifted the folder from my desk—a copy that had my notes and legal definitions written in the margins to help her understand the difficult jargon, unlike the version she had—and I handed it to her. "You have twenty-four hours before this needs to be signed. Take it and get out of here before I spank you so fucking hard that you see stars."

She stood, giving me another angle of that goddamn body and how breathtaking it looked in her dress. "You don't scare me, Dominick. Your threats. Your attention. Your warnings. I'm ready for all of it." She tucked the manila folder under her arm and flattened her palms on my desk, leaning in close to me. "In fact, all it does is make me wetter." She headed for the door, and when her fingers were on the knob, she looked over her shoulder and said, "I'll be back tomorrow to drop off the signed contract."

She didn't say another word.

Except after she was gone, I noticed she'd left one thing behind.

Her scent.

And I was going to smell it all fucking day long.

ELEVEN

KENDALL

Me: Well, it's official. I'm a cast member of Glitzy Girls. I'm holding the signed contract in my hands right now. Insert every excited and terrified emoji. Gah!

Charlize: Hell fucking yes, girlfriend! The world is going to eat you up. You're going to be instafamous in seconds, just you wait. When do we celebrate? I'm ready to shake my sexy ass.

Me: Filming doesn't start for two weeks, and I was fired from my prior job, so ... yeah, any night works for me.

Charlize: That monster.

Me: It's for the better. I keep telling myself that.

Charlize: You're a far nicer person than me. Anyway, fuck her. I'm so happy for you. Like screaming-at-the-top-of-my-lungs kinda happy. Thursday night, I'm coming over and doing your glam, and then we're going out. Drinks, food, more drinks—and no kidnapping by hottie lawyers.

Me: I saw the makeup you did on J. Lo last night for that awards show. The shots you posted on Instagram were stunning, Charlize. You're so incredibly talented. I can't believe you're even willing to glam me up. From J. Lo to little ol' me. Good Lord.

Charlize: Stop! You've got one hell of a canvas to work with, honey. We're going to have so much fun. I'm off to a photo shoot. Kisses.

It was past seven in the evening when I walked into Dominick's downtown office, the time he'd asked me to come in when I texted him this morning about this meeting. I hadn't expected him to have any earlier openings—my research had told me he was the most sought-after entertainment lawyer in California.

When I reached the receptionist's desk in the center of the fancy, large lobby, she greeted me with, "Hello, Miss Roy. Mr. Dalton is expecting you." She pointed at the bank of elevators. "Top floor, last door on the right, in case you've forgotten."

"I appreciate it."

Remembering the journey Valerie and I had taken when we came here yesterday, I exited the elevator at the highest floor and walked down the hallway. As I reached the closed door at the end, I took a few deep breaths before I knocked. I didn't know why, but Dominick still made me so breathless whenever I was around him.

"Come in," he said from the other side of the wood the moment my fingers lowered to the handle.

Once I stepped in, I immediately felt his eyes on my body, the intensity of his stare making my insides tingle.

"What's that?" He nodded toward the cooler hanging on my shoulder, the one I set on an empty chair, taking a seat beside it.

"It's dinner."

He continued to stare at me, reclining against the tall leather high-back, his arms crossing, looking so sexy in his dark gray suit and black tie, the start of a shadow appearing on his cheeks.

"And drinks."

A smile came across his beautiful mouth. "How do you know I don't already have dinner plans?"

The signed contract was underneath my arm, and I placed it on his desk. "I don't, but I'm happy to eat alone in here if that's the case." I opened the cooler and took out two beers, twisting off the caps before I handed him one. "Homemade burritos, guacamole, and salsa. The only thing I didn't cook were the chips." I chewed the corner of my lip before I added, "Tempted, or are you going to pass?"

He clinked his beer against mine and took a sip. "You're extremely persuasive, Miss Roy."

I laughed as I reached inside the cooler again, removing the two dips and the large bag of chips along with the foil-wrapped burritos, setting it all up between us.

He opened the top of the foil, the tortilla almost at his mouth. "Thank you for doing this."

"No bother. I love to cook."

He took a bite, his expression telling me he was savoring it. "Damn it, Kendall. I had no idea what to expect, but it certainly wasn't this." He looked at the burrito as though he'd never seen one before. "This is excellent." He dipped a chip into the guac. "*Mmm*, this is too." He swallowed, washing it down with beer. "You really made this?"

"My talents extend beyond art ... and my mouth. Don't look so surprised."

He chuckled. "You're quick. I like that about you."

"I'm trying to win you over with something other than my pussy."

His stare deepened, a more serious look now crossing his cheeks. "Is that so?" He stilled, the moments ticking away. "Tell me, what is it that you're looking for?" He pulled out a napkin from his drawer, handing me one as well, and used his to wipe his mouth.

I swallowed the bite I'd taken. "More."

"And that is?"

There was no reason to hold it in. I was positive he could see the words before I even said them. If I wanted this to move forward, I obviously needed to be the one to take the first step because I still didn't know if he'd ever planned to call me, and I feared what his answer would be.

"I like the way I feel when I'm with you, Dominick. I like waking up in your bed. I like how I can go from smiling my hardest to dripping wet. So, time, overnights, a commitment—that would be more."

"A relationship."

When he drained the rest of his beer, I got out another from the cooler and gave it to him. "Eventually, yes. Is that something you're opposed to?"

"Kendall ..." He finished chewing the bite and set down his burrito. "Your world is about to become extremely public in ways I can't even describe. Despite offering legal counsel to an array of celebrities, that's not the lifestyle I want. I don't want my personal business blasted all over social media."

"I wouldn't out you, or us, or post pictures of us together—if that's what you're referring to."

His grin wasn't reassuring, especially when he shook his head. "If you hit the level of fame Brett and I are predicting, you won't have to out us. Those pictures will appear online without your knowledge or approval."

I'd seen that happen to Daisy. One of my daily tasks had been to send her the photos that had been posted of her and filter her Google alerts of spreading fake news. When Daisy was rumored to be dating someone, the speculation became almost like an online war, the different outlets vying for the first shot.

I knew what he was talking about.

I just hadn't anticipated this happening to me or affecting my future this way.

"I guess it would be easier if I could walk out of your office and you never had to see me again. But being that you're my lawyer, we're going to be spending much more time together."

"No, you have that wrong." His eyes dipped to my chest, a gaze that was smoldering. "Having you walk out forever would be a real shame."

The icy, sweating glass did nothing to cool down my fiery skin.

"It sounds to me like you're willing to let me slip through your fingers than brave the social media storm."

"Kendall ..."

I'd put my cards on the table along with homemade burritos, guacamole, and salsa.

If he wasn't going to bite, then I was going to show him what he was missing.

"It's all right. I understand. You said the show is going to change things for me, and I'm already getting a sense of that. I'm going to meet so many different walks of life." I winked. "It's best that I go into it unattached and very open-minded."

He ran the napkin over his mouth, a feral look building in his eyes.

I broke our gaze to lift my vibrating phone out of my back pocket. Normally, I would ignore the text, but the timing suddenly felt perfect.

Charlize: I thought the photo shoot was going to last all night, but I'm out and free. I know I said Thursday, but I could definitely use a cocktail. Or seven. You too? Wanna meet?

As I glanced at Dominick, a smile crept over my face. "Looks like those opportunities are already presenting themselves." I collected my beer and the rest of my burrito, and I stood with the cooler on my arm. "Have yourself a good evening, Dominick."

"You're leaving?"

I nodded. "I have plans." When I reached the door, I turned around, filling my lungs with air before I said, "And to think ... I was going to give you one hell of a dessert tonight." My smile still lingered as I closed the door behind me, especially knowing his eyes had been on my ass and I was wearing the tightest jeans I owned.

TWELVE

DOMINICK

"That one," my youngest brother, Ford, said, pointing at a chick on the other side of the bar.

She had tits the size of my fucking head, more makeup on her face than the counter of a goddamn department store.

He knew me better than that.

I took a sip of my whiskey and replied, "No fucking way. She does nothing for me."

"Does she need to?" Jenner asked. "She'll just be a quick fuck for the night." He set down his drink to get a better look at her. "Have you lost your mind? She's smoking."

"Dominick hasn't gotten laid in over a week," Ford said. "You know this is how he gets when he hasn't had pussy. Like a lost fucking bird who can't find his way south."

I wasn't lost.

I knew exactly what I wanted.

What I craved.

Who I needed to pull me out of this rut.

And she was going to be at this bar tonight.

During my meeting with Brett this afternoon, he'd

reminded me that Kendall wouldn't begin filming for another week. Tonight was an obligatory meetup with the crew, so the girls could work on their chemistry and interactions, and the viewers would believe they were actually friends in real life.

In my gut, I had known coming here was the worst fucking idea.

It would do nothing but tease me.

But I just needed to put my eyes on her.

Every time I tried to think of someone else, her body would come into my mind. The sensation of her lips would pass across my skin. I would see the smile that had lit up her face when she sat on the other side of my desk, her mouth full of the burrito she had made for us.

A dinner I had ruined.

Goddamn it, Kendall was a good girl.

Normally, I didn't do good. I found bad and naughty, who didn't give a shit about what happened past the morning, an orgasm the only thing we were both after.

But not Kendall.

She wanted ... more.

Something I'd always avoided, which was why I couldn't understand the reason I was still taunting myself with her. Why thoughts of her were eating away at me. Why the need to see her was consuming me.

"That one," Jenner said, nodding toward the table across from us, where two chicks were eye-fucking my brothers and me.

"Hell no." I glanced at Jenner. "The ginger is not my type, and the other is an old client."

"How old?" Ford asked.

"Not old enough." I twirled my glass over the tabletop. "She switched law firms when my assistant walked in on her and Jeffrey fucking in the copy room."

"Jeffrey, your paralegal?" Ford asked.

I nodded.

"She couldn't hook the lawyer, so she went for the next best thing. Maybe it's time to nibble on her bait," Ford said.

"Jesus." I shook my head, the two of them fucking relentless. I'd heard enough. I got up from the table and said, "I need a drink."

Jenner tapped the edge of my glass. "You have one."

"I need something stronger."

I headed for the bar, where I spotted a vacant seat at the end. Once my ass was planted, without my brothers breathing down my neck, I took a quick scan of the room. Beautiful women were everywhere. That was what this place was known for—a meat factory for singles. But, fuck me, there wasn't a girl in sight who did anything for me, who would make me approach her and cage her with my arms, like I'd done to Kendall on the rooftop of the hotel.

Maybe I just needed a blow job to get her out of my mind. A girl who could suck like her goddamn life depended on it, making me forget what Kendall's mouth had felt like, how her lips had looked when they swirled around my crown.

Yes, that was just what I needed.

And that became my plan—to leave this bar tonight with another woman. A chick I wouldn't even bring home. She'd suck me off in the fucking car, resetting my brain to my old ways so I wasn't just thinking about one girl.

And then Kendall would only be my client, nothing else.

"What can I get you?" the bartender asked, interrupting my brainstorming.

She stood in front of me, her tits high in a corset, her lips glossy and plump.

She was doable.

"Whiskey," I said. "Four fingers, neat."

"And a skinny margarita for me," I heard spoken from behind me.

That voice.

I knew it by heart. The same with her scent as a tropical wave suddenly took over my nose.

It was a sound I yearned for, a smell I constantly found myself searching for.

When my brothers had said they wanted to come here for a drink, I'd suggested a different spot instead.

I had known it was a battle I was going to lose ... because I really didn't put up a fight.

Why the hell had I even tempted myself tonight?

A masochist—that was what I was.

Slowly, I turned toward her, my dick instantly hard as I took in the dress that covered her tight, perfect body. "Kendall ..."

Fuck me.

The sapphire minidress hugged those luscious hips; it stretched across her heart-shaped ass and ended at that beautiful freckle on a high part of her thigh. The material dipped around to her front, cutting off after a heavy dose of cleavage.

Sexy, confident, and fucking delicious.

She stood next to me with her back arched, her hands clenching the wooden edge of the bar, her ass sticking out as though she knew I was staring.

She finally responded to her name, gradually looking over at me, a small smile covering her face. "Out of all the bars in LA, you chose this one. Interesting."

"My brothers wanted to come."

"Of course they did." She licked the inside of her bottom lip, causing my gaze to drop there and me to fantasize. "Things going good, Dominick?"

I didn't do small talk very well. Words, in my field, cost my clients money. Telling Kendall that work had been busy as hell, the weather was sunny, and my brothers were driving me fucking crazy was useless.

Now, her ass was a topic I would much rather discuss.

"Are you filming tonight?" I asked, avoiding her question but initiating conversation I already knew the answer to.

"Just curious ... will you be billing me for this chat?"

"This is off the clock, smart-ass."

"One you clearly love admiring." She straightened her body, changing positions so her ass wasn't so emphasized. "There are no cameras tonight, just a get-together with my costars."

"What do you think of them?"

She turned her body toward me, sending me more of her perfume, the new angle putting her tits in my direct line of vision.

Damn it, she was good, and she certainly knew what she was doing.

"They're fine." She kept her voice low even though the bar was loud, ensuring no one but me could hear her. "They're women I wouldn't normally hang with, but I'm pretty easygoing, so I'm sure we'll get along fine."

"The show is hoping that you don't. Remember, the more drama—"

"The higher the ratings, I know—that's what everyone keeps saying." She twirled a chunk of her wild, long hair before tossing it over her shoulder. "I can already sense the little nuggets dropping. You know, this guy keeps looking at me, but another girl thinks he's hot. That guy is going to ask her out, but he's already dated one of the others. If that's the angst they're looking for, then it's brewing."

It was.

And that was the kind of shit I didn't want to hear—anything that involved another dude even looking at her.

"Skinny margarita," the bartender said, pulling me out of my thoughts. "And a whiskey."

I took the small tumbler into my hand, Kendall already clinking hers against mine.

"Cheers, Dominick."

Even the way she sang my name was fucking sexy.

"Cheers—"

"Ugh, you didn't get me one," a girl asked, cutting me off.

The blonde draped her arm around Kendall's shoulders and lowered her lips to the glass, taking a long pull of Kendall's margarita.

I didn't have to ask who she was. Her appearance told me she was a costar.

"You know I'll share," Kendall said, offering her another sip.

The girl wiped the skinny margarita off her mouth and instantly eyed me up. "Kendall, who's this yummy specimen?" She stuck her hand out for me to shake, fingers bent like a queen. "I'm Delilah, and you are?"

"Dominick."

"My lawyer," Kendall added. "One who charges the most obscene amount per hour."

"*Ohhh*, but it looks like he's worth every penny." She pulled her fingers back from my grip, dangling them in the air as though she wasn't sure where to place them. "Maybe I should have hired you. Surely, someone who's big and burly and dapper, like yourself, could have gotten me what I needed." Her hand landed on my arm, rubbing my triceps as though it were my cock. "And, baby, I need a lot."

"He's single too," Kendall said. "So, have at him."

I wanted to reach across the small space separating us,

wrap my hands around Kendall's waist, and bend her over my knee, where I would spank that tantalizing ass.

But the opportunity ended as she stepped back, adding too much distance between us.

"Good to see you tonight, Dominick. Don't do anything I wouldn't do." She gave me one of her signature smiles, and then she was gone, out of my sight.

Leaving me with Delilah.

"Where were we?" she cooed.

THIRTEEN

KENDALL

Dominick's brothers might have chosen to come to this bar, but there was no question in my mind that he had known I was going to be here. He could have easily convinced them to go to a different place—there were thousands just like this one in LA—but he hadn't.

His stare had told me why.

His eyes devouring me from the moment they landed on mine.

Leaving him alone with Delilah had been too much fun. I'd thought he'd last longer than a few minutes with her, but by the time I made it back to the group, he was already sitting with his brothers on the other side of the room.

Anytime I glanced in his direction, his focus was on me.

And now, it was following me to the dance floor.

After three margaritas, I was ready to shake my butt, the girls joining me out here. The music pounded through my body, the tequila making every part of me want to groove. We were all dancing together, feeling the rhythm, our arms linked to twirl, our hips grinding.

I didn't know if it was all the booze or the pumping music or the fact that I was basking in Dominick's gaze, but I was having the best time. So much so that it killed me when all the drinks had kicked in and I had to excuse myself to run off to the ladies' room.

I finished up in the stall and came out to wash my hands, looking at myself in the mirror hanging above the sink. There was a thin line of sweat over my lip, and my waves needed some taming.

I patted my face dry with a paper towel and ran my fingers through my hair. Even though there weren't any cameras filming tonight, I still added a little more lip gloss, and I smoothed the liner under my eyes. Once I finished, I tossed the napkin and headed for the door.

I wasn't more than a few paces down the hallway when I was forced to stop, a pair of hands clenching my hips, a rock-hard body preventing me from taking another step.

"Dominick ..."

"You've been teasing me all night, Kendall."

A heat moved through me as his hands circled down to my ass.

"That wasn't my intention."

"No?" His lips parted as he looked at me, a hunger taking over his face, more animalistic than it had been earlier. "Isn't that why you went to the restroom ... so I would follow you?"

I laughed instead of answering, and he gripped me tighter.

"Should I punish you for all this teasing and for leaving me with your friend?"

"You wouldn't do that."

He cupped my chin. "You don't know me at all."

Before I could utter a word, I was suddenly in the air, and he was moving me as though I weighed nothing. Seconds later, my feet were placed on the ground, my back now against the wall, his body extremely close to mine.

"Do I eat your pussy until you come on my face?" He paused, grazing his lips across my cheek. "Do I feed you my cock, having you suck me dry?"

I was no longer breathing.

My heart was pounding through my chest.

Wetness was forming between my legs.

My lips opened automatically as his neared, waiting for him to kiss me.

"Maybe I should make the decision for you." His hands moved to my neck, tilting my head back, aiming my mouth toward his. "First, I need to know if you're under any obligation to return to your costars, or can I take you out of here?"

My quick wit was gone.

So was my plan of playing hard to get even though I'd told myself I wasn't going to fall for his fingers, no matter how close they got to me.

But, damn it, here I was, completely hypnotized, his presence making it impossible for me to think straight.

Do I have to return to the girls?

I tried recalling the email the studio had sent this morning as a follow-up for tonight. "No."

I hadn't even finished speaking, and I was already in his arms again. This time tossed over his shoulder, my dangling arms hitting the backs of his knees, my legs bouncing against his chest, his hand holding my butt steady as he carried me through the door that was only a few steps away and into an SUV that was parked outside. We were in the backseat, a driver in the front.

Once the car started moving, Dominick's lips went to my ear, and he growled, "Give me your mouth."

Nothing sounded better in that moment.

I tore at his belt buckle, loosening it enough that I could unbutton his pants and lower his zipper, slipping his cock through the hole of his boxer briefs.

The driver turned up the music just when his tip entered my mouth, a moan releasing in my throat as I sucked on the end.

He gripped my hair like he was holding the end of a rope and guided me up and down his long, thick shaft. I reached inside his boxers again to cup his balls, tickling them as I flicked my tongue over his crown. Even Dominick's skin tasted delicious. And while I used my free hand to pump his base, making sure all of him was covered, I bobbed as deeply as I could go.

His breathing was only loud enough for me to hear, but each exhale caused a tingle inside me. So did the way he urged his hips forward and rocked them back, fisting my hair, showing me how much he was enjoying this.

I went deeper, faster, squeezing my hand a little tighter near the bottom.

And suddenly, there was a change. His dick turned even harder, almost pulsing, his hand tightening around my locks.

"Fuck," he hissed quietly.

In one quick thrust, his hips jerked forward, and a warmth began to fill my mouth. The thickness of his cum coated my tongue, each burst adding more to the pool.

Knowing I had done this to him—I had gotten him off this quickly, that my mouth could give him this much pleasure—was the biggest turn-on.

"Goddamn it, Kendall."

When our movements stopped and I was sure he was finished, I swallowed him in one gulp.

He held my cheek as I wiped him off my face, his eyes all but eating mine.

"You're a naughty fucking girl." He ran his finger over my lips, tugging at the bottom one. "God, I missed that mouth."

Just as I began to smile, the driver pulled up to Dominick's house. Before my feet even hit the ground, he was lifting me from the backseat and carrying me in his arms. He punched in a code at the front door, and we were instantly inside, where he set me on the kitchen island.

"I need to taste you." He knelt on the floor and hiked up the bottom of my dress until it was around my waist. His face moved between my legs, his nose pressing against me since no panties were covering me. "Fuck me, you smell good." Holding my thighs apart, he licked the length of my clit. "I've been dreaming about that flavor for days." He sucked the very top of me into his mouth, flicking the front with his tongue.

"Dominick!"

I pulled at his hair, the same way he had done to mine, the sensation so overwhelming. Pleasure and passion and pressure were spreading through me, and each time I looked down, there was the top of his head buried in the most intimate part of me.

"Oh God." I quivered, my eyes shutting, my neck falling back.

All I could do was try to breathe while his tongue completely consumed me.

When I finally learned his pattern, he would change directions, lowering to the center, rising to the highest point, giving me one of his quick, long fingers.

I was full of him.

Satisfied.

Overtaken by the sweeping movements, the way he was arching his finger inside of me.

He wasn't just circling that ultra-sensitive section; he was using the tip of his tongue to graze across me vertically and horizontally, and then he would surround me with his lips and suck.

"Oh fuck," I moaned.

My knees bent, the heels falling from my feet so my toes rounded over the edge of the counter. My hands were flat behind me, and I leaned into his mouth. Each lick was hard, fast, and my hips thrust forward to meet him, every shift causing the shadow on his cheeks to scrape my inner thighs, only adding to the friction.

The build was there.

Owning me.

Controlling my senses.

It moved past my navel, up my chest, and exploded in my clit.

"Dominick!"

A swirl of sensations was erupting, and that only made him lick faster.

The trembles took over my body, waves of shudders going through me, each one bringing more heat, more ricochets of pleasure.

"*Ahhh*, fuck me!"

I could feel the wetness, the spasms that shot into my limbs, the shaking that continued until his tongue came to a standstill, the tremors inside me finally calm.

"What the fuck was that?" I whispered, trying to fill my lungs.

"The hottest thing I've ever witnessed." He stood, gripping my thighs, his mouth close to mine. "Tasting you while you came ..." He shook his head, exhaling. "Best thing that's ever been on my tongue."

Oh God.

How could a man be that delicious?

One who, only a week ago, had let me leave his office after I asked him for more.

"If you rented out that mouth, you'd make a fortune," I told him.

Quivers moved through my body as he laughed, every part of me still so sensitive.

"Not going to happen. That's something I hardly ever do."

I tried processing his admission and what that really meant.

"Yeah? How'd I get so lucky?"

"Something about you." He traced my lips, and I was learning it was one of his favorite things about me, second to my butt. "I can't help myself." He leaned into my ear, his breaths causing the tingles to return. "When I was watching you dance, all I could think about was how badly I wanted to eat your pussy."

FOURTEEN

DOMINICK

I'd tasted her.

In a way I never normally tasted women.

With my tongue on her clit, my fingers deep inside her pussy, her voice screaming my fucking name.

Watching her shudder wasn't just sexy; it was beautiful.

And even though she'd only been in my life for a short time, the amount of real estate she took up in my brain made it feel like much longer.

But just because I'd caved, that didn't mean she was getting the *more* that she wanted.

In a week, Kendall was going to start filming, and my opinion hadn't changed. Photos of her would drop in the media, and her following would double every day, her popularity soaring.

No matter how I feel about her, I don't need that kind of ride.

And that was what I repeated in my head when I woke up the next morning, her face nuzzled against my chest while she slept.

Damn it, she was gorgeous at this hour.

Her makeup had long worn off, her locks untamed and wild. The tiny freckles on the highest part of her cheeks unhidden. I was just running my fingers through her hair when her eyes fluttered awake.

"*Mmm*," she groaned. "Hi."

"Good morning."

She pulled the blanket up to her neck, covering the body I'd been admiring.

"Did you sleep well?" I asked.

"Too good. What time is it?" She leaned over me, checking the clock on my nightstand. "Nine thirty. Wow, I can't believe I slept this late. I'm usually up so early."

I traced her face, her skin so incredibly soft. "I think that's my fault. I wasn't exactly gentle on you last night."

She laughed, a sound so unique to her. "No, you weren't, and I loved every second." She leaned up on her elbow, holding her face with her palm. "I especially loved how it started with this ..." She ran her fingers across my lips, her exhale emphasizing how much she had enjoyed my tongue.

I lowered to her navel, tightening my grip. "Do you want it again?"

"I can't right now. I really have to get going ... but *yesss*."

I chuckled at her cuteness.

"Dominick, I have so much unpacking to do. I don't even know where to start. I moved out of my apartment a few days ago, and my new place looks like a tornado. My stuff is everywhere, and I need to make it all cozy before filming starts."

"I'll give you a lift home."

She was tickling my chest, rubbing my patch of hair. "You're sure?"

"I carried you out of the bar last night. The least I can do is take you home." I kissed the top of her head and climbed out of bed. In my closet, I slipped on some gray sweats and a T-shirt, sticking on a baseball hat so I didn't have to fuck with my hair.

When I came out, she was leaving the bathroom, wearing that sexy, tiny sapphire dress that showed every dip and curve I had caressed last night.

"Fuck me ..."

She came within reach, and I held her waist to get a better view, my dick already so fucking hard. Wanting to see the back, I turned her around. The fabric stretched across her ass, the outline of each cheek taunting me. I moved in closer, positioning my cock in between them.

"Do you feel what you do to me?" I kissed the back of her ear and down to her neck. "How fucking hard you make me?"

"This dress isn't safe around you."

"It's not the dress, Kendall."

She moaned as my mouth lowered to her collarbone. "I'm never going to get any unpacking done if you take this off me." She arched her back, shoving her ass into my cock.

I hissed from the friction. "Tease."

She faced me, giggling. "I'll go make us some coffee."

While she disappeared to the kitchen, I went into the bathroom and washed up, and when I joined her, she handed me a to-go mug.

"Just creamer," she said. "I remember from my last sleepover."

"You're good." I took a sip, the coffee just the way I liked it. "Really good."

She followed me to the car, and I revved the Porsche as I backed out of the driveaway. "Where's your new place?"

She clipped her cell into the phone holder on my dash, the route highlighted on her screen, the first driving instruction coming through the speaker.

"I have many talents," Kendall said, "but navigating this town and giving directions definitely aren't ones."

I smiled. "Fair enough."

I glanced at her when I came to the first Stop sign. The sunlight was shimmering through her dark hair, her blue eyes so vibrant, even from her profile, her skin glowing with a warm tan.

Some women looked like fucking train wrecks in the morning with bags under their eyes and a weird reddish complexion, terrifying without makeup.

Not Kendall.

I shifted out of neutral, my gaze back on the road. "What's your first day of shooting going to look like?"

"We're all meeting at one of the girls' houses to have a pool day and then back home to get dressed and glammed up for dinner and some clubbing."

"Sounds reality-ish."

She laughed. "Shopping the following day at some bougie boutique, followed by manis and pedis and brunch."

"Doesn't sound too awful."

"No, but hardly the norm. My life is already getting so weird." She rubbed her palms on her thighs, like they were sweaty. "While I was doing laundry in my new place yesterday, one of my neighbors was taking a load out of the washer and whispered to her husband, 'That's the girl who's going to be on that show.' "

I downshifted, looking at her when I replied, "Everyone in your building had to sign a waiver."

She tapped her phone a few times, and a quick glance told me she was loading Instagram. "And word is spreading because I've gone from twelve hundred followers to fourteen thousand." I felt her eyes on me. "Can you believe that many people are interested in my boring life? Because I surely can't."

"Wait until they start promoting the show, dropping teasers from filming. That's when things will really crank up."

She shook her head. "I can't even imagine what crazier will look like when this is already beyond nuts." Her arms wrapped around her waist as her stomach let out a loud growl. "Sorry, it gets cranky when I don't feed it."

"You're hungry?"

"My answer to that question is always yes."

The app on her phone told me we were only a few minutes from her place. "I know you just moved in. Do you have food in your apartment?"

"I haven't been grocery shopping yet." She laughed. "But ask me if I have tequila and wine because, of course, I have plenty of both."

"Priorities."

She lifted her cup out of the holder. "And coffee—I couldn't survive without it."

"What are you craving?"

"Pancakes." Her stomach made a noise again, and she patted it. "I stumbled upon this little restaurant the other day that's about a block away. They have the world's best pancakes."

"Let's go."

"Now?"

I slowed as the light turned red. "Why not?"

"I suppose I could delay my unpacking for an hour or so." She glanced down at her lap. "But I can't go like this. I have to change; I look like a walk of shame."

"We'll fix that." Her building came into view, and I pulled over, parking a few spots from the entrance. "Do you want to go up and change, and when you come back down, we can walk to the restaurant?"

A grin was spreading across her lips. "You know they're not

filming yet." Her fingers trickled down my neck, slowly sliding across my chest. "Why don't we go add to our hunger a bit and break in my bed?"

She knew I wouldn't step foot in her place if the cameras were on. But given that they weren't rolling for another week and she was asking me to fuck her …

"I can't turn down that offer."

"Didn't think so."

I followed her through the front door and into the elevator, watching her press the button for the top floor. Once the doors slid open, we went down a long hallway, and she unlocked the door at the end. I held it open for her as she stepped inside, flipping on the lights. The apartment was fully decorated. I was sure the studio's interior designer had taken care of that prior to Kendall moving in, and I assumed the boxes all over the floor and the couch and the counters were the things she had brought.

"Give me just a second," she said, hurrying into one of the rooms, closing the door behind her.

I hadn't even made it around to the chair, the only surface available to sit on, when the door opened again.

Kendall stood on the inside, her hands above her head, gripping the frame, wearing only a robe.

Nothing else.

No bra.

No panties.

Just nipples and that perfect fucking pussy and eyes that were so goddamn hungry.

My cock throbbed, getting harder by the second. "You're more gorgeous every time I see you naked."

A blush moved across her cheeks. "Dominick, you don't have to just look at me." Her fingers went to her tit, brushing over her nipple before slowly lowering to her pussy, where she began to rub her clit. "You can come touch me too." Her exhale was more like a moan. "And you can feel how wet you make me."

"Goddamn it."

She took a step back and another, sitting at the end of her bed, where she lifted her feet to the edge of the mattress, ready and spread for me. "Come fuck me."

FIFTEEN

KENDALL

Dominick and I were seated in a corner booth of the restaurant, separate from the other occupied tables, the space giving us some privacy. Tall glasses of orange juice were in front of us along with mugs filled to the brim with coffee.

I stared at the menu, groaning at what I was going to get, even though there was no question in my mind. I just wanted to draw out this meal for as long as I could.

It didn't matter that I had a full day of unpacking ahead of me, that we'd just spent the last hour tumbling around in my bed. Time was something Dominick wouldn't normally give me. Now that he was, I was soaking in every second.

I quickly scanned the pancake descriptions, deciding which one sounded the best, and I glanced up from my menu. "Tell me ... why law?"

He looked up. "Where did that come from?"

I shrugged. "Just curious."

He moved his menu aside and surrounded his juice with both hands. "My parents are lawyers, and it was embedded in our heads from the moment we first started talking. Ford,

Jenner, and I have always been expected to take over the firm."

"So, would you call it a passion or a requirement?"

The small laugh told me he liked the question.

"Both." He glanced at the window beside us and back to me. "Law was the language I grew up speaking, and it's all I knew. When you're around something so much, it either becomes a significant part of you or you eventually despise it."

"And you fell in love." His eyes revealed so much. "I can tell."

"It wasn't necessarily the job I fell for; it was the type of law. The three of us focus on our own fields—that was the deal we set before joining the firm." He took a drink. "Ford works in estate planning, and that's a fucking snore to me. Jenner concentrates on real estate and mergers, and I have no interest in that either. I like the thrill or large-scale contracts, the negoti-ation and banter that goes back and forth, winning massive paydays for my clients."

I traced my thumb across the condensation on the juice glass. "At least your parents recognized that you were all so different and allowed you to find your specialty and bring those to their company. What type of law are your parents into?"

"Family law. They're surrounded by divorce all goddamn day." He huffed. "Once I passed the bar, I began building my team, and each of my brothers did the same."

"Have you always worked with Brett?"

"We went to law school together."

My brows rose, as I was surprised to hear this. "He's an attorney?"

"That's what makes him such a good agent. He under-stands the legal parameters, which most agents don't. You combine that with his fearlessness, and he's unstoppable. That man isn't afraid of a fucking thing."

"Are you?"

He laughed again, the sound completely different this time. "Not when it comes to work. I blast right through every boundary in my way, and I believe everything should test me, so challenges are more like games." A small smile was now on his lips. "Most would probably say I fear personal commitments."

My heart clutched, as I knew this was about to get interesting.

"Because you've been hurt?"

"Do you think I'd let that happen?" He paused to take another drink. "When I was growing up, my parents didn't chat about the weather at the dinner table; they talked about the nastiness brewing between the husbands or wives and their clients, the kids who were going to get shuttled between homes, the assets that were getting divided. I came out of the womb with armor on."

Dominick hadn't shown signs that he wanted anything other than sex, no hints that there would be a relationship on the horizon.

He would give me his body, but his heart was off-limits.

I couldn't help but feel terribly disappointed by this news. That what had been building between us was all in my head and it would never amount to anything more.

"A forever bachelor, without kids of your own, sleeping with random women so you never get hurt." I swallowed, and it stung. "That's an interesting way to spend the rest of your life, Dominick."

He was thirty-three years old—an age Google had given to me during one of the times I searched him—and we were in very different places in our lives.

The realization of that gutted me even more.

"Kendall—"

"Have you decided what you'd like to eat?" the waitress asked, now at our table, saving him from having to respond to me.

I handed her my menu. "Blueberry and lemon curd pancakes with a side of extra-crispy hash browns."

"My favorite." She finished writing. "With plain or blueberry whipped butter?"

My stomach growled. "Blueberry whipped, of course."

"And for you?" she said to Dominick.

"I was going to get the eggs Benedict"—he glanced at me, winking—"but you've sold me on the pancakes."

"Same kind?" the waitress asked.

Dominick's gaze returned to his menu. "I'll take the banana and brown sugar."

"Now, that's my son's favorite." She smiled at us. "Cinnamon whipped butter to go with it?"

"Why not?"

"Shouldn't take too long. Let me know if you need any refills," she said and left.

"If you'd ordered the eggs Benedict—which I'm sure is excellent, by the way—I would have felt like I'd failed at describing how amazing these pancakes are. You'd have done yourself a disservice by not trying them."

"I'm not big on sweets."

My eyes widened. "You mean ... at all?"

He chuckled. "At all—for breakfast or dessert."

"I don't know if I can finish this brunch now that this information is in my possession."

His smile didn't fade. "Don't hold it against me." He held his coffee mug to his lips, keeping it there after he swallowed, his eyes really taking me in. "Tell me, what do you think of LA so far?"

"It's nothing like Boston—that's for sure. The Northeast

moves at a fast pace, but everyone does their own thing. Here, the competition starts the moment you open your eyes in the morning—what you wear, how much money you make, what kind of job you have, the car you drive, where you live." I glanced at my coffee. "I cut a Starbucks line, at least twenty people deep, by dropping my sister's name. Bostonians would have let me cut for an emergency, not because I was related to a reality star."

"Different worlds."

"No," I said, finally looking up. "Different planets."

"But it's one you need to get used to. With the path you're on, you're going to be here for a long time."

I didn't know why he had so much confidence in me. But something inside me didn't want to disappoint him and Brett. I wanted to exceed every expectation they had set.

"We'll see," I responded. "I certainly have a lot to prove."

"I was born out here, so I think I'm immune to all the bull- shit." He adjusted his hat, lowering the visor, and then leaned his arms on the table. "The best advice I can give you is, don't listen to the noise. They're going to try to one-up you in every category. Let them talk—they're just words. Keep looking straight ahead. Focus on your goals, your passion. Kendall, it's your heart that's going to take you the farthest."

"And they're certainly going to see it," I admitted, my chest pounding as I thought about the first day of filming. "I'll essentially be baring my soul to the world."

His fingers landed on my chin, his stare moving through me, each of his exhales sending me more hints of last night's cologne and this morning's toothpaste. "The screen is going to be kind to you. You're going to mesmerize the viewers, and they'll want more of your life, your face, your personality. That's what social media will give them—a glimpse at what makes Kendall Roy so fascinating. You've witnessed the rise and success of your sister, but I assure you, she's plateaued. Her fame is going to be short-lived. Not you. They're going to be captivated by your gorgeousness, which stretches far beyond your looks and body."

With the compliments pouring out of him, words were once again failing me. "Dominick ..." I started, but his eyes were making it hard for me to even breathe. "Thank you."

"No thanks needed. I'm just speaking the truth."

"I feel your sincerity." I swallowed, the emotion there—I just didn't want him to see it. "And I appreciate it."

His hand dropped, now resting on the table several inches from mine. He extended his fingers, gently grazing across my knuckles, the sensation lighting sparks through my body.

So many unanswered questions simmered in the silence between us.

How could he have this endless faith in me but so easily let me go?

How could he hold my face and hand, moments that weren't sexual at all, but only want to fuck me?

How did he not yearn for more time, smiles, laughter, mornings where I woke up in his arms?

"Breakfast is served," the waitress said, tearing me from my thoughts as she set our plates in front of us, the stack of pancakes so large that I'd never finish them. "Let me grab the coffee, and I'll top off your mugs. Can I get you anything else?"

I didn't want to release Dominick's stare, but I forced myself to take a quick scan of the table, noticing the extra napkins she had brought and the full carafe of creamer and that we had plenty of butter and syrup.

"I think we're good," I told her.

"Great. Enjoy."

I rested my fork on the side of my plate, watching Dominick cut into his first bite. "I have to witness this. My

113

heart is telling me those pancakes are about to blow your mind."

He chuckled. "Don't get your hopes up. Like I told you, I wasn't born with a sweet tooth."

Underneath that armor of his, I was positive I could find something sweet that he would love even if it wasn't pancakes. Just like I could show him what a relationship would look like, one that wouldn't obliterate his heart, one that wouldn't be anything like the marriages his parents had described over dinner.

A smile began to beat its way through me, eventually tugging at my lips. "I think I'm about to change that, Dominick."

SIXTEEN

DOMINICK

My fork dived into the edge of the pancake stack, drips of butter and syrup falling down the side, a round chunk of banana mashing as I cut through it.

I was more of an egg person.

A breakfast that I could pop into my mouth on the way to the gym or work. I wasn't looking for flavor; I was after the protein, needing all the energy I could get to make it through the day.

That was why I didn't normally eat brunch. Unless I was on vacation with the guys and there had been a night of heavy drinking before, I was usually moving so fast that I didn't have time for this meal.

But it was actually nice to slow down and take a moment to appreciate this.

And the beautiful girl sitting across from me.

The girl I kept tasting again and again, one lick never enough. The same one who had me reaching across the goddamn table, unable to keep my fucking hands off her. The one whose stare told me she was listening and holding on to every word and could probably recite everything I'd ever said to her. The one who subtly glanced at my mouth, licking her own at the same time, wiggling in her seat whenever she laughed or got excited.

Like she was right now, her eyes fixed on my lips as they parted to take in my first bite.

The second the brown sugar hit my tongue, my cheeks almost puckered, but that didn't last as the savory butter kicked in, cutting the sweetness of the banana and syrup.

"Wow." I spoke from behind my hand, taking my time to chew and swallow. "Not at all what I expected."

"Better or worse?"

"Far better." I took another bite, dipping it into the pool of syrup, the cinnamon from the butter still coating my mouth. "I honestly can't tell you the last time I had a pancake, but I can tell you, it didn't taste anything like this."

"Most of them don't. Not even the ones I make." She finally dug into her stack. "They cook the fruit on top of the pancake rather than inside, so it adds a whole different flavor. Then, you add in whipped butter instead of a cold, hard pat, and it's a mouth explosion."

I laughed.

"What's so funny?"

"You." I drank several sips of coffee. "The women I'm around don't talk about food, and they don't eat very much of it."

She shook her head. "Now, that's just a tragedy. Find yourself new women to hang out with, Dominick. There's nothing sexy or fun about what you just described." She wiped a glob of butter off the corner of her lip. "Life is far too short to only eat lettuce."

"That should be your slogan."

She poured more syrup on top of her stack. "Well, unless that lettuce is grilled with pine nuts and feta cheese and a tangy balsamic glaze on top." Our eyes locked, the most enticing charm moving across hers. "And no, that should be your slogan. The next time there's a girl sitting with you, nibbling on a leaf, looking all kinds of miserable, please tell her to order a pancake. Or two."

"You're adorable."

She wasn't just kind and caring. Kendall was real. I didn't see a lot of that, not when I only spent an evening with a woman, most of our conversation superficial and incredibly boring until it was time to fuck.

"I'm just honest." The compliment got to her; I could tell by the color of her cheeks. "I'm curious, what's it like, working with your brothers? Not all siblings can make magic happen— I'm a good example of that—so what's your relationship like with them?"

"We're best friends."

"Now, I'm jealous."

I wiped my mouth, taking a long drink of my juice. "Being the oldest, I've seen them change so much over the years. Sure, there's some friendly competition between us—we're men and athletes, so it's just natural. But we want nothing more than to watch everyone succeed, and we certainly have."

"What are they like?"

I popped a banana into my mouth, the outside caramelized from the sugar, making it taste almost candied. It was delicious, and I searched for another and ate that one too. "Ford's the youngest. He's a single dad to a four-year-old named Everly. She's the coolest kid. Smart, beautiful, sassy, extremely opinionated but endearing at the same time."

"You're smitten with her. I could tell the second you mentioned her."

I knew my lips were smiling. "I see her a lot. I even babysit sometimes."

"Where's her mom?"

I took a deep breath. "That's a complicated story."

She set her fork down and leaned into the edge of the table. "Keep talking about Everly. I like this side of you."

I laughed. "Listen, I'm not even close to being ready for kids, but she's a hell of a lot of fun to have around. When Ford travels for work and his nanny is tied up, she usually stays with me." I thought of our last sleepover and how we had stayed up until eleven, making sundaes, hours past her bedtime. "Uncle D—that's what she calls me, and she crashes in my bed because there are monsters in my guest room."

"Naturally."

"When she wakes up, she has hair like yours, all wild and wavy." I put my hand over my mouth as I chuckled again. "She has me put it into these side ponytails—I don't know what they're called."

"Pigtails?"

"Yeah, that's it." I shook my head as I recalled our last morning together, how the goddamn elastics hadn't matched and she'd thrown a fucking fit. I'd ended up at the store, buying six bags just to make sure I never ran into that problem again. "She loves oranges and eats one every morning for breakfast, but she wants all the pith peeled off. So, before I drop her off at pre-K, we do hair and eat oranges, and I'm almost always late to my first meeting."

"I think I just melted into this booth. Go on."

"I'd give that little girl anything, and she knows she has me wrapped right around her tiny finger." I sliced through a large piece of pancake and brought it up to my lips. "She has a sweet tooth. In fact, she would love these."

"You should bring her here. I'll tag along, being the pancake groupie that I am." While she picked up a blueberry, rolling it between her fingers, I felt her analyzing my expression. "Tell me about Jenner. I met him at the club that night, but we didn't have a lot of time to talk."

"He's fiercely independent. He enjoys being on the road more than in the office and would rather be in an airplane than on land. Real estate law is perfect for him. He can fly to each opening, visiting the hotels and high-rises he scores for his clients."

Her eyes briefly closed while she chewed, a look that told me how much she was enjoying her meal. "So, Jenner is the adventurous one. Always on the go, restless, desperate for new tastes and sounds and sights. Ford is more grounded. As a single dad, he must be sensitive and patient. I would imagine estate planning looks a little like *Groundhog Day*, client after client practically the same, but it requires him to be creative, and that's what fuels him. Where do you fit in, Dominick?"

"That's a good question."

With her elbows already on the table, she dropped her fork, resting her chin on the peak of her fingers. "Can I take a stab?"

"Why not?"

She appeared to be gathering her thoughts, but I knew better. Kendall's theory was on the tip of her tongue. The pause was to keep me in suspense.

To tease.

Something she had become an expert at.

"I don't think your lack of commitment has anything to do with being hurt or the topic of conversations you heard, growing up. I think you've gone after the wrong kind of women, and I think you've done that intentionally." She blinked, marrying her lips as though there were something on them. "A bachelor lifestyle ensures you don't feel guilty when you work too much or when your friends ask you to go on vacation or when you get up extra early to go to the gym and stay longer than you planned. The right woman would change that, so you seek out one-night stands over substance."

She glanced at her fork and back to me. "You've only ever seen lettuce. Globs of butter that accidentally hang from the corners of lips don't happen because the women don't know you, so they're certainly not going to feel comfortable indulging in front of you."

She moved her hair to the side, the locks still a bit crazy from when I'd pulled them earlier in her bed. "You like to know you can have what's in front of you, that nothing is off-limits. You don't know the terms *compromise* or *sacrifice* because you, Mr. Dalton, are used to getting your own way. Control isn't only a desire; it's how you live your life. Maybe that's the lawyer in you, maybe it's that you're the oldest of three, or maybe it's that you fear what would happen if you ever lost your grip. So, as I said, your aversion to commitment isn't due to some dark, ugly past, like some of the bad boys I've met. No, your reason is actually quite simple." She took a long drink of her juice, watching me the entire time. "You just haven't found the right one." She smiled. "How'd I do?"

If I wasn't exerting so much control, I would have dropped my fork.

"Oh, yeah," she continued. "I nailed it, didn't I?"

Every fucking word.

I didn't know if that was terrifying or a relief.

"How the hell did you come up with all of that?"

Her grin grew, as she was obviously satisfied with my response, and she resumed eating. "Creatives are observant people. You know, the kind who goes to a party and ends up being the resident therapist, doing all the listening instead of the talking. Apparently, I have the face that anyone can say anything to." She licked a river of syrup from her mouth before it reached her chin. "People flock to me, especially the tortured souls. I'm not intuitive. I watch and hear, draw a conclusion, and I'm almost always right."

I held her gaze, flipping back through all the years I could remember in detail. "You're the most interesting woman I've ever met, Kendall."

"That's the best compliment you've ever given me—and lately, you've given me a lot." She dug through the side of a pancake until she found what she wanted—what I assumed was the lemon curd—and surrounded her lips over the tines. "I definitely don't want to be ordinary or trite. Most of all, I don't want to be expected."

I exhaled. "You're far from that."

When she set her fork down this time, I could tell how happy my response had made her.

Before I could add to it, the waitress was back. "Can I get you anything else?"

Kendall looked at me, and when I shook my head, she said, "Just the check, please."

The waitress went to drop the billfold on our table, and Kendall snatched it before it even hit the wood.

"My treat." She reached inside her tank top, removing a credit card that had been tucked in her bra.

I held out my hand. "No." When she didn't budge, I reached for the check, and she moved it out of my way, handing it to the waitress. "Kendall, I insist."

"Not a chance. You've already done so much for me. It's truly my pleasure."

Aside from my mother, a woman had never paid for any of

my meals. I wasn't sure how I felt about Kendall controlling that decision, but it was far too late to fight her on it.

The waitress returned with her credit card and receipt.

After Kendall signed her name, she said, "Ready to go?"

I stood, my hand going to her lower back as we walked out of the restaurant.

"What do you have planned for today?" she asked as we headed down the sidewalk.

"Probably hit up the gym at some point, and I have a little work that needs to be done before tomorrow morning. James is filming out of town, so Jenner and I are taking Brett out for dinner."

"That'll be fun."

"Even though we go in with good intentions, it always turns into some form of debauchery."

"Now, that should be *your* motto."

I laughed as I looked at her and realized her building was only a few paces ahead.

She turned her back to the high-rise and faced me. "Thanks for brunching with me. Knowing I converted you makes me the happiest girl alive."

"Converted me?"

She put her hands on her narrow hips. "Into loving pancakes. Sweetness is a religion, my friend."

She was so fucking adorable.

"Get inside," I growled.

"And if I don't?"

I went to rake my hand through my hair, but my fingers hit my hat instead. "You'll never get a goddamn thing unpacked today."

Because I would carry her to my car and have her suck my cock as I drove us to my place, where I would wear out every inch of her fucking body.

Relentlessly.

She took a few steps back, grinning so large that it tugged at my lips. "You say that like it's a bad thing." She blew me a kiss and turned, shaking her ass in those yoga pants. After a few seconds, halfway to her front steps, she glanced at me over her shoulder, unsurprised that I was still staring at her. "See ya around, Mr. Dalton."

SEVENTEEN

KENDALL

"I'd better not lose you once you start filming," Charlize said from the other side of my love seat, a fluffy white blanket covering us, our matching painted toes resting on the coffee table.

"Please. That's impossible. I think I've proven my love to you already." I wrapped my arm through his. "And that love is wicked fierce."

He twirled a chunk of my hair around his finger. "I just needed the reassurance." He leaned forward to refill our wineglasses, draining the last of our first bottle and moving on to our second. "What I didn't tell you while we were getting pedis is that I lost a gig yesterday." He rolled his eyes. "The other artist is super talented, and she's nice and cuddly and all the things, but I'm feeling a little bruised about it."

I turned toward him, gripping my glass. "What? But you're a freaking genius and—"

"*Staaap.* I know I'm fabulous. I'm just a little sour—that's all." His brows scrunched together. "Speaking of sour ... why haven't you brought up the Instagram post that hideous flower shared today?"

I didn't know if it was the wine, but it took me a moment to realize who he was talking about.

"Daisy? No. I've been avoiding her page. Why?"

He pointed at my phone. "Go look."

I set down my wine and lifted my cell off the table, clicking on the app. Her post immediately came up in my feed. It wasn't a photo or video. She'd shared a screenshot of a quote she'd written.

I THOUGHT YOU WERE MY PERSON.
BUT THE KNIFE YOU STABBED ME WITH JUST CUT OFF THE BIG
RED BOW THAT SAT ON TOP OF MY NEW BENZ.
YOU CAN'T HURT THE GIRL WHO'S ON TOP OF HER GAME.
—TEAM LOYALTY
XO

There was no question; that post was about me.

Especially since the one I'd shared this morning on my newly verified account was of the headshot the studio had taken of me and an announcement that filming was starting in the morning and I couldn't be more excited to be representing the show.

"Not very girl next doorsy, is she?"

"No." I pointed at my glass without looking at it. "Fill it to the brim, please."

Once I heard the sloshing stop, I picked it up and downed several gulps, going to Daisy's profile at the same time. It had been several days since I'd looked at it, and I scrolled through her recent posts, seeing photos I hadn't manipulated and videos I hadn't shot.

She had clearly found someone to replace me. I was happy for her; she needed an assistant, and I obviously couldn't be that person. But what my trained eyes saw were videos that were extremely choppy, the cuts not matching, the quality poor. The pictures hadn't been taken in good lighting, and the digital mastering hadn't been smoothed out; it appeared like she was trying to hide her imperfections and had done a shitty job.

I returned to the post from a few hours ago.

The one that was so unnecessary, so callous and self-serving.

"Someone's going for the sympathy vote, huh?"

I sighed. "Yep."

"Should I tell that honey babe that jealousy isn't a good look on anyone?"

My hands began to shake, my stomach churning.

"Do you think everyone knows she's talking about me—but not really talking about me because we both know I didn't stab her anywhere, especially not in the back? I mean, my God."

"I think her stalkers do, but that's it."

I felt my eyes widen. "What does that mean?"

"You just landed one of the biggest reality shows that's ever going to hit TV. It's really peculiar that she didn't congratulate you or share the show, like every other famous sister in her shoes would do." He pushed the wine up to my mouth, encouraging me to take a sip. "She also hasn't posted any pics or stories of you two since you got fired. You haven't liked or commented on her posts, and she hasn't on yours." His fingers went to my shoulders, trying to ease the pain. "Trust me, her loyal fans have noticed."

"Ugh."

My finger hovered above the Following button. If I pressed it, I would unfollow her.

I was sure that would be noticed too.

But in this moment, I wasn't sure I cared.

He took my phone away, setting it on the table. "Don't even think about it. She's the bad guy here, not you, sister."

I shook my head, slumping into the couch. "I know; you're right ... I'm just pissed." I took a drink. "And hurt."

He wrapped his arm around my shoulders, pulling our hips closer, the sides of our cheeks now smashed together. "You know that's her plan, don't you? She wants you to feel like shit while her twelve million followers tell her how amazing she is and how pretty and how she's the best thing since nude gloss." He clinked his glass against mine. "Now, that's a bitch who likes her ego stroked like it's the longest cock in the world."

"If I wasn't so upset, I'd probably be laughing."

"Honey, don't let that hideous flower get under your flaw-less skin."

I turned my face toward his. "She's beautiful."

"Ish, but she's certainly not you."

"God, I wish she'd stop acting like such an asshole." Emotion moved into the back of my throat, and I hated that it was there. "Because she should be here with us, sharing this love seat, celebrating that I start shooting tomorrow."

He clasped his fingers around mine. "You have me, and I'm going to glam you up, so when you go to that pool party tomor-row, you're going to look and feel fabulous."

Each deep breath caused my chest to tighten, but I fought through it, not letting a single tear fall. "I adore you. Hard."

"You know I feel the same."

His phone chimed, and he picked it up off the table, his jaw dropping while he read the screen.

"What's going on?"

"You know how I said the world is soon going to realize how much of a cunt Daisy is? Or maybe I just thought that in my head and didn't actually say those words to you." His lips went wide, showing his teeth ground together. "Well, it's happening."

He handed me my phone from the table, where the latest Celebrity Alert was on the screen.

BREAKING NEWS:

DAISY ROY AUDITIONED FOR A MOVIE ROLE THIS MORNING. TURNS OUT, THE TEARS ARE BECAUSE THE ROLE WENT TO TIFFANY BRYANT, THE REALITY STAR SHE HAD GONE HEAD-TO-HEAD WITH IN LAST SEASON'S SINGLE GIRLS OF LA. LOOKS LIKE THE FLOWER GOT STUNG BY A BEE. BETTER LUCK NEXT TIME, MISS ROY.

"They stole my flower idea."

"I can't even with you right now," I told him and clicked on the alert.

A series of photos appeared above the full article. Daisy was holding a tissue under her eyes, her face in a full-blown ugly cry. I flipped to the next one, a different angle, but this shot showed a close-up of her tears.

There was a girl next to her, holding a notepad and a set of keys. A quick zoom revealed a Mercedes emblem on the fob and Daisy's hot-pink keychain that used to hold the key for her BMW.

That had to be her new assistant.

And in the next picture, it looked like Daisy was screaming at the poor girl.

The last shot was the most interesting. Her assistant was trying to get in the passenger seat of Daisy's new Mercedes while Daisy was driving away without her.

They were all very normal reactions from my sister, the way she acted when she didn't get her way, but this was the first time she had been caught on camera.

"Oh God, she's going to lose her mind over this." I slowly looked up. "And you know she's going to blame me."

She despised Tiffany.

In Daisy's eyes, this was the worst thing that could have happened to her.

Aside from what I'd supposedly done.

I held the glass to my lips and downed several sips.

"Time for a refill?"

I took a few breaths. "As long as your makeup can make this hungover face look halfway decent in the morning, keep pouring."

He wiggled his fingers in the air. "These hands can work wonders, baby."

EIGHTEEN

DOMINICK

"Are you alive?" Brett asked as I answered his call. "Or half-dead, like me?"

I rubbed my temples, staring at the coffee on my desk, wishing it were already down my throat and that the Tylenol had kicked in, this headache relentlessly throbbing. "What the fuck happened last night? I remember dinner and going to the bar. After about our third shot of whiskey, my memory becomes very hazy."

"That's because we finished that bottle." He sighed. "According to the receipt I'm holding, we polished off a bottle of vodka too."

"Between the three of us?"

"I believe Ford showed up at some point, but I'm not entirely sure about that. I could have dreamed it."

"Fuck me."

He laughed. "How's Jenner feeling?"

I'd passed him about twenty minutes ago on the way to my office, his skin as white as the shirt he'd paired with his suit. "Same as us. I think he's flying out in a couple hours—

130

can you even fucking imagine? My head is turbulent enough right now. I certainly don't need to be in the air, feeling like this."

"My day isn't much better. For the last two hours, I've been on set for the *Glitzy Girls*. It's a pool party—think no shade, direct sun, and all heat. At least I'm sweating out all the fucking booze we drank."

"Oh shit, I forgot they start filming today."

If it wasn't for this hangover, I would have remembered. I'd seen the announcement on Kendall's Instagram last night on my way to meet the guys for dinner. I didn't follow her account, but I found myself looking at her posts.

"I sent you a present. Check your texts."

I pulled my cell away from my face, a photo from Brett appearing on the screen.

I shouldn't have been surprised that he'd sent one of Kendall. The guys had nagged me endlessly about her last night. The picture showed her in one of the lounge chairs by the pool. Her body in a tight red bikini, the triangle tops cupping her tits, a small patch of fabric covering that perfect fucking pussy. It looked like she had gone for a swim, her wild, dark hair wet, the drips falling down her skin.

"Fuck me."

"I had a feeling that would make you feel a little better."

I saved the photo. "You're there all day?"

"Why? You want updates?"

"Motherfucker."

He laughed again. "Production will be leaking some shots in the next couple of hours. Once her body hits the internet, you know what's going to happen to your girl."

"Instafamous—and she's not my girl."

I moved over to the window, cranking it open a few inches, inhaling the smog-filled downtown air.

131

"Jesus, Dominick. We can title her anything you want, but it doesn't change the fact that you like her."

I moved the phone to my other ear and grabbed my coffee, nursing the hot liquid past my tongue. "I like the way she looks when her hair is spread over my fucking pillow and her ass is high in the air."

"Brother, you know I was in the same place when James first came into my life. You know I went through that internal fight. I'm telling you, it's not worth the battle. Stop denying yourself and scoop that shit up before someone else does and you hate yourself because you fucking lost her."

I closed my eyes as a breeze came in. "I told you, I refuse to be all over the goddamn internet for reasons other than work."

"You know I felt the same. I still don't want to be the subject of every other Celebrity Alert. But, fuck, it's worth it, man. Trust me."

I knew Brett was coming from a good place, and I remembered the mental battle he'd gone through at the beginning of their relationship for the very same reason as me.

But I'd spent years building my book of business, securing an ironclad reputation, keeping my personal life separate from the celebrities I represented.

Things were just the way they should be.

I didn't need Kendall and her delicious ass to come in and rattle my world.

Is she worth it?

I wasn't even going to let that question simmer, pushing it out of my brain before it had a chance to answer itself.

"Still need some persuading?" My phone vibrated against my cheek. "Go check your texts."

This picture showed her coming out of the pool. Her neck tilted back, hands squeezing the water from her sopping wet hair. The angle was only of her front, as though Brett was standing just a few feet back, and Kendall was nearing the top step. The shot showed every inch of her body, even down to her fucking toes.

And it was one hell of a body.

Flawless, toned, a golden tan on her skin.

"Brett, you're fucking killing me."

"I'm just the deliveryman, and it's nothing you haven't seen before."

I continued to stare at the photo, placing Brett on speakerphone. "How long are you there for?"

"Until they wrap and move locations."

I saved the picture and turned back toward the window, seeing the skyline of LA. "Not a bad gig. Your view is certainly better than mine right now."

"The only thing it's missing is James."

That guy had gone from being one of the biggest players in Miami to moving to LA, so he could become a whipped husband-to-be. He had a pool full of half-naked chicks in front of him, and he was missing James.

Is that going to happen to me?

Once again, I shoved that thought far from my brain.

"Yeah, yeah," I replied. "Your cheesiness is making me fucking queasy."

He chuckled. "Any message you want me to relay to Kendall while I'm here?"

Merciless bastard.

"You need to get off my fucking tip. I'll see you later," I said and hung up.

Within minutes, my phone was ringing again, this time Ford's name on the screen.

"Talk gently," I said, holding it to my ear. "Everything hurts."

"I'm not surprised. The three of you were fucking wrecked

last night. Mom and Dad had Everly for a sleepover, so I swung by the club to have a drink with you guys. I'm shocked you even remember I was there."

I held my forehead, the pressure helping with the ache. "I don't. Brett told me you showed up. I just got off the phone with him."

"Listen, I don't have much time to talk. I'm in Malibu and about to run into a meeting, but I'm calling to see if you have plans on Saturday."

Saturday, Saturday.

I could barely think straight, but nothing was coming to mind.

I pulled up my schedule to be sure. "I'm free. Why?"

"I have to fly to Vegas to meet a client, and my nanny is on vacation all week. You know I wouldn't ask you to take Everly on a weekend unless I was in a real pinch."

"It's no problem. I'll take her."

"You're sure?"

"Yeah, of course."

"You're a lifesaver. Everly is going to be so happy when I tell her."

My phone vibrated once more, and I looked at the screen. This time, the shot Brett sent was of Kendall in the pool. Her back was against the edge, holding what looked like a skinny margarita. The red suit showed her perky, hard nipples, those little peaks fucking taunting me.

I wanted nothing more than to lean forward and bite them.

Her profile was aimed toward the camera, a smile growing across her gorgeous face.

"I've got to run, Ford. Tell my favorite little girl that I'll see her in a couple of days."

I ended the call and held the coffee to my mouth, flipping through the last three pictures.

"Damn it," I growled to myself, taking in her curves and the flatness of her navel, the way the bathing suit dipped over her cunt.

"What the fuck are you doing to me, Kendall?"

Me: I got the contract you sent over for the endorsement deal on the sunglasses. Told you they'd start rolling in the second you started filming. Anyway, today got away from me, and I didn't have a chance to look at it, but I will by Monday.

Kendall: Someone wants to hear the words ... you're right. ;) Take your time, especially if that means you're going to negotiate the deal and get me more money.

Me: That goes without saying. Things going well with filming?

Kendall: Having a blast. I thought of you the other night while we were shooting at Nobu. I remember you saying at some point that it was your favorite restaurant.

Me: That's the only reason you were thinking about me?

Kendall: Are you flirting with me, Mr. Dalton?

Me: Would you like me to?

Kendall: I'd like a lot of things ...

Kendall: Have yourself a good evening. Try not to dream about me.

NINETEEN

KENDALL

F ive straight days of filming, and I finally had a Saturday off. It was time to get some extra sleep and do laundry and get caught up with life. Since we shot at multiple locations each day, running home in between, I was constantly changing my clothes and getting glam done, and my apartment had definitely taken a beating. Clothes were all over the floor of my closet, shoes hadn't been put away, and my kitchen counters held the remnants of every snack and meal I'd tried to scarf down until I ran out of time and had to leave for the next shot.

I'd always been so neat and tidy.

I didn't know what the hell had happened to me this past week.

After making a full pot of coffee and filling the largest mug I could find in the cabinet, I threw on some yoga pants and a tank top, twisting my hair on top of my head to get started on the kitchen. Not having a single moment to cook, everything I'd eaten since I'd moved in was takeout. There were delivery boxes everywhere in addition to the empty wine bottles from when my costars had come over, water bottles, and granola bar wrappers.

I finished the dishes and organized the condiments and leftovers in the fridge, making a list of everything I wanted to pick up from the grocery store. I left the list by my purse, so I wouldn't forget it, and I went into my room to attack the laundry.

I separated the piles and carried them down the hallway to the laundry room. There were several machines, and most were available, so I loaded the colors into one, the whites into another, and while I was putting the towels into a third, there was someone whispering behind me.

When I'd walked in, I remembered seeing a couple standing in front of the dryers, folding their clothes on the closed lid. The sound had to have come from them.

I finished dumping in the soap and turned around, waving once I made eye contact.

They waved back, and the woman said, "Are you Kendall Roy?"

I was surprised to hear my name. "Yes."

"I thought so," she said. "I'm Elizabeth, and this is my boyfriend, Doug. We live five doors down from you."

I smiled. "Nice to meet you both."

"We saw you filming in the lobby the other day," Doug said. "When is the show going to air?"

"It's a big surprise, even for us." I tossed the now-empty laundry bag over my shoulder. "I think they're afraid we'll tell everyone, but I'm hoping it's in the next couple of months."

"Doug just opened a mobile detailing company," Elizabeth said. "You know, maybe you could mention something about it on the show or give him a shout-out on social media?"

"Elizabeth—"

"What?" she said as she looked at her boyfriend. "The girl's about to be super famous—she practically already is. Can you imagine what that could do for your business?"

Another thing I'd noticed about this town: no one was afraid to ask for favors.

"Give me one of your cards," she said to Doug.

He reached into his wallet and removed a business card, and she came over and handed it to me.

"All of his info is on there. We'd really appreciate whatever you can do for us."

I checked out the logo and website, and when I glanced up, she hadn't moved, her expression telling me she was expecting an answer.

"All of the products mentioned on the show are paid placements," I told her, tucking the card into the top of my yoga pants. "But I'd be happy to send your info to the studio, and they'll get in touch."

She laughed like I'd said the stupidest thing she'd ever heard. "We can't afford what they're going to charge. What about your social media?" She crossed her arms over her chest. "Or are you going to connect me to your publicist, so she can tell me how much your fees are?"

Is this what celebrities deal with every day?

I was just an entry-level reality star, and I still couldn't believe what I was hearing.

I turned to the washer again, pouring in the fabric softener I'd set in between the machines, and when I faced her, her hands were on her hips.

"So?"

I took a deep breath. "I'll see what I can do."

I was walking toward the door when she said, "Can you give me an approximate date?" She smiled. "I'd like to keep an eye out, so I can make sure to share your post."

When I glanced at her boyfriend, he looked appalled, silently apologizing for her behavior.

"Congratulations, Doug," I said to him from the doorway. "Starting a business is no easy feat, and I wish you the best of luck. When I have a minute of downtime, I'll reach out and book you for a detailing. My car could certainly use it."

Before Elizabeth could say another word, I went back to my apartment, phoning Charlize the moment I got inside.

He answered with, "Morning, sugar."

"I have a question for my LA expert."

"Talk to me."

"When you have the tiniest bit of fame—I'm talking miniscule amounts, like myself—does everyone and their mother come out of the woodwork and want something from you?" I slumped into the couch, kicking my feet onto the coffee table. "I just got cornered in the laundry room by a not-so-nice girlfriend who would have given her soul for an Instagram plug. P.S. I haven't even brushed my teeth yet."

"One, don't ever walk out the door until those suckers are polished and minty. And two, yes. Be prepared to hear it all. People have zero shame in their game."

"Ugh." I buried my head in the fluffy throw pillow. "I liked it much better when people asked for favors because they genuinely needed them. This whole *what can you do for me because you have social media followers* is too much."

"It's just getting started, baby."

My eyes rolled. "Everyone keeps saying that, and it's somewhat terrifying."

"We'll get through it, promise. How was the club last night? I tried to make it, but I was so tired when I got home from the photo shoot that I took a bath and climbed my perfect ass straight into bed."

I laughed. "It was fun—drank, danced, the usual. I wish

you had been there. I certainly missed you, and the girls did too. They love you." I peeled myself off the couch and went into my room to make the bed.

"Now, I really wish I had gone. What's on the agenda for this evening, Miss Fabulous?"

I finished pulling back the comforter and fluffed the pillows, heading into the bathroom to clean the counter. "Nothing. Doesn't that sound glorious?" I tossed a handful of makeup-coated tissues into the trash. "I'm going for a long run, finishing up my laundry, going to the grocery store, and cooking something yummy, followed by a Netflix marathon of something worth bingeing."

"I'm coming over."

I paused, the trash bag half-tied in my hands. "Really? That would seriously make me the happiest."

"Then, why didn't you just ask, silly girl?" I heard a honk in the background. "I just hit all kinds of traffic. I've got to run. I'll see you around seven."

Before I hung up, I said, "Can't wait."

A few hours later, I was on the couch, folding the clean laundry on my coffee table, when my phone rang. Frantically searching for my cell, I found it on the kitchen counter, Dominick's name on the screen.

He'd said he would have my sunglasses contract reviewed by Monday, but it was Saturday, a little past eleven in the morning, and my gut told me this had nothing to do with work.

"Hello?"

"What are you doing right now?"

I glanced around my apartment as though that would help answer his question. "You mean, this second?"

"Yes."

"I'm deep in the trenches of laundry and cleaning."

"Come downstairs."

My chest tightened, the tingles sparking in my stomach. *"Downstairs*, downstairs? As in ... my lobby?"

He laughed. "Yes, Kendall. I'm parked outside."

He'd seen me the morning after an all-night sex session, and I'd probably looked a lot worse than I did now. But still, I wanted to shower and brush my hair and put something on besides workout clothes.

"Is there any way you can give me thirty minutes? I look like death, and I really need—"

"I'm with Everly, my niece. We're going on a pancake date, and we'd like you to join us."

He'd brought out the big guns.

Fuck.

And he'd remembered when I told him I wanted to be his pancake groupie when he took Everly to have some.

The tingles had moved into my chest, the rest of my body melting into the couch cushions, feeling like a big pile of goo.

"Give me two minutes," I said, rushing into the bathroom. "I'll be right down."

TWENTY

DOMINICK

Kendall walked out the front of her high-rise in a pair of tight black yoga pants and a light-blue tank top, the same color as her eyes. Her hair was high on her head, messy, the silver aviators showing a reflection of my car on the lenses.

Goddamn it.

There was nothing sexier than a woman in athletic gear with not a single drop of makeup on her face.

That was her this morning.

And if my niece wasn't in the backseat, singing to the tunes that were playing, I would fuck her in my Range Rover, her palms flat on the tinted glass, her legs spread wide, riding me in my seat.

"Hey, guys," she said as she climbed into the passenger side, smiling at me. She immediately turned around to greet Everly. "I'm Kendall." She stuck out her hand, my niece gently grabbing it. "It's very nice to meet you. I've heard lots of things about you. Your uncle is a bit of a bragger when it comes to you."

"That's 'cause I'm his favorite." My niece giggled. "I'm

Everly, but Uncle D calls me Eve sometimes. He says you're pretty cool."

"Is that so?" Kendall looked at me. "She's the cutest."

"She's excited about these pancakes." I pulled away from the curb, the drive only a block from her building.

"Has your uncle told you about all the delicious flavors they have?"

I watched Everly from the rearview mirror as she nodded, the side ponytails bobbing, one several inches higher than the other.

"I did her hair."

I felt Kendall's smile on me when she said, "I can tell."

"Uncle D says they're scrumptious."

"Did I really use the word *scrumptious*?"

"Don't know." She shrugged, her doll falling in the seat beside her, her little legs kicking as she reached for it. "That's what it sounded like, and I like everything to be extra scrumptious."

"Me too, girlfriend. Me too," Kendall said.

I parked in a spot right in front and helped Everly get out. She grasped my hand the moment her feet touched the ground, and before she even took a step, her other hand was holding Kendall's.

The sight made me smile as we walked to the restaurant and again when Kendall said, "Thank you for the invite."

"I'm glad you were free."

"This is the first free morning I've had all week." She grinned as she gazed at my niece. "And I get to spend it with you. Do you know how excited that makes me?"

"Yippee," Everly sang as we lifted her off the ground, swinging her body in the air. "You're *sooo* fun."

Kendall laughed as she replied, "I'm happy you think so."

"Higher! Higher!"

We lifted her several more times until we walked inside, and I said, "There's three of us," to the hostess.

With menus and crayons, she led us to the same section we'd sat in before. "Your waitress will be right with you."

Everly, still holding Kendall's hand, tugged her toward the other side of the booth. "I want to sit next to you." She slid in first, and Kendall followed.

"You're ditching me?"

"Don't be sad, Uncle D." She wrapped her arms around Kendall's and rested her face on Kendall's shoulder. "I just like her. Lotskies."

"At least someone does." She winked at me. "And I like you lotskies too." She opened the menu in front of them. "What's your favorite kind of pancake, Everly? Like the one you'd pick over all the others?"

Everly's eyes went wide. "Chocolate chip. Those are the very best."

Kendall tightened the ponytails on each side of Everly's head. "What do you think is my favorite kind?"

"Berry."

"Berry?" Kendall inquired.

My niece pointed at Kendall's tank top. "Berry for blue."

"Berry does sound pretty good, and I do love blueberries, but that's not my favorite."

Everly pointed at Kendall's necklace. "Gold?"

She reached for Everly's belly, tickling her. "Who's ever eaten gold pancakes?"

Everly was laughing so hard that little snorts were coming from her mouth.

"You're just the silliest," Kendall said.

The girls quieted as the waitress approached. "What can I get you all to drink?"

"Coffee," Kendall replied.

"Same," I told her. "And milk for the little lady."

"Hey!" Everly chimed. "Daddy says I'm not so little anymore. He wishes I were though; he says I was way less sassy then."

The waitress chuckled. "I have a daughter about your age, and she's also quite sassy. That's one of the reasons we love her." She smiled. "I'll grab those drinks, and I'll come back to take your order."

I opened the menu, knowing they had chocolate chip, but I confirmed just in case it had changed. "Eve, you're in luck. They have exactly what you want."

"*Yuuum.*"

"Do you want a single or a stack of three?"

I already knew her answer and that her eyes were far larger than her stomach.

"Three, Uncle D."

"Someone's extra hungry today."

Her nod was overexaggerated, making her hair flop in her eyes. "With lots of syrup and butter." She drew a circle in the air and poked the center. "Daddy always puts a big glob right in the middle."

Kendall took out one of the crayons and began drawing on Everly's place mat. "Sounds like your daddy knows how to make amazing pancakes."

"Don't tell Daddy this," Everly whispered, her voice carrying across the table, "but they used to be kinda icky. Now, they're way better."

I thought of Ford in his kitchen, a disaster in front of him, flour and eggshells everywhere as he tried to make his baby girl happy. "Your secret is safe with us, sweetheart."

Everly tapped Kendall's arm. "You know what? Uncle D makes really good pancakes. He's gotten way better too. At first, they were kinda hard, but now, they're perfect. Sometimes, when I go to his house on the weekends, he makes them for me, but today, he wanted to come here with you."

"Is that right?" Kendall inquired.

"*Mmhmm.*" She grabbed the red crayon from the package and began to color between the lines that Kendall had drawn.

A four-year-old who didn't miss a goddamn thing.

"Everly, can I tell you a secret?"

The little one placed her ear toward Kendall's mouth, cupping her small hands around it. Unlike my niece, Kendall kept her voice down, making sure I didn't hear anything, but the entire time she whispered, her eyes were fucking glued to mine.

Once Kendall pulled away, Everly's mouth dropped.

"Don't say anything," Kendall told her. "It's our secret."

Everly wiggled, shaking her short arms like there was music playing. "Okay!"

"So, the two of you are keeping secrets from me?" I crossed my arms over the table, attempting to look pissed. But that was hardly the case. The two of them couldn't be more adorable together.

Everly was enamored with Kendall.

"It's a girl thing," Kendall told me.

"And I'm a big girl now," Everly added.

The waitress dropped off Everly's milk and our coffees and cups of water and said, "What can I get you to eat?"

"Cinnamon roll pancakes for me," Kendall said. "I'll take the cinnamon whipped butter as well."

"And for you?" the waitress asked me.

"The strawberry almond pancakes, and this one"—I nodded toward Everly—"will take the chocolate chip, the full stack. Whipped butter and syrup on both."

As soon as the waitress left, I looked at Everly and said, "Do you know that Kendall is going to be on TV?"

Her eyes widened again. "Like in the movies? With the princesses? And the mermaids?"

"No." She shook her head. "Not anything that fabulous. Just a TV show."

"Uncle D, can I watch it? Pretty please?"

I chuckled. "You're going to have to ask your father."

"I'm going to tell all my friends at school to watch you. There are lots and lots of big kids there, and everyone is going to know you're my friend."

Kendall ran her hand over the top of Everly's head. "That's very sweet of you."

"Did you ever think the highest-watching demographic of *Glitzy Girls* would be Everly's pre-K?"

Kendall gazed at me, those beautiful cheeks reddening. "I'd die." She looked back at Everly. "Make sure you and your friends cheer extra loud for me, okay? I need all the support I can get."

Everly clapped. "We will. We're good clappers. We can do it really loud."

Kendall picked up the yellow crayon and began drawing large circles, which Everly filled in with different colors.

"I wish I had more friends who were as cool as you. I've only met one really good friend since I moved here. His name is Charlize, and he's the best. He even does my makeup for me."

"Really? Wow." Everly looked up. "But Uncle D is your friend. He invited you for pancakes."

Kendall grinned. "He did—you're right—but Uncle D is my lawyer."

"Daddy says lawyers can be nice sometimes."

I took a drink of my coffee. "I think half the world would probably argue that point."

"How about Daddy? He'll be your friend."

"Not that kind of friend," I said to my niece. "We're going to keep your dad far, far away from Kendall."

"But why?"

Kendall's arm went around Everly's shoulders, and she attempted to reply, but I chimed in first with, "Because your dad has so many friends; he doesn't need any more."

When Kendall looked at me, I winked.

"I think you just need to be Uncle D's friend. He can make you a sundae when you stay the night, and for breakfast, he'll peel your oranges, and he'll take all that icky white stuff off."

Kendall watched me as Everly spoke, her eyes full of warmth. "Uncle D hasn't ever made me a sundae or peeled my oranges when I've stayed over."

"Uncle D, no sundaes for Miss Kendall? That's a bad friend!"

Something inside me wanted to reach across the table and put my hand on Kendall's. To graze her knuckles with my thumb, to inhale the tropical scent from the inside of her wrist. To have those tiny hairs that had fallen around her face tickling my cheeks as I kissed her.

My thoughts were interrupted as the waitress appeared and said, "Here you go, young lady. Look at that gooey chocolate stack."

Everly's face brightened up, her eyes so large that they looked like they were about to pop. "Holy bananas."

"I even found some whipped cream for you." The waitress placed a bowl in front of my niece.

"What do you say?" I reminded Everly.

"Thank you." Everly grinned at her. "It looks scrumptious."

We laughed as the waitress handed out the rest of the plates.

"Can I get you anything else?"

"We're good," I told her and thanked her.

Everly dipped her fork into the whipped cream and spread it over the edge of the pancakes before attempting to cut off a bite. She pushed down too hard, causing a chunk to go flying into her hair, another landing on her shirt, where the chocolate left a streak as it fell to her lap. "Oopsie."

I was just about to help her when Kendall leaned over Everly's plate and started to cut up the stack.

"It'll taste even better if it's in small pieces," she told Everly.

Once she chopped up the section in front, knowing that was more than enough, Kendall took the crumbs out of Everly's hair.

"How is it?" I asked as she took her first bite.

"*Whoooa.*"

"That good?"

"Uncle D, *sooo* good."

I dug into the strawberry almond stack, this flavor full of tartness, not nearly as sweet as the banana and brown sugar had been.

And it was fucking delicious.

I could tell Kendall really liked hers by the way she was groaning as she chewed. When she swallowed, she said to Everly, "Can I try some of yours? I've never had their chocolate chip, and it looks delicious."

"*Mmhmm,*" Everly replied with her mouth full.

Kendall took one of the pieces she'd already cut, her eyes closing the moment it hit her lips. "Oh my God." Her head leaned back, like the night I'd gone down on her. "Everly, this is the best pancake ever. It's like cake."

"Want more? I'm a good sharer."

She laughed. "No, honey, you keep eating, but thank you for offering."

"There's so much chocolate. Yummy!"

A chip was on the corner of her mouth, somehow smearing toward her cheek every time she chewed. It now matched her shirt, and I had a feeling more was on her lap.

I would need to hose her off before she brought all that stickiness in my car.

"A girl after my own heart," Kendall said, wiping Everly's face with a napkin she had dunked in her water glass. "Chocolate is my favorite kind of cake."

"Me too!" She reached for her milk, leaving chocolate handprints on the cup. When she finished drinking, she dumped another spoonful of whipped cream on her plate, her lips forming a big circle, full of excitement. "When are you going to be on TV? I need to remember, so I can ask Daddy if I can watch."

"The TV cameras are following her around now," I said.

"NOW?!" Everly shouted across the restaurant before realizing how loud she had been and laughing at herself.

"Not *now*, now," Kendall said. "But they have been over the last week, and the show will probably come on in a few months."

"Uncle D, make sure to tell Dad that, 'kay?"

"Of course."

Everly wiggled as she ate, the thrill not even close to wearing off and the sugar just starting to kick in. After a few more bites, she flopped back against her seat. She patted her belly. "Umph. I'm stuffed."

"That makes two of us, girlfriend."

I was feeling full myself and set down my fork, lifting my coffee to sip. "Was it better than you thought it would be?"

Her bangs bounced when she nodded. "I wanna come back next weekend, and I want Kendall to come."

"What if she's busy and she can't make it?"

"I can certainly make time to have brunch with you two,"

Kendall replied.

"It's a date," Everly said.

Kendall looked at me. "I'm not sure I'd call it that ..."

I held her gaze and then waved over the waitress to get the check. Before she even pulled it out of her apron, I handed her my credit card. "Do you mind boxing up these leftovers?"

"Of course. Let me run this"—she held up my card—"and I'll be right back."

Kendall put her arm around Everly, pulling her against her side. "This has been a blast. Maybe next time, I'll bake you something chocolaty to eat with your pancakes."

"Like cake?"

Kendall laughed. "Sure, I can make you a cake."

"Uncle D, can Kendall come over and bake a cake? And I can help her decorate and frost and stuff?"

My eyes were back on Kendall. She was making a promise she couldn't renege on, but her expression told me she wouldn't. She'd fallen for Everly, like I'd had a feeling she would.

"We can arrange that."

"Yay!"

Kendall smiled, using the same wet napkin to clean off Everly's face and hands. "We'll plan a time really soon. How does that sound?"

"Fantabulous."

The waitress delivered the receipt and returned my credit card and boxed each of the leftovers. I signed the bottom of the slip, and we got up from the booth, leaving the restaurant.

"Fly," Everly said, holding out her hands.

Balancing the boxes, I held one, and Kendall gripped the other. We lifted her into the air, her giggle louder than the traffic that passed.

Even though Kendall was looking at Everly, I couldn't take

my eyes off her.

Something had told me she was going to be wonderful around kids. But seeing her interact this way with my niece was an entirely different feeling. A deeper one, something I couldn't translate into words.

But I felt it.

Right in my goddamn chest.

Kendall, what the fuck am I going to do with you?

I couldn't get enough of her, couldn't keep her out of my mind.

Each time I tried, she found her way right back in.

More.

But was that something I could really give her?

Now?

Everly rose into the air one last time before we reached my SUV, and I got her set up in the backseat.

Kendall stayed beside me, and when I finished, she gave Everly a hug. "I'm going to walk back to my apartment, so I'm going to say good-bye now."

"*Nooo.*"

Kendall pulled back to look at my niece's face. "I promise you'll see me soon. I'll have Uncle D set up a cake date for us, all right?"

I heard the sadness in Everly's voice when she said, "*Okaaay.*"

Kendall gave her a final wave and shut the door. "Thank you for brunch. It was perfect in every way."

"Are you sure you don't want a lift? I'm passing your place on the way."

"It's only a block, and it's so nice out; I'd rather walk." She reached forward, her fingers gently touching my chin, her eyes searing through me. "I'll talk to you on Monday regarding that contract?"

"Out of all the things you could have chosen to have during that hour I blocked out for you, you want my negotiation skills ..."

She laughed, her hand dropping. "In front of your niece? Shame on you, you dirty man."

I watched her take several steps down the sidewalk before I climbed into the driver's seat.

"She's way awesome," Everly said as I shut the door.

The doll had returned, perched high on Eve's lap.

"I'm glad you liked her."

I pulled out of the parking lot and onto the main road, catching sight of Kendall's ass. Fuck, it looked so good in those pants, heart-shaped and luscious.

I honked as we passed and glanced in the rearview mirror as Everly waved through the window.

I waited to take a few more turns before I said, "What did Kendall whisper in your ear, the secret you're not supposed to tell me?"

"I can't tell, Uncle D."

I knew if I started a tickle war, the words would fly out.

But this was more fun.

"What if I promise a big sundae with tons of hot fudge for after dinner?"

"*Ohhh*. I like extra fudge." A smile moved over her face, and she squeezed the doll in her arms, wiggling in her car seat. "She said she likes you very much."

"Is that right?"

She gave me a big nod. "And she wishes you would be her friend already."

"She said that, huh?"

She yawned, resting her chin on the doll's head. "Uncle D, what in the world are you waiting for?"

I laughed, shaking my head.

TWENTY-ONE

KENDALL

"Who is that?" I whispered to Delilah as we sat on one of the couches in the VIP area of the club, the cameras pointed directly at us.

With the microphone taped to the inside of my dress, catching every word I said, there was no reason to keep my voice so low. Undoubtedly, this conversation would air on the show.

"Girl, you don't watch *Sky House*?" She waited for me to shake my head before continuing, "That's Presley Jordan, the lead in that show. Isn't he positively delicious?"

I hadn't asked because of his looks; I had asked because every girl in this club was gawking at him.

Presley Jordan.

That name did sound familiar.

The more I thought about it, I realized that it was because of Daisy; she had mentioned him in the past, saying how sexy he was. At one point, I could even recall Googling him just to see who she was talking about.

Presley didn't have that super-manly, husky handsomeness

like Dominick. But he was certainly cute in that boy-next-door kind of way, and the women in here were gushing over his smile, a set of white pearls that glowed, even in this dim room.

"Oh, honey, you're interested, aren't you?"

I looked at Delilah. "Me? No."

"*Riiight.*" She rolled her eyes. "Do you see all those girls flocking around him? They're not interested either."

"Why aren't you part of that group?"

She put her hand on my shoulder. "I don't like my boys clean; I like them bad. And Presley is so far out of that category."

I laughed as he happened to glance away from the girl he was speaking to, slowly looking around the room until his eyes landed on mine. His gaze was so intense, so heated, that I had to look away.

"My God, he can't take his eyes off you. *Daaamn*, that's a fuck-me stare if I've ever seen one."

"Don't be silly." A quick peek in his direction showed he was still studying me. "I'm sure he just recognizes me from somewhere—that's all."

But that wasn't the truth because I was positive we had never met before.

"I don't think so, babe. That man is practically stripping off your dress with his eyes."

"I'm definitely not interested in that."

"Show me who you would be interested in. Who in this club revs you up?"

I did a quick scan of the space around us. There were several celebrities, each of them so done up. Like Presley, every strand of hair had been perfectly placed, every accessory on point, as though their stylist were on standby, prettying them up between conversations.

That wasn't my style.

I wanted someone who could throw on a baseball hat and sweatpants and have breakfast with a little girl who was covered in chocolate chip pancakes. Someone who was as real on the outside as he was on the inside, who could be sensitive when it was required and rough when I demanded him to be.

Only one man fit that description.

"Not a single one," I finally replied.

"*Whaaat?*" She shook my shoulders. "Come on, girl. There has to be someone in here you find hot as hell."

"What can I say? I'm picky as fuck."

She was silent for a few moments before she said, "How about him?" and nodded toward the guy who had just walked into the VIP area. "I get the sense he'd be your type."

That man was Jenner.

"No." I laughed as I shook my head. "I know him, and he's not my type at all."

"Who is he? 'Cause, girl, maybe I need to know him."

"Remember my attorney, Dominick? That's his brother Jenner. He's a lawyer too. They're partners at their family law firm."

She was ready to pounce, especially when she said, "He's everything—provocative, sexy, and full of dick."

I tucked my clutch under my arm. "Go talk to him."

"You don't have to tell me twice." She pushed herself to the edge of the couch. "Do you want to come and introduce us?"

I smiled. "I don't think you need me to break the ice." I got to my feet, my ankles wobbling from the combination of sky-high heels and skinny margaritas. "Besides, I'm going to run off to the ladies' room before I hit up the dance floor."

"I'll meet you out there."

I nodded, and we parted ways. Delilah headed for the bar, where Jenner was sitting, and I went to the back, where I'd seen the sign for the restroom. As I was nearing the entrance, I felt a hand on my lower back, and I turned around.

A gasp left my lips when I saw who it was.

"Hi," Presley said. "Finally ... it's you."

I smiled at his weird choice of words. "Me?"

He reached for my hand, holding it between his. "You, the girl I've been staring at since I got here. In my head, that's what I was calling you until I found out your name."

"I'm Kendall."

"I know. I asked around." His smile grew. "You're even more gorgeous than I thought."

He still hadn't released me, so I turned my fingers, quickly shaking his, and pulled them back. "Thank you. It's nice to meet you, Presley."

His smile was certainly charming. The guy could probably teach a course on how to entice women. It just wasn't what I was looking for.

He glanced to his right, where a cameraman stood halfway between the couch and restroom, his lens aimed at us. "I was wondering if we could talk when the cameras weren't filming."

"Sure. Do you want to take down my number? We can chat—"

"Kendall, I'd like to talk to you now."

Now?

Without cameras?

I couldn't think of a single reason why he would want to have a conversation with me, but I was semi-curious, even more so because I hoped it had something to do with work.

"Were you about to go into the ladies' room?" he asked.

I nodded.

"Then, I'll go with you. I know the cameras aren't allowed in there."

Before my brain could even think of a response, his hand

was on my back again, and we were moving into the restroom. Once we were inside, I reached into my dress and turned down my microphone. The show allowed for privacy during bathroom breaks, so this was something I would normally do anyway.

He checked the stalls, each door unlocked and open. "Good. We're alone." He closed the distance between us, leaving less than a foot. "I know that won't last for long, so I'll be quick. Kendall, I'd really like to take you out. Not when there's cameras following you or when there's paparazzi tailing us. Just me and you, in a restaurant off the grid, where we can talk and get to know each other."

I was sure the shock was registering on my face, his suggestion the last thing I'd expected.

"I'm sorry ..." I took a breath. "I'm just a little surprised."

"I can tell. Why?"

"I don't know." I glanced around the small room, trying to get my thoughts straight. "I guess I assumed this had something to do with your show or mine or something like it in the future."

He laughed, moving a little closer. "That would come from my agent, not me." His knuckles grazed my cheek, a tender embrace that sparked nothing. "The rumor is, you're single, so what's the harm in grabbing something to eat?"

Direct and to the point—I couldn't knock him for that.

I had taken the same approach with Dominick.

Dominick ...

The man who was teasing me to death. Inviting me to hang out with him and his niece, where I'd fantasized about his hands as he held his fork, his lips as he ate those strawberry almond pancakes. My ovaries exploding every time he'd looked at Everly with all that love in his eyes.

"There's no harm in that," I replied. "But I don't think dinner is a good idea."

"We can skip dinner and go straight to dessert if you'd like." He added more charm to his grin. "When are you free?"

Never was the answer I wanted to give. I just didn't want to come across as rude.

"Can I look at my schedule and get back to you?"

He laughed, now his face full of shock.

I was sure no one had ever said that to him before. Most women would probably be lowering their dress right now.

"This show has so many unexpected, unplanned shoots. I'd most likely have to cancel our date, and that wouldn't be fair to you. When things are more confirmed, I'll have a better idea of when I'm available." I didn't want to lead him on, but I wanted to soften the blow in case I ran into him again. "I know your schedule is nuts, too, and you can relate to the madness of filming."

"I can. I get it." His hand had left my face and was now palm up in the air. "Give me your phone."

I reached inside my clutch and gave it to him, watching him press the screen and type.

"I saved my number in your Contacts. Call me when you're up for that date."

"Thank you," I said softly. I glanced at the door. "Should we get out of here?"

His gaze deepened. "Unless you'd like to stay ..." When I didn't reply, he added, "After you."

I stepped toward the exit, and the moment I opened the door, there was a flash in my face, followed by what felt like hundreds more, especially once Presley was directly behind me. The light was blinding. The questions—*Are you dating Presley Jordan? What were you two doing in the restroom? How long have you been intimate with one another?*—being shouted was completely overwhelming. I didn't know how many people were surrounding us, trying to see what the commotion was about, but it seemed like a gang and that they were all rushing at us.

Air was stuck in my throat, and I couldn't take a deep breath, my stomach in knots, my chest pounding.

I used my purse as a visor, trying to create some darkness so I could see, and I pushed myself away from the light and the people, moving against the nearest wall.

"How the hell did you get in here?" a bouncer shouted at a man, grabbing him by the neck and dragging him out of the VIP area.

The paparazzo.

He was still trying to take pictures, wrestling with his camera, even though he was being kicked out.

"Are you all right?" Presley asked, joining me.

I searched for my breath, trying to calm myself down. "I think so. That was a lot."

"The bouncers don't normally allow them in this area. That bastard must have somehow snuck in." He clenched my shoulder, smiling. "Call me, all right?"

I nodded, and as he disappeared into the crowd, I headed toward the bar, gripping the wooden top the moment my hands landed on it.

"What can I get you?" the bartender asked.

"Skinny margarita. Extra tequila, please."

A hand was on my back again, this time the sensation making me jump.

"Jesus, are you okay?" I heard.

I turned, and Jenner was behind me. "It's you—thank God."

"What happened back there?"

I shook my head. "One minute, I was leaving the restroom. The next, I couldn't see anything, and all these words were being screamed at me."

"Celebrity life. Here, drink some." He handed me his scotch, and I took a sip. "Being with Presley Jordan only fueled that fire. The paps love him; they follow him everywhere."

My stomach dropped once more, this time for an entirely different reason. "It wasn't how it looked."

He put his hands up, like I was pointing a gun at him. "I'm not here to judge."

I swallowed another sip and returned the drink to him. "Is he here?"

His eyes told me he knew who I was asking about.

"No."

I didn't know why I had this immense urge to see Dominick. I just felt like he could make this moment better somehow.

"Here you go," the bartender said.

I wrapped my fingers around the glass, and as I turned toward Jenner, he was taking a few steps back.

"I'll see you later, Kendall."

I waved, bringing the drink up to my lips, swallowing a huge gulp. I only had the chance to take one more sip before Delilah was at my side.

"I thought you weren't interested in him, you slut."

"I wasn't." That hadn't come out right. "And I'm not. We just went to talk, and a circus erupted."

The camera crew was nearby, catching every second of this. One of them signaled for me to turn my mic back on, but I didn't. I needed a minute to try and relax before they caught every word I said.

"You come out of the restroom—the ladies' room no less—with Presley's hand on you, and you expect me to believe nothing happened?" She snorted. "*Okaaay.*" She put her arm around my waist, clinking our glasses together. "Girl, you can't fool me, but I'll give you props for trying. Come on. Let's go dance."

I couldn't even imagine trying to do that right now.

There was a tightness in my chest. An uneasiness moving through my body that I was hoping this tequila would erase.

"I'll meet you out there."

"Suit yourself," she replied, heading for the other girls.

I took another drink and found my phone, searching my Contacts for Dominick's number. The clock on my screen showed it was past midnight. I could only hope he would answer.

"Kendall," he said in a rough, gritty voice.

"I woke you. I'm sorry."

"It's all right. What's going on?"

I moved to the side of the bar, positioning my back against the wall, giving it most of my weight. I knew the camera was catching this, too, so I tried to keep my face as emotionless as possible. "I don't know. I just needed to hear a familiar voice."

"You have mine."

"Dominick ..." My lungs felt like they were going to explode. "Everything is so crazy right now. I don't know how to navigate this—the cameras, this weird fame I'm experiencing, all these flashing lights."

"What happened?"

"This guy, he brought me into the restroom and asked me out on a date."

"Why are you telling me this?"

"Because ..." I paused to try to breathe, and a sound came through my cell, one that was specific for Celebrity Alerts.

I pulled the phone away from my face to read it.

BREAKING NEWS:

SHE MIGHT BE RELATED TO A FLOWER, BUT SHE'S QUITE
THE BEAUTIFUL GEM HERSELF.
WE'RE TALKING ABOUT MISS KENDALL ROY, ONE OF THE
FABULOUS SIX FROM GLITZY GIRLS, WHO WAS JUST SEEN
GETTING COZY WITH NONE OTHER THAN PRESLEY JORDAN.
AND BY COZY, WE MEAN, FINDING THEMSELVES IN A STALL
IN THE LADIES' ROOM.
PINK LOOKS MUCH BETTER ON KENDALL, DON'T YOU
THINK, MR. JORDAN?

My hands shook as I pressed the alert, a series of photos now loading that showed Presley and me coming out of a door clearly marked as the ladies' room. My skin appeared flushed, like something naughty had been going on in there, my hair a little disheveled.

Even my lipstick was smudged.

Whoever had Photoshopped these pictures, they had taken the lipstick from my mouth and smeared some on Presley's lips to make it look like we'd been kissing.

My knees felt weak as I read the alert again, my stomach churning, every emotion plowing into my chest. "Oh my God."

Dominick.

I moved the phone back to my ear just as he voiced, "I thought you said he only asked you out in the restroom?"

No.

No, no, nooo.

"Kendall, did you fuck him in there?"

"Hell no," I growled. "You know me better than that." My face dropped, my entire body shaking. "How did this happen? I ... I didn't even say yes to having dinner with him. Dominick, you have to believe me."

A few seconds of silence passed.

"Can you get a ride to my house?"

163

I glanced up, and two cameras were pointed at me, a lighting guy standing only a few feet away. I was sure they'd all read the alert and they were trying to film my reaction.

My stare moved farther across the room, and that was when I saw Jenner standing in a group, where he was talking to another guy.

"I'm pretty sure I can," I replied.

"Make sure no one follows you. Call me if you need me."

I set my drink down and hurried past the cameras and lighting team, and when I reached Jenner, I wrapped my hands around his arm and whispered in his ear, "Will you take me to your brother's house?"

I knew this was going to get me in trouble with production. I had to get it cleared before I left a set for any reason, but I didn't care about that right now. I just needed to get out of here.

He looked down at my face, and I felt so many other eyes on me.

Everyone in this room had seen the alert.

They were all assuming the same thing.

So was the entire world. In the next few minutes, every media outlet would be posting the same photographs.

My family would see. My friends in Boston.

I felt sick.

"Please," I begged. "I need to go, and I know you'll get me there safely."

He handed his drink to one of his friends and took off his jacket, giving it to me. "I'm parked out back, but put this on over your head. There's going to be paparazzi everywhere outside, and they're going to want to get more shots of you."

TWENTY-TWO

DOMINICK

I was reading the Celebrity Alert again when the gate outside my driveway began to open, the monitor in the kitchen showing Jenner's car driving through.

He'd asked me to go out with him tonight, and I'd chosen sleep. I could only assume he'd ended up at the same club Kendall was at and that she was the passenger in his front seat.

I met her at the door, holding it open enough for her to slip inside, and I waved at Jenner as he reversed out of my driveway. Once I locked up, she was sitting on my couch in the same dress that had appeared in the photos. Her hair wasn't as wild as it had looked in the shots, her skin not as flushed.

She didn't have any lipstick on.

"Do you want some water?"

She nodded, and I went into the kitchen, grabbing two bottles that I brought into the living room, handing her one. I took the blanket off the back of the couch and spread it over her.

"Tell me what happened."

Photographers manipulated their shots before they sold

them to online outlets. Responses and situations were almost always taken out of context. I knew because these were things I fixed for a living, suing photographers and media sources when I could prove fraud.

Before my hands went anywhere near Kendall, I needed to get to the bottom of this.

And I needed to hear it in her words.

Her knees were pressed against her chest, arms wrapped around them; she looked even smaller than she already was. "I've never experienced anything like that before." She put her head down, and when she finally looked up again, I saw the emotion. "The lights, the screaming, all the rushing around me. It felt like I was being attacked."

I sat beside her, resting my fingers on the back of her neck, feeling the heat on her skin. "It can get intense, I know."

"It all started when Jordan approached me in the VIP area," she began, and she went on to explain how he'd led her into the restroom to ask her out on a date. She described their conversation, how he'd come on to her and the way he had touched her face. She even told me the excuse she had given him and how he'd programmed his number in her phone.

She put down her water. "I mean, God, there were hundreds of other stunning women there tonight. Celebrities. Industry peeps. I didn't think he'd be interested in me."

It blew my mind that she had no idea how beautiful she was. That she didn't believe a cocky son of a bitch like Presley Jordan could want her.

But it wasn't the right time to tell her this.

"I don't like him—you need to know that, Dominick. I'm never even going to call him." She opened her bag and took out her phone, showing me his number. "See, I'm deleting his info right now." She tossed her cell against the couch, her eyes taking in mine. "Photoshop is what I know best, and I can promise you with everything I have that those shots were edited. I wasn't even wearing pink lipstick tonight."

I believed her.

Not a single part of this story surprised me in any way. This was Hollywood; these were the things that happened to make money and sell stories and gain popularity.

But there was one thing that needed clarification. "Why did you call me?"

She released a long exhale, her legs dropping from her chest, her hands folding on her lap. "When that happened, all I wanted was your voice. Your protection. Your arms around me." She ran her hand through her hair. "Then, you seeing that alert and thinking I would do that, that I would so easily be with someone else when I had all these feelings for you, was something I couldn't handle."

"Kendall—"

"No," she said, grabbing my arm, "let me finish." She took another breath. "I don't know how else to tell you this or how to show you I'm nuts about you, but I am. I know this life isn't what you want, and I understand now why that is. If tonight showed me anything, it's that. But somehow, someway, I believe we can make this work if it's something we both want." Her eyes were pleading with mine. "And it's what I want, Dominick. More than anything."

What she wouldn't let me tell her was that when that alert had come across my phone and I looked at the photos of Kendall and Presley, how they had been made to look like Presley's hands and mouth had been all over her, I'd wanted to fucking throw my phone across the room.

All I could hear in my head was Brett's warning, repeating on a continuous loop.

"Stop denying yourself and scoop that shit up before

someone else does and you hate yourself because you fucking lost her."

I knew this wasn't going to be easy. It would take some maneuvering and hard planning to keep this relationship private for as long as we could. Dating was something I never did, especially with a celebrity-to-be, but there was no way I could let this one go. No fucking way I could let another second pass without this stunning girl knowing exactly how I felt about her.

"Get over here." My eyes narrowed as I took her in, deciding that if she didn't move closer in the next few seconds, I was going to lift her myself.

"Dominick, I don't—"

My hand tightened on her neck, and I growled, "So I can put my lips on you and show you that you're mine."

Slowly processing my words, she threw herself in my arms, clutching my waist with all her strength. My hands became lost in those unruly locks as I held her even tighter against me. For the first few seconds, she squeezed me with all her strength, and then her body turned limp, allowing me to move her, protect her, hold her the way I wanted.

"Baby," I whispered, pulling her head back, locking our stares, "I'm fucking crazy about you. When I'm not with you, you're all I think about, wanting to be closer, wanting to wrap you against me." My lips pressed to her cheek. "Wanting to be inside you."

I took several breaths, inhaling her tropical scent, and leaned back to look at her again. "You were correct when you said I hadn't found the right one. But that was, until I met you, Kendall. That's when everything changed—when I started to change."

I held her face, scanning each of her eyes. "I fought this because I knew it was going to get heavy and go against everything I believed." I shook my head. "But I can't fight it anymore. I can't take the chance of losing you." I swiped my thumb across her bottom lip, my favorite of the two. "You're perfect. And you're perfect for me."

"You're ... mine."

A smile moved across me. "In every fucking way."

Her arms found their way around my neck, and she moved over my lap, her legs straddling me. I gripped her ass, hissing when I didn't feel any panties and again when I felt the bump of her microphone pack.

"It's turned off; don't worry." She reached into the top of her dress and moved the piece that was taped inside along with the wire and the hardware it was attached to, setting the whole device on my couch.

I held her face still. "You need to make me a promise. No more photos of you and Presley or some other dude coming out of a restroom—or anywhere for that matter."

"Was someone a little jealous?"

I rubbed my nose over hers. "I didn't like it."

"At the thought of him touching me or that the world would assume the two of us were together?"

"Both." My fingers tightened, and I felt the need to repeat myself. "You're mine, Kendall. All mine."

With her legs still over me, she positioned her pussy directly over my hard cock, rubbing herself back and forth across me. "This was what I wanted when I called you from the club. The side of you that goes all alpha and territorial and doesn't want to share me with anyone."

I cupped her ass. "How much of that side do you want right now?"

She moaned, "Every inch of it."

I lifted her dress over her head and unclipped her bra. Now that she was naked, I held her head back, elongating her neck so

I could kiss all the way down her throat, across her collarbone, stopping at her tits.

I pulled one of her nipples into my mouth, sucking the end, grazing it with my teeth.

"Oh my God, yes."

She quivered beneath my mouth, her pussy grinding over me as though she couldn't stop.

What I needed was to be inside her, owning the deepest part of her body.

But I was going to take my time in getting there.

I sucked away, massaging around her tit while my mouth focused on just the center. After several laps of my tongue, she got more of my teeth, giving her that small burst of pain I knew she liked.

But as much as I fucking loved her nipples, I needed to taste her.

I set her back on the couch and dragged my lips down her navel, pausing at the top of her pussy. Her inner thighs were wet, showing me how turned on she was. My nose pressed against her clit, breathing her in.

"Fuck, I missed this scent."

Her fingers dug into my hair, her hips tilted upward, both movements urging me to lick.

But I stayed right where I was, swallowing her aroma. "Mine," I growled.

"Yours."

That earned her two fingers, the tips circling her until I knew she was ready, and I slipped them inside her. Her tightness immediately closed in on me.

"*Ahhh*. Fuck!"

"I know you like that." I went in as far as my knuckles, turning my wrist and pulling back, her wetness coating me as I plunged in.

With each dip, her hips swayed, her breathing became louder, her hand tugged even more of my hair.

I hadn't even licked her yet.

But it was time.

I flattened my tongue, swiping the whole length of her, spreading her wetness. At the very top of her clit, I made my tongue into a point and flicked back and forth.

"Dominick!" She trembled and rocked against me. "Yes!"

She was getting my fastest speed, every twist of my fingers, the full power of my tongue.

And I knew what it was all doing to her. I could hear it in her moans. I could feel it by the way her clit was hardening. I could taste it as her wetness thickened.

"Your mouth," she cried. "Oh *fuuuck.*"

She rubbed her cunt over my face, the build so present in her body, and when I knew she had reached her peak, she began to shudder, screaming my name at the same time, each syllable drawn out. Waves of tremors shot across her stomach, and I licked and swallowed her until she stilled.

"*Mmm.*" When she calmed, I kissed around her pussy, slowly pulling my fingers out and licking those too. "I could do this all fucking day."

Our eyes met.

"I might ask you to."

I kissed up her stomach and across her tits, stopping at her mouth. "You won't have to. It's going to happen whether you want it or not."

"You"—she shivered—"are everything."

I lifted her off the couch and into my arms and carried her into my bedroom, setting her on the bed. I left her for just a moment to grab a condom from my nightstand, and when I returned to her, I dropped my sweatpants and T-shirt on the floor. While I tore off the corner of the foil packet, she surrounded my crown with her mouth.

"Goddamn it, that feels good."

With her eyes on mine, she pumped the base of my cock with her fist, her lips wide as she took in the rest of my shaft.

"Suck it."

And she did, like it was hers, like she couldn't get enough of it down her fucking throat.

"Fuck yes."

She was squeezing with the right amount of pressure, swirling her tongue over my tip and down the sides. She wasn't just bobbing; she was closing her cheeks in around me, giving me the friction I needed.

I could easily come.

But I needed her pussy tonight.

I pulled out and held the condom over my crown, rolling it over me.

"If I'm really yours, you don't have to use that."

My gaze hardened as I took in her stare.

"I'm on birth control, Dominick, and I'm clean. As long as you're not going to be with anyone else, I'd rather not use one."

I knew what this meant—now and for our future.

And I was ready for it.

"Yours," I repeated for both of us to hear, and I tossed the condom on the floor, moving directly between her legs.

It had been a long time since I'd been inside a pussy uncovered, possibly as far back as high school, and the anticipation was overwhelming. With her legs spread wide, I positioned myself, devouring her lips while I dived in.

"Fuck," I bolted out when her wetness covered me, a heat I didn't normally feel, a tightness that hadn't ever been this intense. "Kendall ..." I pulled back, my nose pressed to hers, and I stayed buried, her pussy clutching me. "Jesus Christ."

172

"I know."

I reared back and thrust in again, her legs widening around my waist. Her back lifted off the bed as she met me in the middle.

There was such a difference, and I felt it each time I sank into her. So many fucking sensations—a narrowness, a pulsing, a goddamn dripping.

"Kiss me," I barked, her mouth being the only thing I wanted to taste in that moment.

She instantly sucked on the end of my tongue. I could feel the desperation in our mouths, the need to be closer even if that was impossible.

She released a long, pent-up sigh the second our lips separated. "Your cock, Dominick ... fuck."

And then she gripped my face as though I were going to pull away. I had no intention; I needed her mouth as much as her body. To feel every part of her, her lips being the most intimate.

Air stopped moving so easily through my lungs. A build was working its way through me, consuming me. Somehow, I needed more, and the only way to get that was to free up my hands.

I flipped onto my ass and moved her onto my lap, her legs on either side of me as I pressed my back against the headboard.

She knew what this position meant, but I still ordered her to, "Ride me."

When she rose, her pussy clenched my cock, her wetness sucking me in as she lowered.

"Yes," I roared. "Fuck me."

I roamed her body, starting with her tits, rolling them, pinching, the hardness growing. They each got a quick lick, but that wasn't enough. I breathed against her nipple, pulling the tip with my teeth.

"Oh God, Dominick."

When she stalled, I knew the sensations were grabbing ahold of her, the stillness as intense as the grinding. And when she kept me in and rotated, hitting her inner walls, I fucking lost it. The motion was rubbing her clit against me, so I didn't touch it, but the moment she lifted, that was where my fingers went. I didn't need to spread any wetness—my girl was already sopping.

She moaned, "Yes! You're going to make me come."

I wasn't far behind, but I couldn't give up this feeling. I needed more of her. "Not yet."

I leaned her back, her elbows falling to the mattress, catching her weight, and I rose to my knees, holding her legs around my waist. This new placement opened her hips, allowing me to get in deeper, feeling an endless surge of pleasure.

"Oh fuck." She quivered, her eyes feral and stunning. "This isn't going to stop me from coming—I can tell you that right now."

I gave up on wanting her to wait.

In fact, I wanted to feel her cunt squeezing my cock even tighter.

While holding her, I reached down and rubbed her clit, giving her the pressure she needed, arching my hips at the same time and driving back in.

"Dom-i-nick," she panted.

She was on the ride.

The one where there was no stopping, no turning back.

All she could do was hold on.

And she did, her eyes glued to mine while I dominated every part of her.

But as she began that climb—her body responding, allowing

me to feel each change—it all felt too fucking good. To the point where I couldn't hold back.

"Kendall," I roared, nipping her hip with my fingers, her cunt pulsing.

"Harder."

That was what I gave her. A pace that sent her soaring, a power that pounded into her, taking over every one of her senses.

She gripped me as she fucking screamed, "Dominick," and she completely lost herself.

And I got to watch.

Each shudder that passed through her came with a different feeling, one that held me inside, milking me in a way that it hadn't ever before. She was drawing my orgasm closer, teasing it, each moan and throb bringing it toward the surface.

A rush of her wetness coated me.

"*Ahhh*! Yes, Kendall!"

And that was when I lost it.

"Fuck me." Not able to hold back for a second longer, the burst came through my balls, up my stomach, and peaked. With her face too far away to kiss, I gnawed her nipple as the pleasure ascended through my body. I treated her nipple as though it were her lips, licking across it, sucking like her cunt was doing to my cock.

The first shot made me fucking shudder, moaning, "Kendall," as my hips thrust as hard as they could.

A tightness moved through me, followed by an immediate release, each pump filling that beautiful fucking pussy with more of my cum.

"Yes!" I continued to hold her, breathing out my orgasm, my movements slowing once the sensation began to pass. The moment I finally stilled, I rested my face on her stomach, exhaling over that warm, soft skin. "Christ."

We stayed in that position, locked, until I settled my head on the pillow and rested hers on my chest. Her legs tangled with mine, her arms holding me in a way where I didn't want her to let go.

"You're an animal." She took several breaths. "A wild, erotic, unsatiated animal."

I traced down her back, her goose bumps meeting my fingertips. "Wait until I fuck your ass. Then, that term will have a whole new meaning."

She tilted her neck to look at me. "I've never done that before. Should I be nervous?"

"Do you trust me?"

There was no pause when she answered, "Yes."

I softly surrounded her top lip and bottom with my own, giving her the smoothness of my tongue. "I'll be gentle."

Her reply came out as a laugh and then a long, deep moan.

TWENTY-THREE

KENDALL

"Hello?" I whispered into my phone, the head of production appearing on my caller ID, but I still kept my voice low so I wouldn't wake up Dominick.

"Kendall, it's Shane."

I'd expected one of the assistants to phone me, not the boss. If Shane was calling, that meant I was in serious trouble.

And I deserved to be.

"Hi."

"We need to talk about last night."

I hurried out of Dominick's bedroom, so he wouldn't hear me, and I took a seat on the couch in the living room.

"Before you say anything, I'm sorry I left the club and that I didn't tell anyone I was going or get it approved by production. It was wrong, and I know it goes against every rule. That was extremely irresponsible of me."

I looked at my hand, remembering how they had shaken when the alert came through my phone. "There's no excuse for what I did, but I want you to understand where I'm coming from. Having a Celebrity Alert so inaccurately portray a situation, one that affects me so personally, was something I'd never experienced, and I know I didn't handle it right, but I was overwhelmed, and I reacted." I flattened my palm against my chest, the memories from last night resurfacing.

"I know I signed up for this show, I know I agreed to air my life, and I'm sorry. All I can say is that it won't happen again."

He was quiet for a moment. "I appreciate you taking responsibility."

I walked over to the sliding glass door, watching the sun rise higher in the sky, peeking through the wispy clouds. "There's no one else to blame other than myself."

"You know your contract states that we can fine you for this type of behavior, and I'm not going to waive it. The full amount will be docked from your check. I don't want the other girls to think we tolerate these kinds of actions. We don't, in any capacity, but you took accountability for your infraction, and that's all I can ask for."

"I understand."

"Filming starts in three hours. I assume you'll be there?"

"Yes. Of course."

"Good. We'll need you to go straight into an interview, where production will ask you to discuss the alert and your reaction to it. Once we have that documented, you'll join the other girls for brunch. Do you have any questions?"

"No." I turned around and walked back toward the bedroom. "Thank you."

He said good-bye and hung up, and I climbed back into Dominick's bed.

"Do you have to leave?"

I wrapped my arm over his abs, my face pressed to his chest. "Not yet, but that was Shane, head of production. He wasn't happy, but he didn't fire me, so that's a good thing. And now that that's taken care of, I have to tackle my parents and explain the whole night to them, so they don't think their daughter turned into this promiscuous minx when she moved out to LA."

"That sounds less than fun."

I ran my hand through his hair and around his face, his whiskers so rough and delicious. "They have an idea how all of this works. I mean, my sister has definitely prepped them for the Hollywood madness. Plus, they know me. I'm no prude, but banging in a public restroom isn't my style."

He took in my face. "Can I make a suggestion?"

"Please."

He rolled toward me, resting his arm across my hip. "Do you have photos of yourself from last night, prior to when things had gone down with Presley?"

I nodded. "The girls and I took several while we were in the limo and a bunch more while we were inside the club."

"At some point today, once you get your thoughts straight, go to your Instagram and share one of those pictures. It'll show what you really looked like last night, and in your post, say that it was wonderful to meet Presley, but photos aren't always the way they seem, especially the ones that have been digitally retouched." His thumb traced my lips. "Then, end it with something personal and cute, like you hope the next time you find yourself in a Celebrity Alert, it's due to your philanthropical work. That the ninety-year-old you're teaching watercolor to looks much better in pink."

My chest instantly started to loosen.

I hadn't even thought of that, but he was absolutely right.

"You're my hero."

His stare was so intense, endearing. "I've been in this business a long time, baby. These are just tricks of the trade." He leaned down, grazing his nose over my cheek, as though he was inhaling me. "I need to tell you something."

I was silent while his head returned to the pillow, his arm going behind it to prop himself up.

"I assigned Daisy to one of the attorneys on my team. If she's unhappy with the transition, she can find herself a new law firm, but I won't represent her any longer."

My heart clutched, and I pushed myself up onto my elbow. "I'm not asking for that. I hope you don't feel pressured because of what happened."

His fingers soothed those thoughts as he caressed my face. "I'm dating her sister now, so it's a conflict of interest, in my opinion. Not to mention, she's been a fucking cunt to you." His grip tightened. "But I can see that you're worried, and I assure you, anyone on my team will take excellent care of her."

"Good."

He shook his head, sighing. "You're nothing like her."

It killed me that we still hadn't spoken. That I would have to be the one to reach out if things were ever to get fixed. But she'd want me to take the blame for our spat, and I didn't think that was fair.

"No matter what, I'll always love her and care about her. I truly want the best for her, Dominick."

"Even if she treats you like shit?"

I thought about his question. I let it simmer, and eventually, I nodded. "Yes. She's my family."

"I have news," I said to Charlize, standing outside my building after Dominick dropped me off. "It's top secret—you can't share it even if there's wine or a gun is being held to your head—but I have to tell someone before I explode."

I couldn't go inside and talk to him. Every word would be

caught on camera, and I just wanted this moment of privacy before I went upstairs and got ready to film.

"Does it have to do with Presley Jordan? Because I was texting you all night, and your MIAness has made me CRAYness."

"You know those pics are fake, and that alert couldn't have been further from the truth."

"I figured. Homegirl does not have the right skin tone for pink—no offense. Besides, I know you're not moving on that fast from Daddy Dominick."

I laughed, walking on the curb that framed the side of the building, balancing on it like it was a beam. "There's no moving on. We're together."

"*Whaaa*? Damn, I'm happy that man finally came to his senses. He was about to earn himself a slap for being so ridiculously stupid. When did this all go down?"

"Last night, I darted out of the club and went to his house."

"You've officially scored yourself the hottest man I've ever seen in a suit. So, how's this all going to play out? I mean, you're on camera, and that hasn't changed."

I paused the pacing, teetering on my heels. "We're going to keep it a secret for as long as we can. If that means date nights at his house, I definitely have no objections to that. As for outings"—my chest tightened a little as I thought of the upcoming events I had, things I wanted to share with him, like the red carpet for opening night, the photo shoot I'd soon be having for the sunglasses deal—"we'll figure it out as we go."

"Honey, those are just details. It doesn't take away from how happy you sound right now."

The smile was already there, his words causing it to widen even more.

"I am, like almost-tearing-up kind of happy."

"You know that means another celebration." He giggled.

"It's a hell of a good thing they have a lot of tequila in this state because I see years of skinny margaritas in our future."

My eyes closed, a warmth filling every part of me.

The move had brought some heartache—leaving my friends and family in Boston, having a falling-out with my sister, the world thinking I'd slept with Presley Jordan—but it had brought so many wonderful things into my life as well.

"I'm lucky to have you," I said, the tears making their way down my cheeks.

"No, babycakes, I'm the lucky one."

TWENTY-FOUR

DOMINICK

"I'm one lucky motherfucker," I said as I opened my front door while the most gorgeous girl stood on the other side, dressed in a pair of cutoffs and a tank top with flip-flops on her feet and not a drop of makeup on.

She waited for my eyes to return to hers after they traveled the length of her body before she replied, "Two rounds of hair and makeup today and six outfit changes. My body is tired of clothes, and my face needed to breathe."

"You're more than welcome to show up naked. No need to get dressed for me." My hands went to her waist, pulling her inside. "And I prefer you without makeup."

She dropped her bag on the floor, her arms circling my neck. "*Mmm*," she moaned as she kissed me. "I've been thinking about your lips all day." As she pulled away, she touched hers, first the top and then the bottom, as though I'd left something behind.

"My lips?"

She nodded. "They're soft and so dominant. I know exactly how you're feeling by the way you kiss me."

"How about tonight?"

She smiled. "Hungry."

I chuckled, shutting the door behind her. I then took the overnight bag from the floor and placed it on the couch, returning to her side.

She linked her fingers through mine. "I used to have to dream about them, fantasizing about their taste and feel." She rose on her tiptoes and pressed her mouth against mine. "Now, I can kiss you whenever I want, and I love that."

I cupped her ass, searching for a panty line. When I didn't feel one, I growled at the thought of her bare pussy rubbing against her shorts.

"My face isn't the only thing that likes to breathe," she whispered. "That's why I never wear them."

"And you expect me to get through dinner with that knowledge in my head?" I squeezed her ass even harder. "That I just have to take these off and your pussy is ready for me to eat."

"Let's see how long you can make it." She smiled. "Besides, it would be a shame to skip dinner. I'm sure whatever you cooked is going to be incredible."

I could say the same thing about her cunt, but I held her face still and kissed her instead.

When our mouths separated, my grip dropped to her chin, taking in her beautiful eyes. "We're having barbeque."

"Yum." She nibbled her lip. "And I brought dessert."

I rubbed that forbidden spot between her cheeks. "I hope it's this."

She laughed as she walked over to the couch, removing Tupperware from her bag. "I baked." She opened the lid to show me.

Inside were several rows of chocolate-covered balls. I grabbed one and bit off half.

"What are they?" It took a moment before the inside melted over my tongue. "Jesus, this is fucking good."

"Aren't they heavenly?" She popped a whole one into her mouth. "They're cake balls, and it saddens me that you've never had one before."

"You know I'm not into dessert."

She winked, handing me another. "And you know I'm determined to change that about you." She pointed to the new one in my hand. "That's red velvet. I wasn't sure what kind you'd like more, so I made a few different flavors. The first one you had was peanut butter, obviously. There's also Oreo and butter cake."

"When did you have time to make these?"

"At three this morning."

"Kendall ..."

"You're worth it, so don't even."

I kissed her again, giving her a taste of the red velvet I'd just finished devouring. "They're really excellent. Gooey cake, balled up and dunked in chocolate. Fucking genius."

"Thank you." She put the lid on the container. "We'll save these for after dinner." She nodded toward the kitchen. "Put me to work. I want to help with what you've got going on in there."

I held her against me for several more seconds, needing to feel more of her body. "I was waiting for you to get here before I threw the steaks on the grill. Veggies are going on there too. Potatoes are in the oven."

"Sounds like you've got it handled. I'll set the table."

"Already done."

I brought her into the kitchen, where the meat was sitting in a pool of marinade, rising to room temperature—a trick I'd learned from my father that made the beef juicier. The vegetables were next to it, all cut to the size I wanted.

She eyed up both and wrapped her arms around my waist. "I'm impressed. Admittedly, I semi-expected your chef to be here. I'm really happy he's not."

My thumb traced her bottom lip before I kissed it.

The truth was, our chef was tied up at Ford's house tonight, but I wouldn't have used him. I knew my cooking would mean more to Kendall than having my chef here.

"Hungry?"

"Starving."

"I'll start grilling."

She loosened her arms, and I took the meat and vegetables outside. There were four different cuts of beef that I set on the grill—my goal was to give us a variety of flavors. On the other side of the flames, I lined up the large mushroom caps and cubed onions that I wanted caramelized for the steaks along with bell peppers and jalapeños. I made sure the temperature wasn't too high and shut the lid.

"Thirsty?"

I nodded. "There are limes by the bar and several different kinds of tequila on the shelves. If you're feeling wine, there's red in the racks and white in the fridge below."

"Fresh lime juice. God, you're amazing." Her fingers went to my face, and I kissed them before they landed. "What can I get you?"

"Red. It'll go perfectly with dinner."

"I'll be right back."

She disappeared inside, and through the windows, I watched her walk to my wet bar. She looked so natural in my house, like one of the floor-to-ceiling art pieces that decorated the walls in my home. And, goddamn it, she was stunning. She put her back to me as she scanned my wine collection, reading a few labels before choosing one and pouring it into two Bordeaux glasses.

She handed me my drink when she came back outside, clinking our wines together. "To our first home-cooked meal."

"Our second."

The sexiest smile stretched across her face. "I would hardly call eating Mexican at your desk a home-cooked meal."

"I would." I grazed her chin with my fingers. "And it was fucking amazing."

"Okay, okay, to our second meal, then." She took a drink. "But now, I owe you something really tasty if I'm going to compete with what you've done here."

I set the glass on the counter of my summer kitchen and checked the food. "Whatever you make, I'm positive I'll enjoy it."

She closed her eyes, inhaling the scents wafting off the grill. "I know exactly what I'm going to do, but I'm going to need to borrow your kitchen since we know date night can't happen at mine."

"It's all yours. You can make yourself at home."

She leaned into me, hugging our bodies together. "I like the sound of those words."

My lips went to her neck, where I devoured her scent, taking several whiffs before I surrounded her earlobe. "You know what I like? The thought of you in my kitchen."

"Dominick," she breathed, quivering, "if you keep that up, we're definitely skipping the eating part of this meal, and that would be a real travesty because I'm dying to attack that rib eye."

As she moved to one of the lounge chairs, I poked the meat with the tongs, checking the texture to see what temperature it had reached. "Five more minutes."

"Whatever you say, chef." She held her wine against her chest, her legs curled underneath her, feet bare and crossed. "I want to ask you something. I'm not trying to dampen the mood, but I have to know." She stopped to take a breath. "Did you talk to Daisy about the attorney stuff?"

I sat in the lounge chair beside hers. "Yes."

"I need more than yes, mister. I need details."

I'd planned on telling her later tonight. I was just waiting for the right moment.

But when it came to Daisy, I was learning there never was a right time. All she did was cause Kendall anxiety and anguish, and I couldn't fucking stand it.

"I didn't think it was professional if the conversation took place over the phone or through email, so I had her come in today."

Her eyes widened. "And?"

For confidentiality reasons, I couldn't say Daisy had immediately blamed her, how she went on the attack, ranting about Kendall before I kicked her ass out, telling her my firm would no longer represent her anymore.

I wouldn't tolerate that behavior, no matter who it came from.

And I wouldn't sit there and listen to her accuse my girlfriend of something that wasn't her fault.

Instead, I told Kendall, "It went exactly the way you'd expect."

"I'm assuming that means, she lost her mind?"

"The Dalton Group won't be working with Daisy. Ever again."

Streaks of emotion shot across her face. "Dominick, I'm so sorry."

"Baby, for what?" I reached across the space between us, grazing the back of her arm. "You've done nothing wrong. This is all on her."

She was silent, staring at the pool, at the hills of homes across from mine. "I feel responsible for her actions. I mean, if it wasn't for me, she wouldn't be having these outbursts." She glanced at me. "Which, I assume, was ugly?"

When I wouldn't give her a confirmation, she looked away again, tucking her legs against her chest.

"Have you heard from her?"

She continued to look straight ahead when she replied, "No, but I'm sure it's just a matter of time." She sighed. "I don't want this. I know you know that, but I still need to say it." She wrapped her arms around her knees. "She had a crush on Presley Jordan, so she must be beside herself over that Celebrity Alert. She lost her unicorn agent and manager, followed by her incredible attorney. It seems like I'm trying to steal everything away from her, and that couldn't be further from the truth."

"She knows about us."

Her head turned so fast; she could have gotten fucking whiplash. "How?"

"I don't know."

"Dominick ..." She dropped her feet on the pavers, taking several drinks of her wine. "She went from being on top of the world to feeling like she was going to lose it all, and that happened the moment I got just the tiniest bit of attention."

"It's getting worse."

She stared at me for several moments. "What do you mean?"

"At the beginning of this week, I heard she lost one of her endorsements. Apparently, an incident had happened on set while they were shooting a campaign, and they paid her what they owed her and canceled her contract."

"You're kidding?"

"Brands keep things quiet. They don't like drama—it hurts business—so you won't hear about this unless she tells people, which she won't."

"Oh my God." Her hand went to her forehead. "I used to pay her bills and balance her checkbook; I know how much income those sponsorships generated. And now ... they're all going away."

"And it's her fucking fault." I moved over to her chair, extending her legs across my lap. "Baby, you'd better not take a single second of blame for this. Hollywood might appear big, but the industry is tight, and people talk. Your reputation is all you have, and the moment you start treating people like shit and acting like an entitled cunt, people notice. Everyone is replaceable, and Daisy Roy is getting what she fucking deserves."

"But she's worked so hard to get here." Her voice was only a little above a whisper.

"Then, she needs to start appreciating what she has and respecting those who have helped her." I rubbed the bottoms of her feet. "And that includes you."

TWENTY-FIVE

KENDALL

Dominick returned to the grill to finish cooking our dinner, leaving me on the lounge chair with a tornado of thoughts in my head. Most of them picturing Daisy in her giant house, alone, drowning in her avalanche that seemed to be gaining more momentum each day.

Maybe I really did need to reach out, to try and find a way to be there for her. It was too late to even consider leaving the show—I was under contract, and it was ironclad. My first endorsement had come in, the deal signed, and Brett had emailed the details of another one, which had been sent to Dominick this morning for him to review.

Was it too late to stop it all just to please my sister?

Did I even want to?

And just when I thought things couldn't get worse, it did the moment my phone vibrated from my back pocket.

Daisy: You're ruining my whole life. I hope you're fucking happy. And I hope you're fucking proud of yourself.

My entire body shook as I read her text, my heart pounding as though I'd been running.

I glanced at Dominick. He was standing at the grill, flipping the meat, so I turned my attention to my phone, fingers hovering above the screen.

She was so angry, and it was my fault.

Somehow, I had to make this better.

Me: I'm not happy. I'm not even close to happy. It kills me to know that things are going wrong in your life. I love you, Daisy. Let's talk and air everything out.

Daisy: You mean, you'd step down from your high horse and meet with little ol' me? Never.

Me: You know it's not like that. You know I would do anything for you.

Daisy: I asked you not to do the show, so that's a lie—you wouldn't do anything for me. What else have you lied to me about? Oh, let's see. 1. Your desire to get into acting. 2. Your attraction to Presley Jordan. 3. Your attraction to my attorney. I could keep going, but my fingers are getting tired of typing.

Me: Now, you're just being catty.

Daisy: Six weeks since you moved to LA and you've already destroyed my life. SIX FUCKING WEEKS. Go fuck yourself, Kendall.

"Hey ..."

I looked up, and Dominick was standing in front of the chair, the meat on one platter, the vegetables on another.

"You're texting her, aren't you?"

I took a big, deep breath, slipping the phone back into my pocket. "How could you tell?"

"Your expression. It's also telling me the conversation didn't go well."

I tried to find my breath, stopping the tremors from racking my body. "She told me to go fuck myself."

His jaw flexed as he ground his teeth together.

I would never take for granted how protective he was. It was one of the traits I loved most about him.

"Fuck her. Everything she's saying is bullshit—you know this. So, stop focusing on Daisy and what you can do to repair things. It takes two, Kendall, and she's made no effort. Instead, all she's done is blame you for everything." He nodded toward the house. "Tonight is about us, not her."

He was right.

I couldn't sit here and dwell on something I had no control over. When Daisy was finally able to see that she wasn't the innocent party in this mess, maybe that was when things would change between us. Until then, we'd just have to continue with the way things were.

That made me even unhappier, but I had no other choice.

I gave him a smile, knowing that was what he wanted to see. "Let's go eat."

I followed him inside, draining the rest of my wine, and headed straight to the bar to retrieve the bottle, carrying it to the table. When I noticed Dominick's glass on the counter by the grill, I went out and got it, filling both as I came back in.

He'd set the platters in the center of the table, all four of the steaks already sliced.

"I'll get the potatoes," I said, rushing into the kitchen, sticking them on a plate that I carried into the dining room. When I returned, he filled my dish with a little of everything, the aroma almost overwhelming as I sat in my seat. "I'm so ridiculously impressed right now."

He picked up his wine, smiling. "Wait until you try it."

I started with the baked potato, my knife sliding right

through the skin. "It's cooked perfectly." I added the necessary condiments and took a bite. *"Mmm*, yes."

While I chewed, I cut off a chunk of rib eye, the edges richly seared, a medium temperature in the center, a thick seasoning coating the outside. "Oh my God, Dominick." I barely had to chew—the meat practically melted, the flavors exploding on my tongue. I added a few pieces of onion and mushroom into my mouth and moaned.

"You seriously know the way to my heart." I pointed at my plate. "Food will always be my love language."

He was holding his fork but stayed still, watching me dig into the jalapeño and place some over the tenderloin.

"Wow, that was just as good," I said from behind my hand. "The spice and savory meat—now, that's an unforgettable combo."

Leaving his plate untouched, he set down his fork and lifted his wine, his eyes never leaving me while he drank.

"Why aren't you eating?"

He didn't immediately answer, but there was a grin on his face, an intensity in his stare that made me feel emotions I hadn't expected. "Watching your happiness is better."

My mood had turned the moment he'd put food in front of me.

Not just any meal would have done that. I was positive I would have still felt the slap of Daisy's words had we been at a restaurant. But tasting Dominick's love in each bite was what I'd needed.

And he had known that.

"You know, I remember the private jets and the five-star vacations and all the gifts Brett had bought James when they first started dating. Girls like her want to be lavished. Not that there's anything wrong with that, but it's just not you."

"No, it's not me."

He reached under the table, his hand on my leg. "My time and attention make you smile the biggest."

"And your cooking."

He laughed. "Baby, you can have as much as you want of all three."

Hours after we finished eating and devoured my dessert, we were lying by the fire, sharing a glass of wine, the moment building between us.

The one where Dominick wasn't going to wait another second to have me.

There were blankets beneath us that he'd arranged, and the gas fireplace released heat and beauty from behind the glass. The back side of his hand, the part that wasn't covered in gym calluses, rubbed over my bare shoulder. There was a quick graze of his lips along my collarbone.

He knew how to make me feel my best.

How to turn me on.

How to work me up to the point where I was leaning into his touch for more.

My hands ached for the feel of him, so I pulled at the thick metal of his belt buckle, loosening the notch. I unbuttoned his jeans and lowered his zipper, reaching into his boxer briefs.

That thick, long, perfect cock was waiting for me.

"Oh God, yes," I breathed, wrapping my fingers around it.

When I rose to the top of his shaft and dropped to his base, the same sound came from him.

"I can't get enough of you," I admitted.

I was already wet.

I had been since I'd felt his lips across the top of my back, minutes before he kissed my shoulder.

"Kendall ..." he exhaled over my neck, chills bursting through me. "I'm all yours."

Those were the sexiest words I'd ever heard.

Dominick Dalton was mine.

Every part of him.

Every inch.

And I was going to count each one as it passed through my lips.

I got onto my knees and surrounded his tip, his crown dominating the top of my mouth.

"Oh fuck," he hissed.

I circled my tongue around the edge of his dick and across the center.

His moans were deep and guttural as his hand held my hair, urging me up and down as though I was going to stop.

But I was just getting started.

"Fuck yes, baby."

I loved those noises.

That I could make him feel good.

That his hips were rocking forward for more of my suction.

Aside from him touching me, those were the things that made me wetter.

I placed my hand at his base, covering that section while I dived over the top. I tightened my grip on him, meeting in the center, sucking in my cheeks to give him the feeling of a vacuum, swirling my tongue at the same time.

His thickness was filling, consuming me.

And with each plunge, I couldn't stop thinking about what this was going to feel like when it was inside of me. That deep, overwhelming satisfaction I could only get from his dick. It was that need, that burning desire, that caused my speed to increase.

He twisted my hair around his wrist, grunting, "You're going to make me fucking come."

That sounded like a challenge.

But I knew he wasn't going to let me bring him there because I was positive he had much more planned for tonight. And seconds later, I learned I was right when he lifted me in the air and set me on my back, hovering over me while he stripped off my clothes.

The only thing that remained on my skin was the heat from the fire and his scorching gaze.

"I'm going to fucking devour you."

I shivered.

From the anticipation.

From the look of hunger on his face.

From his feral lips as they moved down my chest, surrounding my nipple, repeatedly tugging it with his teeth. Each pull lifted me higher, my back arching before I landed.

"Oh God."

Suddenly, he was moving lower. My stomach the next target, pecking around my belly button and across to each hip, pausing at the base of me.

His nose wedged between my lips.

"Fuck me." He breathed in more of me. "I can never get enough of that scent."

He didn't move. He just replicated the same action.

In and out.

As though I were his oxygen.

And then I was suddenly on my knees, straddling his face, his mouth beneath my pussy.

"*Ohhh.*" I shook.

In one quick swipe, he had me trembling even harder from

his tongue, from the new angle, from the totally new feeling it caused.

He curled it to a point, tracing my clit, flicking it in different directions.

The moment I finally found air, when I stopped moaning long enough to fill my lungs, he inserted two fingers, turning them inside me.

"Dominick," I hissed.

I couldn't form any other words.

I couldn't think.

He was completely controlling my body, reaching that spot deep within me that no one else had touched before. And each graze caused everything else to intensify, especially after every lick, every sweep of his tongue.

"Oh *fuuuck*."

His speed increased, the build coming on like a storm. "Come on my fucking face."

I couldn't stop what was happening. I couldn't slow it down. A surge was roaring through me, causing my muscles to contract, my back to lift off the floor. It stretched through my whole body and once it reached the highest peak, my stomach shuddered from each blast.

"Dominick!"

I gripped his hair, needing to hold on, to balance what was happening while I rode this out. When the calmness eventually came through, his licking slowed, his breathing now making me extra sensitive.

"Fucking beautiful." He kissed the top of my clit. "That's what you look like when you come."

I was all tingles.

They didn't ease up, still holding me captive. Every time he breathed against me, a wave would pass through my navel.

When he pulled out his fingers, I gasped from the quakes they left behind.

But his hand didn't go far, spreading my wetness.

Lower.

In an instant, I knew where he was going.

"I'll be gentle."

It was as though he could read my mind.

His lips touched me again, this time halfway down my clit, his tongue leading the way, adding more to the wetness already there. Each dip caused my breathing to turn more rapid, my heart to race.

I didn't know what to anticipate. I didn't know if I could handle it.

His size.

His strength.

What if he's too much?

"I'm going to take care of you," he whispered across my pussy. "You're soon going to enjoy this so much that you'll be begging me for it."

He moved us, setting me on my back, where he knelt in front of me. The richest desire bored through my eyes. He pumped his cock several times and spread my legs even further apart.

"Don't move," he ordered.

As he left me on the floor, the air hit between my legs like a cold slap, showing how wet he'd made me. I barely had time to inhale before he returned, a tube of lube in his hand.

He squirted some over his shaft, adding more to his tip. "This will help."

He covered two of his fingers with the gel, and suddenly, they were probing that hole, a feeling that almost made me pucker. There was slickness and sliding, an acceleration of this enjoyable agony.

"This is going to feel so fucking good."

It already did. Even more so as he twisted his wrist, giving me a slow, steady plunge.

But it didn't last.

I held in my breath as his hand left me, lining up his tip, my ass opening to allow him in. "Dominick ..."

With his eyes on mine, he held my face, making sure I didn't move, that I stayed focused on him. "I'm not going to hurt you, Kendall, but I need you to breathe."

I trusted him.

And I believed him.

I exhaled as deeply as my lungs would allow, and just as I inhaled, he went in deeper.

"Ah!" I squeezed his shoulders, sharing some of the burning and pain as I stretched around him.

"Trust me." He kissed me. "It will get better."

There was a heat that got worse, the farther he went in. A burning, like a blaze was igniting inside me, each inch adding fuel. When I tried to hold in air, putting my mind somewhere else, he would bring my attention back to him.

And he would remind me to, "Breathe."

His lips pressed to mine, his hands now framing my face, his tongue circling. When he pulled back, he dived into my neck, kissing up my jaw and over to my ear. "You're almost there."

I wanted to close my legs, the invasion too much, the irritation spreading through my whole body, increasing the more he moved. But with his mouth parked on the outer edge of my ear, I listened to his whispers, encouraging me to relax until I finally heard what I'd been waiting for.

"You have all of me."

Once he stilled, the heat died, but the aching was there.

"Tell me how you feel."

I waited until the nerves calmed in my chest, when my brain could form words. "Full."

He growled, "That's because you're so fucking tight." He kissed me. "I'm not going to move. I want you to get used to this feeling first."

This was certainly more than I had been ready for, but it wasn't getting worse. I was adjusting, widening a bit more even if that happened slowly.

He exhaled against my face, the titillation so clear in his sounds. His tongue swept through my lips. "Tell me when you're ready."

He was so big that I worried the friction would hurt worse than what I'd already experienced. I didn't know if he'd fit back in, if I would need him to stop.

"Trust me," he repeated against my mouth, his mind inside mine. "I'm not going to hurt you."

I didn't know how much time had passed, but I took several breaths, staring at his incredibly handsome face while I whispered, "Okay." I swallowed. "I'm ready."

He gradually reversed, and an entirely new feeling came over me; the same happened when he smoothly dived in. There wasn't a heat, only stretching that was far more tolerable than before. The sharpness dulled; the fullness became less overwhelming.

"Fuck," he hissed. "You're fucking pulsing."

I could feel it.

The narrowness of my body.

The pressure didn't change, even as he pumped me. But what loosened was the discomfort, the tiniest hint of fervor there instead. And that grew when his fingers landed on my clit, rubbing.

"Dominick ..." My nails bit into his skin.

"That feels good, doesn't it, baby?"

Small, intimate bursts were sparking inside me.

"*Yesss.*"

It wasn't the same intensity like when he was in my pussy or when his mouth was between my legs. This was subtle but definitely present. And it increased a little with every thrust, especially when his thumb stayed on my clit, but then a finger slipped inside me.

"Oh God."

My mind was so jumbled with what was happening; my body was trying to catch up to all these unknown feelings. There was so much movement, so much back and forth; I couldn't distinguish one part from the other.

"Goddamn it, Kendall."

He pulled one of my nipples into his mouth, flicking the tip, and I reached into his hair and tugged.

"Fuck," I moaned.

He was pleasuring every sensitive spot on my body.

He didn't leave a place untouched.

And all his attention was working. The tingles in my stomach were exploding. The build was coming. I didn't have to reach for it or search.

It was already there.

Surfacing.

Peaking.

"Dominick ..."

His tongue stilled from circling my nipple. "Tell me."

I was sure he could feel the words. He knew what they were going to be before I shouted them.

And when he bit down on that sensitive point, he knew more than a moan was going to escape.

It happened so fast.

"Fuck!" I screamed. "I'm going to come!"

His palm ground against my clit while two of his fingers

thrust inside me, his teeth nipping my nipple, my ass full of his cock, the combination urging my climax.

He was fully dominating me.

And all I could do was hold on.

"You just got tighter," he barked.

My eyes closed as the first shot barreled through me. "*Ahhh!*" It was paralyzing, a crushing mix of shudders and tingles. "Dominick!"

Something was clawing through me, each layer causing me to yell louder, to tremble harder. This wasn't an orgasm I was used to. This feeling came from everywhere, in each part, in waves and gusts that refused to die, instead growing taller and heavier.

"Fucking Christ," he moaned against my breast. "You're going to make me come."

Even though I was lost, I felt him go deeper, his movements rougher, more powerful.

That only heightened the sensations inside me.

He rocked his hips in a more forceful rhythm, his kisses needy and demanding. "Your fucking ass"—he gave me his tongue to suck on—"is milking me." His pattern changed to short, intense strokes, and I finally started to come down. "Fuck!"

I watched the satisfaction spread across his face, moans releasing from his lips, a warm thickness filling me.

"Kendall." He shuddered, his hands framing my cheeks. "My fucking Kendall." He was falling apart, using slow, breathy sounds that I wanted to savor for the rest of my life. After several more spasms, his kisses were his only movement. "Fucking amazing."

I hugged him against me, needing him closer. His hair tickled my chest, his whiskers a coarseness that I loved. "I never expected it to feel like that," I breathed into the top of his head, my eyes closing. "For it to honestly feel that good."

He lifted his face, giving me his eyes, an emotion passing through them that I hadn't seen in him before. One that was soft and endless. "I told you ..." He rested in my neck, and I cupped the back of his head, a tenderness in each of his breaths. "I'll never hurt you."

TWENTY-SIX

DOMINICK

A fter two weeks of traveling, Jenner was back in town, and Ford had gotten a babysitter for the night, meaning only one thing.

We were going out.

And the place they'd chosen was one of the most popular clubs in Hollywood.

The same one where Kendall would be filming tonight.

I didn't like the idea of being in her space while the cameras were rolling, not being able to talk to her, not being able to put my fucking hands on her.

Watching her act as though she were single.

But I had no choice. We had a secret to maintain, and that was the path I'd chosen.

I wasn't surprised when the guys had picked a table in the corner of the bar, a spot that allowed us to see the whole VIP section, Kendall and her costars and their entire production crew in the center.

It was fucking excruciating to watch her from this far away, seeing how goddamn beautiful she looked in that red dress. I couldn't touch her upper thigh when the material rode high on her legs or squeeze that perfect fucking ass that I'd been thinking about nonstop since she'd let me fuck it.

I couldn't whisper in her ear, inhaling her scent, feeling the softness of her skin against my lips.

I could only observe.

With my hands to myself.

And I had to make sure I didn't flirt with her from all the way over here, so the producers didn't pick up on any signs. Raising their attention was the last goddamn thing I needed.

So, instead, I drank, the waitress topping off my glass with the bottle we'd ordered whenever she came over to check on us.

But that didn't stop my brothers from fucking ogling at her cast, giving me their thoughts on each member.

"That one," Ford said, nodding toward Delilah, "she's fire."

"And trouble," I warned.

"Oh, yes, I can attest to that," Jenner said. "A bite that's not worth the bark."

Ford looked at us. "But her tits"—he shook his head—"they have to be at least triple Ds."

"There's no denying that," Jenner agreed. "But trust me, man, stay far away."

I held the glass against my lips, tasting the sourness of the lime as it floated on top of the ice cubes. "Unless you want to be in my kind of hell, dodging the cameras, avoiding outings"—I knew my brothers felt the same as me about being in the public eye—"you should keep your distance."

Ford looked away from her. "You're right ... I'm good." He took a long drink. "But Jesus, fuck, she's hot."

"They all are," Jenner responded.

"Nah." I glanced at the wild-haired beauty in the middle, the one all the girls flocked to—my fucking queen. "None of them even compare to Kendall."

"Our brother has finally found himself a girl after how many years?" Ford stopped to jokingly count on his fingers and added, "You know we're not going to comment on her."

"I'm steering clear from that as well," Jenner agreed. "But I will say"—he punched my bicep—"you did well, Dominick. Really fucking well."

"I second that," Ford said.

Brett was suddenly standing in front of our table, his hand pounding each of our fists before he sat. "What are you mother-fuckers doing here tonight?"

We hadn't had a chance to speak today, so I hadn't realized he would be here, but I wasn't shocked at his presence. He tried to stop in wherever his clients were shooting.

"The boys and I came by for a drink," I told him.

"For someone who wants to keep things wrapped up, you chose an interesting location for vodka."

I pointed at Jenner and Ford. "It's their fault."

He laughed. "Oh, I'm sure they handcuffed and dragged your ass here, and you had no say in this whatsoever."

"Listen"—I chuckled before I took a sip—"she's been filming all over town, and I haven't visited any of the spots until now."

He squeezed my shoulder. "I'm just giving you a hard time, buddy." He looked in Kendall's direction, but my eyes stayed on him, where it was safe. "You plan on dancing with her tonight?"

"Hell no."

He laughed again. "I was in the production office this morning, watching some of the footage they were editing from the earlier shoots. The executives are pleased with her performance." He sighed, grinning. "I'm talking, really pleased."

I added more tonic to my glass. "That means two things, my

207

man. More fucking money that we can negotiate and more endorsements that'll be rolling in."

He nodded. "A contract came in this afternoon; I haven't even had the chance to tell her yet."

"Anything good?"

He pulled out his phone, tapping the screen, scrolling. His brows rose as he looked at me. "Balmy Hard Seltzer. Isn't that the brand that just dropped Daisy?"

I crossed my leg over my knee, resting my drink on top of it. "Yes. Fuck."

"Apparently, they want to keep it in the family." He shook his head. "I'm not even sure what to say about that."

"Kendall won't do it."

"No?"

"Hell no. She won't stir the pot." I stole a quick glance at her. She was standing with two of the girls, dancing in front of the couch, their arms around each other. "We'll wait for the next deal and get that brand to double their offer."

Ford poured himself more vodka. "I fucking love those words."

I turned to him. "Because you know I'll make it happen, brother."

"You've got that right," Brett said. "I'm going to make her famous, and you're going to make her rich as fuck."

"Now, that's one hell of a team," Jenner said.

We all laughed, and Brett continued, "Since you told me things were moving forward between you guys, I haven't asked how it's going. I'm assuming all is good?"

"Very fucking good." I didn't want to glance Kendall's way again, but I had to. Just a taste. A tease. *Fuck.* "She's everything I didn't know I wanted."

"Never thought I'd hear you say that," Jenner responded.

"That makes two of us," Ford said.

"Hey," I said, looking at Ford and then Jenner. "Neither of you has a reason to talk. I don't see either of you in a goddamn relationship."

"We're definitely not denying that." Jenner chuckled.

"But you will be," Brett said. "Like I told Dominick, once you find the right one, they change everything. Every view you ever had, every direction you thought you were going in. That's what James did to me"—he stared at me—"and what Kendall has done to you." He pointed at my brothers. "You bastards are next." And then out of nowhere, his expression dropped, and he groaned, "Oh, fuck me ... not now."

I followed his gaze, leading me to the entrance of the VIP section. "You've got to be fucking kidding me."

"What's going on?" Jenner asked.

"Daisy fucking Roy just walked in," I said across the group.

The moment the words left my mouth, her eyes connected with mine, and a grin spread across her face.

One that told me her presence was going to be nothing but trouble.

"Play nice," Jenner said. "I don't care if that girl's up to no good; you won't stoop to her level."

I needed the reminder because as she walked toward me, I could see her fucking claws.

"Gentlemen," Daisy said to my brothers as she stopped in front of our couch. "Brett," she voiced in the slyest tone. Her stare moved over to me. "Dominick."

This girl had some fucking balls.

Not only to show up to where her sister was filming, but to also come over here and speak to me.

And to look at me with such distaste and resentment.

"Daisy," I replied.

"How's everyone doing this evening?" she asked.

She held her hips, exuding such confidence on her face.

Except this girl was a nobody and soon-to-be nothing and I had a front row seat to her vanishing career. One movie deal lost, followed by an endorsement. The rest, I was sure, would disappear just as fast. The final straw would be when her show didn't renew her contract.

She'd be forced out of Hollywood.

It was only a matter of time.

And her fucking time was up.

"Why don't you cut the bullshit and tell us what you want?" I said.

She glanced around the club as though this were her living room. "Oh, Dominick, what do you mean? Can't a hardworking girl go out to enjoy a cocktail or two, like you're doing with your boys?"

She was fucking poison.

"We both know that's not why you're here."

She crossed her arms over her fake-as-fuck chest. "I can't believe you listen to her. Don't you know my sister is a compulsive liar? I would have thought you would have figured her out by now." She scolded me by shaking her finger. "I thought you were a better lawyer than that."

I laughed, realizing comedy was really the avenue Daisy should be pursuing. "You're pathetic. It's sad really."

"What's sad is how badly she's manipulated you. That you're so blinded from sleeping with her that you can't see her motive. She's outsmarted you." She pointed at Brett. "And you too." She grinned. "And now, she has you both right where she wants you."

I had to give her credit; she was certainly creative. While sitting in that fucking house, alone, she derived scheme after scheme.

She had the goddamn brain of a psychopath.

"Is that what you tell yourself when the cancellations keep rolling in? You know, to keep fueling your narcissism?"

She smiled even wider. "My dear Dominick. Since your simple brain can't seem to figure it out—really, I'm not surprised by that; you do earn one of the cheapest hourly rates in the business—I'll fill you in. She's playing you, baby." She wiped her lips as though she'd just finished eating. "Just like I would have, but I wouldn't have needed to suck your dick."

I ground my teeth together. "Get the fuck out of here and stay away from Kendall."

"Is that a threat?" Her voice softened, like she was narrating a bedtime story. "I would hate for the cameras to catch my sister's boyfriend being hauled out of the club in handcuffs." She twirled a piece of her hair. "But that would make for some good reality TV, wouldn't it?"

"I'm not playing, Daisy. Leave her the fuck alone."

She waved her hand in the air by bending just the top of her fingers. "Good to see you all."

As she began to walk away, I looked at the group and said, "That girl is a fucking monster."

"A raging cunt," Brett added, and then he looked at me. "We need to keep an eye on Kendall tonight. Daisy is here to start some shit, and we can't let it go down."

I set my drink on the table and tore at my hair. "I'm getting her out of here."

Brett's hand went to my arm, stopping me from standing. "You can't. That'll be strike two, and production won't let that one slide."

TWENTY-SEVEN

KENDALL

Dominick's eyes were on me.

I felt them every time I smiled. Every time I faced my back toward him, feeling his gaze lower to my ass. Whenever I spoke closely to one of the girls and particularly when I danced.

His text had told me he was coming here tonight.

But I hadn't anticipated how difficult it would be to see him and not be able to show him any love, to inhale the spiciness of his cologne even though I'd been searching for it in the air all night.

I tried so hard to keep my stare away, but he was a magnet.

His eyes, his demeanor, his presence—all of it was tempting me to get closer to him, to wrap my arms around his deliciously handsome neck that I had woken up kissing this morning.

That was what I really wanted—or to be sitting on his lap, or watching a movie in front of his fireplace, or tucked in his bed.

I would prefer any of that over the distance between us now.

And the drama that was scheduled to go down this evening.

Two of my costars, Asia and Monica, were angry with each other for sleeping with the same guy. Production had been poking both ladies about it all night, instigating an eruption.

Delilah had taken each of the girls into the restroom to tell them, every bit of the tell-all caught on camera.

It didn't matter that neither girl even liked the guy; their emotions were on the verge of exploding.

But before the fight really got brewing, the staff wanted to make sure we all had plenty of alcohol in us, so there was potential for even more drama. Our VIP table was covered in bottles and mixers along with every kind of garnish, and now, there was a waitress pouring us shots of tequila.

She didn't stop at one.

Once we downed the contents of the small glass, she'd immediately return to give us more. By the third shot, I could no longer feel my feet, but I knew my body was swaying to the beat, my butt grinding against the leather seat beneath me.

"Let's go dance," Erika, a costar, said, her fingers now linked with mine.

If I went out onto the dance floor to shake my ass, it would warm up Dominick for what I had planned for later tonight. We hadn't talked about what we were doing after filming, but since he was here, there was no way I was going back to my apartment.

I needed him.

His mouth on every part of my body, starting with that sensitive place between my legs.

I looked at Erika and replied, "Ladies' room first. Then, it's on."

"Hell yes, girl."

With our arms now looped together, we got up from the

couch, clinging to each other as we wobbled in our heels, hurrying toward the restroom.

I'd never been to this club before. I had no idea where the restrooms were located, but it appeared as though Erika did, and she led us toward the back of the VIP section.

The camera and lighting techs followed, knowing they had to wait outside until we were done.

The moment I walked in, I reached into my dress and turned off my microphone, and Erika and I released each other, going into our own stalls. That was where I worked my contortionist magic to hover over the bowl.

Erika and I came out at the same time, but I was sure she wasn't shocked to see the person standing in front of the sinks, facing us.

Not like I was.

Daisy.

My entire body began to shake.

Even more so when the restroom door opened, the camera and lighting guys stepping inside.

What is she doing here? Why would she come into the restroom? Is she really going to start something in front of the cameras?

"Kendall, my dearest sister." Her arms crossed, her butt now leaning against a sink. "Not returning my texts, not answering my calls. I had to come all the way here just to tell you how much I've missed you."

She always wanted to seem like the good guy, especially when the cameras were pointed at her.

God, she was clever.

But I wasn't going to let the world know our business. I wasn't going to feed into her nonsense, her goading, regardless of how much I'd had to drink.

That was what she wanted, and I refused to cave.

Even if that pissed her off more.

I rushed forward, closing the distance between us, and threw my arms around her neck. "Daisy!" I shouted, like I would have months before. "Oh God, I've missed you so terribly much."

Her hug was weak, and she pushed me away after a second. "Really? You could have fooled me; since you've gotten a taste of fame, you've been completely ghosting me." Her expression was full of pain and agony. "I've needed you; you're my best friend, and you haven't been there for me. At all." She wiped her eyes. "This show has made you so popular; it's like you can't be bothered with me anymore. Kendall, do you know how much that hurts?" She clutched her chest. "Oh God, it aches." Her head dropped. "You went from being there for me every second, my person, even my assistant, to being way too good for me." Her tone was so full of sadness that it was like I was squeezing her voice box.

No matter what I said, I would look like the bad one.

My truth wouldn't justify the facade she was putting on. The fake tears she was shedding. The script she was reciting that she'd probably written in the car on the way over.

She wasn't just mean.

She was vindictive.

"Daisy—" I started but was immediately cut off as the restroom door swung open, Dominick barging his way through.

The look on his face was lethal.

"I warned you," he said to Daisy.

He warned her?

I had no idea what that meant, but I couldn't believe he had come in here and risked being filmed even though they couldn't air the footage because he wouldn't sign a waiver. But he was still putting himself next to me, taking the chance of the crew and Erika finding out that I was more than just his client.

Daisy looked at him, seething but hiding behind her tears. "Kendall, your boyfriend doesn't need to come rescue you. I was just purging my heart to you. I've done nothing wrong—unless you count needing my sister as a punishable offense."

She hadn't waited more than a second to out us.

I shouldn't have been surprised.

But I was.

"That's your boyfriend?" Erika asked. "But I thought you were single?"

"She told you that?" Daisy inquired, shaking her head. "No, honey, Kendall lied to you, then."

Dominick grabbed me by the arm, gaining my attention. "You're coming with me."

My heart was beating out of my chest.

My body was numb and so incredibly heavy.

I didn't want to get in any more trouble with production. I'd already been fined once for leaving. I didn't know what would happen a second time. But more conversation and having those words aired could be detrimental in so many ways.

I wasn't willing to take that chance.

"You know I love you more than anything," I said to my sister.

"You say that now, but does that excuse what you've done to me?" Her voice was turning sharp. "How you've treated me?"

Dominick positioned himself between Daisy and me. "We're leaving."

"If you've done nothing wrong, then why do you need your man to put out your fires?" Daisy asked. "For someone who's so innocent, you surely look guilty from where I'm standing."

"Don't respond," he whispered even though the camera and microphones the crew were holding caught every word.

"I get it; you just prefer to do your dirty work behind the scenes. That's it, isn't it, sister?" She moved to Dominick's side to get a view of me.

"We're out of here," Dominick said, his hand on my back, guiding me to the door.

A production assistant moved in front of us, stopping me from taking another step. "We need to speak to you. She can't just leave."

"I'm her lawyer, and she's getting verbally assaulted. I would like you to show me where in her contract it states that she can't leave for her own safety and comfort."

"Assaulted," Daisy gasped from behind us. "That's what you're calling my tears? I'm the one who's being assaulted here."

Dominick glared at the production assistant and said, "Move out of our way."

The assistant looked at the cameraman. "Shane is going to blow his lid over this."

"Tell Shane he can fucking call me," Dominick snapped.

My brain was spiraling.

I couldn't even begin to process what Daisy had tried to start tonight, the way she had spun things, that Dominick had flown into the ladies' room, breaking every one of his personal rules. And then there was the show, the way Shane was going to react, and the phone call I was most definitely going to get later.

"I can't believe you're going to let your boyfriend control you," Daisy said. "Our parents raised us better than that. Don't you have a voice, or did he take that away from you too?"

I went to turn around, to say something, anything that would just make her stop.

But Dominick cut me off and said, "Don't. We're leaving. Trust me, it's not worth it."

With his hand still on my back, he led me out of the restroom, the cameras following us through the VIP section and down the small staircase, all the way out to his car. The light was so blinding that I used my hand as a visor, trying to block some as it came in through the tinted glass of his window.

"Are you all right?" he asked the second we were away from them, speeding out of the parking lot, toward the road.

"I don't know."

Once he shifted, his hand went to my thigh. "I saw her the second she came in, and I warned her." He shook his head. "I fucking warned her, Kendall, and she didn't listen. I saw her go into the restroom after you, and I tried to get there as fast as I could." His fingers moved to the back of my head. "Jesus, baby, I'm so fucking sorry she did that in front of the cameras."

"Me too."

The emotion was moving into my throat, the reality of what had happened finally sinking in. I couldn't halt the tears that were falling. I couldn't make my chin stop quivering.

This hurt.

"My sister," I whispered. "My goddamn fucking sister. I don't understand why she did this."

"She's losing everything, and she's desperate to get it back."

And her attempt was going to play out on TV, and it would slap even harder when I saw it on the screen.

Before that happened, I would have to deal with the ramifications of tonight, the Celebrity Alert that was probably going to be released, either announcing my relationship or how awful I'd treated my sister.

I hated this.

And I hated that she had caused this.

He looked at me when he reached the red light. "Tell me what I can do to make you feel better."

My heart was pounding, aching. My body still trembling. "You're already doing it." I wrapped my fingers around his. "You protected me; that's all I could ever ask for."

TWENTY-EIGHT

DOMINICK

"Drink this," I said, holding a glass of wine in front of Kendall.

She wrapped her fingers around the stem and held the drink against her chest, tucking herself in the corner of my couch, where I covered her in a blanket.

She'd been shaking the entire drive to my house, still was by the way the blanket appeared to be moving. At least the tears weren't running as fast. I hated more than anything to see them. Kendall was strong, resilient. I knew she would get through this.

But I also knew she was hurting something fierce.

Battling a sibling, someone you were supposed to be able to trust, wasn't easy.

And Daisy had taken things to the next level. That bitch would be the first person to stab Kendall in the back, and she wouldn't even feel remorseful about it.

I pulled her against me, holding her back, rubbing my palm across it. "While I was getting your wine, I called Shane."

She tilted her neck to look at me, her eyes widening from the news.

"Brett gave me his number. I wasn't going to wait for him to reach out. This shit needs to get squashed before morning."

"What did he say?"

"I realize I didn't get to the restroom immediately; therefore, I'm sure there's dialogue that I'm not in. But for the majority of the footage, I'm present, and I told him I'll file suit if they release any of those shots. I don't care if they try to blur me out or disguise my voice. I won't stand for it."

"Does that mean they can't air that scene?"

"That's exactly what it means."

"What about the conversation prior to you coming into the bathroom?"

"I dare them to try to release it." He paused. "I'll get it all tossed, don't worry."

Her head fell back against my chest. "That's such a relief."

It was for Kendall, but Shane had been fucking pissed, especially when I'd told him that my suit for defamation would exceed the insurance policy they'd taken out on the show and then I would come after the studio for the balance.

I didn't care what I had to do to protect her. I wouldn't stop until I got my way.

She was still breathing so fast, her tears leaking through my shirt and onto my skin.

"Kendall," I whispered, holding her tighter, "tell me what I can do."

"Nothing." She gave me her eyes again, the pain inside them hitting me right in the goddamn gut. "I'm just struggling."

I positioned her across my lap, so I could wipe the wetness that fell. "With the show? Your sister?"

"All of it." She sighed. "Since the show started, it's just been ... a lot. Things with my sister erupted. I have no privacy anymore. I have to worry about everything turning into a Celebrity Alert, including our relationship when we were really hoping to keep that under wraps." My hand moved to her cheek as she added, "It's more than I imagined, and most of it isn't good."

"And I'm responsible."

"No." Her fingers found mine and clamped down. "I made the ultimate decision. I signed the contract. This is absolutely not your fault."

"I'm not stopping with production. I'm going to take it further."

She searched my eyes, her lips parting but nothing came out. "I don't know what you mean."

"I mean, I'm going to talk to Daisy." She tried to cut me off, and I stopped her. "This is getting out of hand, and I'm not putting up with her bullshit anymore. You have two more months left of filming. If I have to hire a fucking bodyguard to shadow you around town, I will, but I won't let it get to that because I'm putting an end to this."

She sat up, setting her glass on the table, her arm then returning to my shoulders. "Didn't you hear her tonight? She thinks you fight my battles for me. Talking to her about this will only make her angrier."

I smiled, visualizing the way it would play out in a meeting. "Not when I sit her down with her manager, agent, new attorney, and I describe in detail the libel suit I'm going to build against her. She's trying to hurt your reputation, Kendall. It's not going to happen; I won't let it."

"Dominick ..."

I pressed my lips to hers, trying to calm her a little. "I won't have to file suit; it won't come to that. She just needs to be put in her place, and if I show her what she's about to lose, she'll re-shift her focus back to her career rather than concentrating so hard on you. Trust me on this." I caught several more drips that were about to fall from her eyelids.

"I'm so lucky to have you." She circled her other arm around me, hugging her body against mine, her breathing finally starting to slow.

I didn't care what she said. I'd brought her into this, I'd created this mess, and I was going to fucking fix it.

"I'm going to take care of everything, baby; don't worry."

In the meantime, I wanted to make her feel better.

I wanted to take her mind off what was happening, to ease the tension in her body.

In the past, there was only one way I knew how to do that. That was by lifting her dress over her head and thrusting my cock inside her tight, wet pussy.

That wasn't to say I wouldn't try that in the morning.

But tonight, I was going to do something different.

With her already on my lap, I slid my arms under her body and lifted her off the couch. "You're coming with me," I said, kissing her forehead while I carried her to my bathroom.

I set her on the lip of the jetted tub and turned on the water, finding the right temperature before plugging the drain. I added in some of the oils and bubble bath the interior decorator had placed nearby and got her a towel.

"Don't move," I ordered and grabbed a lighter from the kitchen to ignite the candlewicks that surrounded the tub.

When the water was several inches deep, I loosened the straps of her heels and slipped them off her feet. I then lowered the zipper of her dress, pulling the red material down her beautiful body. Once I unhooked her bra, I held her hand to help her step in.

She leaned her back against the jets, the bubbles rising to her chest.

I took a handful and rubbed it across her neck. "Let's try to forget about tonight. I want you to relax and clear your mind."

"Okay."

She sank further into the water, extending her legs, her toes breaking the surface, covered in suds.

"Do you want your wine?"

She nodded, and just as I went to leave, she grabbed my hand and said, "Thank you. For everything, Dominick."

Even the smallest grin that glowed across her gorgeous face made me smile.

"I'll be right back."

As I went into the living room to get the glass from the coffee table, my phone chimed from my back pocket. I pulled it out and looked at the screen.

BREAKING NEWS:

A LITTLE BEE TOLD US AN INTERESTING ALTERCATION
WENT DOWN TONIGHT IN A LADIES' ROOM AT CLUB HUB.
THIS ONE WAS BETWEEN DAISY AND KENDALL ROY.
SOUNDS LIKE THERE'S TROUBLE IN SISTERLY PARADISE, AND
SOMEONE IS FEELING A LITTLE STUNG.
WE ALSO HEARD KENDALL IS DATING DOMINICK DALTON,
THE LAWYER TO MANY HOLLYWOOD STARS, INCLUDING
KENDALL AND DAISY. DALTON AND KENDALL WERE SEEN
LEAVING THE CLUB TOGETHER TONIGHT.
HEY, DALTON, DO THE SISTERS QUALIFY FOR A BOGO?
WE SURE HOPE SO.

Those motherfuckers.

TWENTY-NINE

KENDALL

The sun was just coming in through the blinds when my eyes opened, my body sore but extremely relaxed from what Dominick had done to me in his pool last night. That was what happened when I went to his house after a long evening of filming and complained I was sweaty.

I'd found myself in his infinity pool.

With him.

Naked.

The two of us creating even more sweat.

I tightened my thighs together, still feeling our sex, the coarseness of his whiskers when he'd gone down on me underwater. The heaviness of his tongue on my clit while I had gripped the edge of the shallow end, trying not to scream too loud across the Hollywood Hills.

I'd never met a man like him before.

Dominant.

Protective.

Ridiculously handsome.

And someone who truly wanted to take care of me.

As I glanced toward the other side of his bed, where he was asleep on his stomach, I still couldn't believe he was mine. Now that the whole world knew we were together, courtesy of a Celebrity Alert, we found no reason to hide our relationship. Dominick still didn't like the limelight—I certainly couldn't blame him—but when we went out for lunch or dinner, there were shots of us holding hands. When I'd attended an industry event last week, he had been right by my side on the red carpet. He was along for the ride, and he wasn't allowing anything— paparazzi, online pictures, articles, alerts—to get in the way of us.

I was running my fingers through his hair as he stirred, slowly opening his eyes, reaching for me. "Morning, gorgeous."

"*Mmm.*" I felt the smile on my lips as I looked at him, the tousled hair he always woke up with, the shadow on his delicious cheeks—a sight that wouldn't stop turning me on. "Good morning."

"How did you sleep?"

I stretched my arms over my head, adjusting the fluffy pillow. "Aside from hurting everywhere"—I laughed—"really well."

"I was a little rough on you last night."

I winked. "A little?"

"That wasn't my plan." He cupped my breast, grazing my nipple back and forth. "Sometimes, you make it impossible to go easy on you."

"I loved it—you know that."

He grabbed my chin before lowering to my waist. "What time do you have to film?"

"Not until two." I yawned. "I have the whole morning off."

"Do you want to get some breakfast?"

I nuzzled my face against his chest. "I would really love that." A thought came into my head. "Except the only thing I have to wear is that purple dress I came over in last night, and you know how I feel about the walk of shame. We'll just have to stop by my place first."

He kissed my cheek, just below my earlobe. "You left some running clothes here last week. I had my housekeeper wash them for you. They're in the top drawer of the island in my closet."

I remembered that outfit—the yoga pants and tank top and sports bra I'd forgotten and been meaning to grab. Now, they were in a drawer along with his things.

I really liked the direction this was going.

"Even better," I whispered.

With his hand on my face, he traced my bottom lip. "I'm going to wash up and make a few phone calls. We'll leave in thirty?"

I nodded. "Perfect."

I watched him get out of bed, and that delectable, long, thick cock bounced with each step, the muscles in his arms so defined as they hung at his sides, his tight, rippled abs flexing as he walked.

Good Lord.

I went into his massive closet, finding the drawer in his center island, and put the bra on over my head, followed by the pants and tank top. Using the mirror along one of the walls, I twisted my hair into a messy bun and tied it with the elastic I kept on my wrist. By the time I exited, he was coming out of the bathroom, still not a stitch of clothing on his body.

I stood frozen next to his bed, watching him head to his closet.

He laughed as he neared. "Can I get you something?"

I shook my head, and then I changed my mind and nodded instead. "You."

A smile joined his face. "I think I've met my clone."

227

He continued walking, his incredible ass in my view.

"I was never like this before you," I told him. "You've ... ruined me."

"Ruined?"

"Yep." I went into the bathroom. "Now, all I think about is your dick."

I shut the door, and at the sink, I covered my finger with a line of toothpaste, brushing it across my teeth and finishing off with a swish of mouthwash. I quickly scrubbed my face next and dried off with one of his extra-soft towels.

When I made it back into his bedroom, I could hear Dominick in his office, which was only a few doors down. Before I went into the kitchen for coffee, I found my purse and took out my phone to check the texts that had come in overnight.

Charlize: Loved hanging with you at the club last night.
Me: SO happy you came. Filming is much more fun with you around.
Charlize: Just one more month, babe. Then, we'll only have to worry about the paparazzi and not those god-awful cameras that add ten pounds.
Me: The countdown is already happening in my head.
Charlize: At least things have been Daisy-free. That must be somewhat of a relief?
Me: The sit-down with Dominick and her team worked, I guess. But you know her silence bothers me as much as her nasty words.
Charlize: I know, but we're focusing on the good—like the whopping hangover I woke up with this morning because of YOU. Are you not dying too?
Me: Dominick drained all the alcohol from me ... in his pool.
Charlize: Slurp. I'm obsessed with that man.

*Me: That makes two of us. Dinner tomorrow night? Off camera,
obviously.*
*Charlize: We're on, girlfriend. But first, I'm coming over to raid
your closet to find something to wear. While I was there
yesterday, I saw that the studio had delivered the new Gucci
blazer, and I'm dying to get my hands on that sucker.*
Me: It's yours. XO

"Are you ready?"

I glanced up from my phone and joined Dominick in the doorway. "Yes, and I'm starving."

He grabbed my ass and kissed me. "Good. Let's go."

I followed him to the garage and climbed into the passenger seat.

"Pancakes?" he asked.

I was already dreaming about the cinnamon roll stack I'd had there the second time I went, the cream cheese icing falling off the sides in globs. "It's like you know me or something."

His hand went to my thigh when he wasn't shifting, and since he lived so close to me, the café only a block from my place, it didn't take long before we were there. He parked in front, clasping my hand as we walked in. The hostess led us toward the back and into a booth along the wall of windows.

"Coffee?" the waitress asked as she came to our table.

"For both of us," Dominick replied. "And some orange juice as well."

"I'll be right back with your drinks and to take your orders."

I read the menu even though I already knew what I wanted. "What are you feeling?"

He sighed, crossing his hands under his chin. "You've got me craving all this sweet shit, so what the hell do you think?"

I giggled. I'd known I would eventually convert him. "I love that I've had such a profound effect on you."

"In more ways than just food."

Right after I leaned across the table to kiss him, the waitress delivered our drinks and took our orders, and the moment we were alone again, an alert came through my phone.

It was the specific ringtone that I feared. During most occasions, I wouldn't immediately reach for my phone, but what followed the alert this time was an incessant dinging of texts.

From Dominick's cell.

And mine.

"What the hell is going on?" I said, unzipping my bag. The second I saw my screen, my mouth fell open. "Oh my God."

BREAKING NEWS:

WE'VE GOTTEN OUR HANDS ON SOME STEAMY PHOTOGRAPHS. ONES THAT STAR KENDALL ROY. WE DON'T KNOW WHO THE LUCKY COSTAR IS, BUT WE DO KNOW SHE LOOKS AS GOOD NAKED AS SHE DOES AT THE CLUB. IF YOU WERE WONDERING IF SHE'S SWEET OR SPICY UNDER THE SHEETS, IT LOOKS LIKE WE'VE GOT OURSELVES A JALAPEÑO, FOLKS.

"I'm going to be sick," I whispered, my hands trembling as I clicked on the link.

There were pictures of me standing in the bedroom of my apartment, my back to the camera as I walked over to a man lying on my bed.

His face and body were shaded out, so he couldn't be identified.

But I knew it was Dominick.

They weren't so kind when it came to masking me. Although parts were blurred, I could still see the outline of my breasts, my bare ass, the dip of my hips, the arch of my back.

In the shots, I was riding Dominick; in others, he had me

positioned doggy style. There were even some of me on the floor, Dominick sitting on the edge of the bed, my hands and mouth around a dark blur that I was obviously sucking.

"I'm going to fucking kill someone," he barked, causing me to look up. "Wring their goddamn necks until they can't take another breath."

He was clearly looking at the same site.

"Who would do this to me?" Bile was working its way up my stomach, my eyes filling with tears, my mouth on the verge of dry-heaving. "Why is this happening?"

I couldn't put the pieces together in my head.

Dominick had only been to my place once, and that was before filming had even begun, when I was free to do whatever I wanted in my apartment, the cameras not on.

Or so they had promised.

My stomach lurched again as I read the text underneath the photos.

First, she was with Presley Jordan, their mouths smeared in pink.
Then, she landed Dominick Dalton.
Is this mystery man one of the above or someone new?
What we do know is, we like what we see.
Keep up the good work, Miss Roy.
Meow.

THIRTY

DOMINICK

Once I had Kendall back at my house, making her as comfortable as possible in my bed with a bottle of wine and a glass of water next to her—whichever she needed most—I got in my car and drove straight to the studio.

Fuck calling.

I needed Ted's fucking head in my hands, and a conversation over the phone with the studio's CEO wasn't going to give me that satisfaction.

I was only a mile past my driveway when I phoned my assistant. Once she answered, I ordered, "I need Brett Young and my brothers on a conference call immediately. I don't care if they're in meetings; haul their asses out."

"Give me two seconds. I'm just going to put you on hold while I call them."

I was driving double the speed limit, barely braking around turns, running yellows that changed to red.

"Dominick," my assistant said through my car speakers, "I have them all on the line. I'm going to connect you now."

I heard the click and said, "Brett? Jenner and Ford?" When

they confirmed, I continued, "I know you all have seen the alert. I've gotten your voice mails and texts. It's easier to have this conversation all together."

"Jesus, brother. I pity the fucking asshole who's about to get the wrath of you," Ford said. "What do you know so far?"

"First, it goes without saying that it's me in the photographs."

"Never questioned it," Jenner said. "I just want to know who the fuck I'm about to sue."

I slowed down at the next red light, my foot feeling heavy enough to run it. "I was only at Kendall's place once—the day before she started filming. We stopped by, so she could change her clothes before we went to brunch, and the obvious happened. The contract was clear—I'd read it with my own goddamn eyes—and the cameras weren't supposed to be on until filming began."

"That's correct," Brett said. "I read the same verbiage."

"Then, how the fuck did this happen?" Jenner asked.

"I'd like to know the same thing," Brett replied.

"I'm going to tie up that studio in so much legal, that show is going to sit on a hard drive, collecting twelve inches of fucking dust."

"Should I start the proceedings?" Jenner asked.

I blew through the next yellow, turning onto the street where the studio's executive offices were located. "Not yet. I'm headed there now for answers. I'm bypassing Shane—that motherfucker can't give me what I want—and I'm going straight to Ted."

"Going right for the big dog—I like your style," Jenner said. "But be prepared. I'm sure their legal counsel is on his way there as well. They don't want litigation or their name tied to this. If they're responsible for the leak, they're going to offer a private settlement before this goes to court—I can promise you that. And they're going to do it quickly; they don't want anything or anyone delaying the airing of this show."

I laughed. "It's far too fucking late for that."

"Do you want me to meet you over there?" Brett asked.

"I'm not dragging you into this," I responded.

"What do you think happened?" Ford asked. "Do you think it's to garner attention for the show? Or something else?"

Since I'd read the alert and viewed the photographs, that question had been fucking eating at me.

I had theories, but I needed proof.

"I don't know," I told them. "But you bet your ass I'm going to find out. I'll call you once I leave the studio."

"We're on standby," Jenner said.

I disconnected the call and turned up the music, pounding my fist on the steering wheel, my mood bubbling like I was standing on burning coal.

This was bullshit.

There shouldn't be naked photos of my girlfriend online, causing her to throw up her coffee at breakfast.

I shouldn't have to worry about her safety or her unpredictable fucking sister.

Kendall was right; the show had changed so much.

And I was responsible for all of it.

Now, the aftermath was tucked into my bed, sobbing her fucking eyes out.

I had to fix this.

I parked in front of the studio's entrance and rushed inside the lobby.

I walked past the three receptionists who were sitting behind the desk and said, "I'm Dominick Dalton. You can let Ted know I'm on my way up."

I stepped into the elevator, pressing the button for the top floor, the lift instantly rising. Once it opened, I headed for his office, passing another receptionist on the way.

"Excuse me, Mr. Dalton—"

I held up my hand. "If he's in a meeting, tell him to end it."

I continued past her toward the end of the hall, clenching his doorknob and pushing it open. Ted was behind his desk, the CFO also in the room, the COO in another chair, and a fourth guy, who I assumed was their legal counsel.

"Dominick," Ted said as I entered, a man I'd had drinks with many times at social events around town, "we've been expecting you." He pointed at the only empty chair. "Take a seat."

I planted my ass down and crossed my legs. "I want answers. Now."

"We've spoken to Shane Eldridge—the head of production, as you know—and he's working with the production staff to see what he can find out," Ted said, folding his hands on top of his desk. "The alert was released only two hours ago. You know there are protocols in place and proper procedures that we have to follow. We need more time."

"Here's what I know ..." I glanced at each of their faces. Their lawyer had coached them to stay aloof, revealing nothing that could hold them accountable. "The leak had to come from your studio. Whether it was from the executive side or from someone in the editing room or the production team, it doesn't matter. Their intention and their actions hurt my client."

"We're not in the business to hurt anyone, Dominick. I assure you, we want answers as quickly as you do."

Ted was filling me with meaningless corporate jargon. Words I would have told my client to say if one of them were sitting on the other side of this desk.

"We both know you're in the business to make money," I barked. "Whoever sold those photos hit a large payday—not to mention, the media attention the show has gained as a result." I gripped my armrests before I pounded my fists on his goddamn desk. "Kendall Roy has been violated. She put her trust in your studio, and you've destroyed that trust. She won't be stepping foot on any of your sets or in front of any of your cameras until I'm satisfied with the answers you've provided."

"She's under contractual obligations—"

I cut off the attorney with, "We both know I can tear up that motherfucking contract."

"Dominick," the CFO started, "I need to remind you, Kendall was warned that whatever occurred in that apartment, including each of the rooms inside, would be on camera. That footage is accessible and legally allowed to be shared."

The anger in my chest was fucking erupting.

"Photos of her ass, of her on her goddamn knees, are not in the realm of appropriate, and apparently, I need to remind you of that."

"But still ... permitted," he continued.

That footage wouldn't have made it past the editing room. If it did, possibly airing a ruffling under the covers or a seductive pose prior to any physical engagement, her body would have been blurred. Pornographic material in any capacity was not authorized to be aired.

He knew that.

They all fucking knew that.

I pushed myself to the end of my chair. "Let's cut the bullshit right now. Even if the photos weren't timestamped, I know the date those still shots were taken. I know because it's me who's in them."

All four men glanced at each other, their expressions unchanged.

"The date it took place was prior to the start of filming, a date when you were not supposed to be recording any material in that apartment." I stared into Ted's wrinkled fucking face. "I need answers. I need names. And I need to know how you plan to make this right."

"We're working as hard as we can, Dominick. You have my word."

I could wipe my ass with Ted's word.

In this building, he represented the studio—our social interactions counted for nothing.

I stood. "You have forty-eight hours."

As I began walking to the door, Ted exclaimed, "Forty-eight hours isn't nearly enough time—"

"Not a second more," I said, and I shut the door behind me.

THIRTY-ONE

KENDALL

I waited until the call connected and whispered, "Mom," into the phone. I envisioned her seeing my name appear on the caller ID, taking a seat at the kitchen table, where she took all her phone calls. Her short light-pink-painted nails drawing circles over the worn tabletop. "Oh, Mom."

"Honey ..."

"Things are such a mess right now."

I hadn't planned on what I was going to say to my parents. I didn't know how to even address the photographs. But I'd had several missed calls from them, and I knew I couldn't avoid this conversation any longer.

"Are you all right, Kendall? I need to know that first."

"Yes ..." I took a breath. "No." I wiped my eyes, glancing around Dominick's bedroom, pulling the comforter up to my chin. "I mean, I'm safe. I'm at Dominick's house, and he's at the studio right now, trying to get answers. But, Mom, I hurt." My chest tightened to the point where it felt like it was going to crack. "I hurt in a way I can't even describe. And I'm angry, and I feel violated. I can't believe this happened to me—that the whole world is seeing those photos ... I just want to disappear."

"I'm booking a flight to LA. The minute we hang up. I'll hopefully be there before tomorrow morning."

I tucked my knees to my chest, dropping my face against them. "No."

"No?"

"The paparazzi are already outside Dominick's house, waiting to get a shot of me." I stared at the closed blinds, unable to even keep them open because their lenses could see me behind the glass. "I can't subject you and Dad to this media stalking. Please just stay where it's safe and quiet and where your privacy won't be jeopardized the minute you step off the plane."

"Kendall, the thought of not being there with you is making me sick."

I gripped the blanket, knowing I needed to explain, the thought causing my stomach to act up again but there was nothing left in it to throw up. "Those pictures, Mom"—I swallowed as my mouth watered—"they were private moments between Dominick and me that weren't supposed to be captured on film. It doesn't matter that I'm on a reality show; this isn't reality. This is an invasion. They've painted me in a way where I look like a slut—first with Presley Jordan, which was so far from the truth, and now, this." I tightened the ball I was in, rocking over the mattress. "I'm disgusted—over all of it."

"Baby, I don't think for a single second that this is your fault or that you could have somehow prevented it. The only thing you can do is find out who's at fault, and then you can make sure the world knows who that person is."

"Dominick won't stop until that name is in his possession."

The entire time I'd been speaking to my mom, my phone had been vibrating.

I quickly went into the settings and silenced all the notifications.

I couldn't read another one.

I couldn't see another headline.

I couldn't respond to any more texts.

I needed it all to stop.

"Has your sister reached out?"

My parents knew things weren't good between us. We'd individually told them the minute the tension started brewing, and once the Celebrity Alert had aired about our argument in the restroom, we'd each given them our version of what had happened.

They didn't choose sides; they just encouraged us to speak to each other.

But it was no use. Daisy still blamed me for everything, and I didn't believe I owed her an apology.

"No," I replied. "And I don't expect her to."

She sighed. "Maybe you should come home. I can't imagine the paparazzi will follow you all the way to Boston."

There were paparazzi in Boston too. It didn't matter where I went, they would find me in the States.

I used the back of my hand to wipe what had dripped from my eyes. "Home doesn't feel like the right place for me now either."

Nowhere did.

Except for this bed with the shades drawn and the room filled with total darkness.

"I'm here, Kendall. So is your father. Whatever you need, whatever we can do, you just say the word."

There was a fire in my throat as I thought of the way those photos had hurt them too.

At the conversations they'd have to have with our extended family and friends.

Our neighbors.

My brain was on a course, and the scenery wasn't pretty.

"I love you, Mom. Tell Dad the same. I'll be in touch the second I know something."

"We love you, baby. To the moon and back."

As I hung up, the screen showed all my missed notifications. Even though their appearance no longer made a vibration, there were hundreds. Maybe thousands. And they were coming in from news outlets and social media apps, texts, even voice mails.

I tossed the phone onto Dominick's nightstand, the screen facing down, and just as I was pulling the blanket over my head, he walked into the bedroom.

He came over to my side, sitting on the edge of the bed, framing my face with his palm. "How do you feel?"

I adjusted the pillow behind me, repositioning the blanket so it covered my neck. "Like there's a knife in my back and it's twisting around and around and around."

He took off his shoes and climbed over me, resting across the open space, where he pulled me against his chest. "I don't have answers yet, but I gave them forty-eight hours."

I was silent while I let that number digest. "This is going to be the longest two days of my life."

He rubbed across my back, kissing the top of my head. "What can I do to make you feel better?" He exhaled, his air heating my hair. "Whatever it is, I'll make it happen."

I looked up at his face, my eyes pleading with his. "Can you make me disappear?"

THIRTY-TWO

DOMINICK

"When I asked you to make me disappear," Kendall said from the edge of the pool, overlooking the lapping waves of the Atlantic, "I definitely wasn't expecting this."

Keeping her locked in my house without any fucking sunlight wasn't going to be healthy. She needed air, relaxation, a place where she could unplug from all the bullshit.

My parents' vacation home in Bimini was the answer.

When any of us wanted to go off the grid, we came here.

After a quick call to my assistant, who'd reserved the company jet and shopped for the clothes and bathing suits Kendall would need for this trip, we'd immediately boarded the plane.

Kendall glanced at me from over her shoulder, the water running in droplets down her back, her soaked hair clinging to her skin. "It's so incredibly beautiful here. Thank you, Dominick. You've done so much already. This is just"—she paused, shaking her head—"beyond what I was anticipating."

I wrapped my hands around her slim waist, holding her ass against me. "You were destined to come here sooner than later anyway." I kissed her neck, taking in a deep breath of that ocean breeze, realizing it was the same as her scent.

She turned around, her hands clinging to my neck. "I wish it were under better circumstances." The pain was so evident in her eyes; it punched me in the fucking gut. "That doesn't mean I'm not grateful or I don't appreciate this trip."

Kendall couldn't ever be an attorney. She wore her heart on her sleeve, and that was something I really liked about her. When it came to her emotions, I didn't have to dig. If she was upset, I saw it. If she was happy, she showed that too.

But what I saw now didn't settle well with me.

Even her voice had changed, an ache in every syllable she spoke.

"Listen to me ..." I gripped her even tighter. "For as long as we're here, I want you to forget about what's happening. Consider this your bubble. No one will find you, and you don't have to hide." I aligned our mouths but didn't kiss her. "And no one can hurt you, not while you're with me."

"It sickens me to know what they're all saying about me, what they think about me." Her chest rose and fell so fast that I could tell she was trying to fight off tears. "Those are the thoughts that haunt me."

I turned her around and lifted her into my arms, moving my back against the pool, waiting for her hands to drop to my shoulders and her legs to circle my waist. "You can't change the way people think, how they feel, the way they react." I kissed her chest, right along her heart. "You can only control what's in front of you." I then moved to her lips, pressing mine against them, stalling there for several seconds. "Being here. Enjoying the escape." My mouth found hers again. "Us."

"You're right."

"Once we know the truth, we'll come up with a plan, a statement will be made, and you'll get an apology—whatever it looks like. But that's when you'll gain back some power, when you can control things from this end."

With her facing the beach, she broke eye contact to look at the water, her eyelids closing, the sound of the waves so prevalent, the perfect soundtrack. "I'm going to try." She finally looked at me. "I promise."

I was going to do everything I could to help her keep that mindset.

But that didn't mean my brain wasn't on fucking overdrive, scheming what I was going to do to the bastards responsible for this.

And how deep I was going to bury them.

"You and your family have something really special here," Kendall said, setting her fork down after taking a bite of her fish. "A private chef." She nodded toward the plate. "A yacht." She pointed at the boat that was docked out front. "Aside from your house in LA, this is the most beautiful home I've ever been in." A hint of a smile crossed her lips. "And, my God, that sky."

The sun was just setting, reflecting across the ocean.

But there was a sight more beautiful than anything she could ever list. "None of it compares to the girl sitting across from me." A blush moved over her cheeks as I added, "You have no idea how gorgeous you are, Kendall. Your humbleness is something I love about you."

"The way you look at me ..." She paused, like she was almost speechless. "It sometimes makes it hard to breathe." She lifted her wineglass, and I could tell there was far more on her mind. "You know, when you left me at your house and you went to the studio to talk to the executives, my mind went wild with thoughts. One of the worries I had was if you were going to want to be with me anymore."

I reached across the table, grabbing her hand off her fork and holding it in mine. "What would make you think that?"

She took several deep breaths. "That Celebrity Alert made me look like a whore, someone so unlovable, and when you combine that description with those photos, I thought maybe you wouldn't want to be seen with me anymore."

She'd thought I'd be ashamed of her.

Embarrassed of the way she had been portrayed.

I got up from my chair and moved over to hers, kneeling so our faces would be close. "Never—do you hear me?" I gripped her cheek. "When I made the decision to be with you, I knew what it would entail, how public things would become. With fame comes scandal, and no matter how much you try to avoid it, the media brings it on. I didn't expect this to happen, but that doesn't mean I care any less about you. If anything, it makes me care more."

"I don't understand." She searched my eyes. "Why?"

"Because it's showing me how tenacious you are. Do you know how sexy that is?" I gently kissed her. "You had your ass kicked emotionally, but now, you're ready to kick someone's ass, and I can see that in your eyes."

Her teeth sank into her lip as she stared at me. "Man, I'm positively crazy about you."

"Baby ..." I whispered, about to fucking devour her at this table.

But I couldn't.

The chef's assistant appeared to refill our waters, removing some of the plates we were no longer using and the homemade bread. "I hope you've saved room for dessert," he said. "The chef has prepared his own spin on cake balls." He smiled before he went back inside.

I lifted Kendall from her seat and set her on my lap, rubbing the center of her stomach. "Do you still have room?"

"For cake balls? Of course." She winked. "It's really adorable that you had him make that dessert—along with the rest of dinner. The fact that he served all my favorites didn't go unnoticed."

"I'm glad you enjoyed it." I kissed her and turned us toward the water, so she could watch the ocean if she needed a break from my stare. "You know, you have a lot of decisions ahead of you, and one of them is whether you want to continue shooting. If you want out, all you have to do is say the word."

"I didn't know that was even an option."

I nodded. "Your contract was breached; therefore, you're going to have many options, Kendall." I took a drink of her wine and handed her the glass, so she could have some. "If the studio is found liable, then you have to decide what you want for restitution. Is it a public apology? A check? Both? Remember, you're going to get the power back, and with that comes decisions."

She ran her hand through my hair, and I could tell it gave her a chance to get her thoughts straight.

She nursed the wine before eventually returning it to the table. "Money has never been what motivates me. Was I excited to see the salary the show was offering? Definitely. I have student loans and a car loan and credit card debt, and my life would be easier if I didn't owe so much. But it's just money, Dominick. It's not what makes me happy."

"Tell me your dreams." I kissed the end of her nose. "What you want, what you see happening in the future."

This was when her stare moved to the ocean, her expression matching the contentment she saw in the water. "I've always been my happiest when I'm volunteering, teaching art to seniors." She glanced at me again. "Those are the times I look forward to the most every week."

"Is it the teaching or being around old people, or is it the art?"

Her eyes closed, a warmth coming across her face. "The combination of all three. I love coming up with the ideas each week and being surrounded by these seasoned, brilliant souls— people who don't just inspire me, but also teach me about life. The art takes them on these powerful, moving journeys, and I love that. So much."

This was the Kendall I wanted. The one whose face shone when she spoke about her job. Who found meaning in her work, who was able to make a difference.

There was a greater purpose for her, and it wasn't to be the lead of a reality TV show.

"Regardless of what happens," I said, "the show must pay you your contracted amount. You could earn a settlement as well. I would imagine that figure would make a considerable dent, if not cover all of your financial obligations." I held her cheek, my lips moving to her ear. "And rent is off the table; you'll no longer have to pay for that."

"Because landlords are suddenly so forgiving when it comes to reality stars?"

I tugged her earlobe into my mouth. "Because you'll be living with me." Her eyes made me chuckle when I leaned back to look at them. "Don't be so surprised, baby. You stay most nights at my house anyway. Moving in wouldn't be much different; you'd just have more than yoga pants in my closet."

She searched my face, and the only word leaving her lips was, "Dominick ..."

"What I want is to wake up next to you every morning." I nuzzled her neck, tightening my grip around her. "To hold you like this when we go to bed every night."

"You're ... heavenly."

"Then, there's nothing to think about. We'll make that happen the second we return to LA."

I was just pulling my mouth back from kissing her jaw when the chef's assistant returned. He had a bottle of champagne, two flutes, and a large plate of dessert in his hands.

"The chef says the champagne will pair well with the flavors he's prepared."

He poured the bubbly and removed our dinner plates and went back inside the house.

I continued holding Kendall on my lap, handing her a glass. "To moving in?"

She clinked her flute against mine. "Hell yes." She kissed me. "Now, let's dig into this dessert before it melts everywhere."

The chef had added heavy scoops of ice cream to each corner of the dish, the balls in the center covered in chocolate, and there were small bowls filled with dipping sauces.

She grabbed a cake ball and lowered it into the chocolate sauce, adding some strawberry ice cream before taking a bite. "*Ohhh.*" Her head tilted back, and she groaned, "It's velvety and perfect."

Nothing made me happier than watching her enjoy herself.

I dipped mine into the white chocolate and coffee ice cream and bit off half. "Yours are better." I continued to chew, the rich cake and toppings certainly sweet and delicious but not as decadent as Kendall's.

"Come on. That can't be true."

I finished the bite and wiped my mouth. "He's the best chef on the island. He's worked for my family for years. But you put love into cooking, and I can taste that when I eat your food."

"You're sweet."

I sipped on my champagne while she ate another one, licking her fingers.

"I'm beyond stuffed."

"You did well."

She laughed. "An appetite isn't something I ever lack."

"Another thing I like about you."

I lifted her from my lap and set her on the deck. "Come with me."

She followed me across the patio and down to the dock.

When we reached the beach, I instructed, "Leave your shoes here."

I slipped out of mine and waited for her to be done. Then, I took her onto the sand where the waves met.

I faced her, holding one of her hands against my heart, wrapping my other arm around her waist. "Dance with me, Kendall."

A smile moved across her gorgeous face. "But there's no music."

I dipped down to kiss her, tasting the chocolate on her lips, the island scent on her skin. "Just listen to the waves."

She moved to the beat of the Atlantic, and every exhale drew her closer to me.

THIRTY-THREE

KENDALL

My cell had been on silent since before we even left for Bimini. Periodically throughout the day, I'd check it to make sure there wasn't anything vital I needed to reply to—aside from responding to the texts from my family and Charlize. I kept it in my purse on the far side of the bedroom, away from my line of vision, ensuring I wouldn't be distracted by the notifications.

But something woke me up at two in the morning, and it wasn't my quieted phone or the breeze coming in through the open balcony or the feel of Dominick's arms around me. It was something in my gut, telling me I needed to look at my phone.

And it was strong enough to make me rise out of bed and hurry across the room.

Daisy: I need to talk to you. It's important. Whenever you see this, call me. I don't care what time it is.

Since Dominick was still asleep, I walked into the living

room and out to the back porch, taking a seat in one of the large, overstuffed chairs that faced the ocean.

The way she had worded the text caused so many questions, each of them circling, nagging, tightening my body from the inside.

I didn't like the feeling in my stomach.

What could you possibly want, Daisy?

Dominick would tell me not to call her, that she had already done enough. I was in the Bahamas to stop hurting, and all she did was cause pain.

But he wasn't out here.

And he wasn't related to my sister.

With tension pounding through my muscles, my hands slightly shaking, I found her number in my Contacts and held the phone up to my ear while it rang.

She answered, "Hi."

Her tone was ice, as though she were in the middle of something much more important than me.

I shouldn't have been surprised.

But still ... I was.

"Hey, Daisy. I just got your text. I know it's late—I guess not as late there as it is here."

"Here?" she asked. "You're not in LA?"

"No."

She cleared her throat. "I'm not shocked you fled. I mean, the entire world is talking about you right now and saying—"

"Daisy," I interrupted, not needing the recap, "you asked me to call. What is it that you want to tell me?"

She sighed. "I'm sure your attorney boyfriend is going to be investigating, so I thought I'd throw you a bone."

My stomach clenched, the knots inside grinding together. "Okay."

"I was at a bar a few weeks back, hanging, whatever, and

after a couple drinks, this guy started telling me he works for Happy Lite—you know, the studio that owns *Glitzy Girls*."

Our perfect dinner began to churn in my stomach.

"Well, come to find out, he works in the studio's editing room. How ironic, right? And he has access to all the shows and their footage and yada, yada, yada."

I could sense where this was heading, and I suddenly felt like I was on fire, my lungs screaming to breathe, so I stood and paced the patio.

"The next thing I knew, we were on a date, and he asked about you. I told him the truth—how you wronged me, how you shouldn't be my competition but that you were ruining everything for me. How you took the team I'd worked so hard for, the team I deserved—not you."

I felt sick.

"Daisy ... no."

"I had three glasses of wine, and you know that third one makes me extra chatty." She paused for several seconds. "Anyway, a few days later, the Celebrity Alert came out, and once it aired, the guy sent me a text with a copy of the photos he'd submitted to the site along with the confirmation that they were going to share them. His next message asked if what he'd done would score him a second date." She laughed. "Can you imagine? He actually thinks he's good enough for me. Seriously, I can't even with some people."

I didn't know whether to dry-heave or start sobbing.

But my entire body was now shaking, even my feet as they stepped over the tiled floor.

"You're disgusting," I whispered, my throat not allowing me to speak any louder.

"Hold on. I came to you out of the kindness of my heart, and I'm the disgusting one? I didn't have to help at all. I could have let your ridiculous boyfriend spin every one of his wheels and come up empty-handed, but I didn't. I helped. And now, you're turning this around on me?"

"Kindness?" I snorted, but not a single bit of this was funny. "You think you're showing me kindness? Kindness would have been asking how I was doing the moment you answered the phone. Kindness would have been standing by my side when this media storm erupted. Kindness would have been *not* talking shit about me to a complete stranger, *not* dropping nuggets in his brain, so he couldn't do something this horrific to your sister." I stopped pacing, holding the wooden pole at the end of the patio, clinging to it like the ground was falling. "But there isn't a fucking kind bone in your body."

"I literally can't believe what I'm hearing right now."

"Were you the one who sent the photos? No. Were you the one who tried to ruin my life? Not directly. But you're not taking a single bit of accountability here. You're throwing the facts at me like you're doing me a fucking favor and washing your hands of this mess. Well, guess what. You don't deserve to walk away innocently; you don't get the fucking medal of honor for reaching out to me."

Something was tearing through my chest, and I couldn't stop it. This wasn't a PMS beast that reared its claws every month. This was years of frustration that had peaked since I'd moved to LA, and I couldn't hold it in any longer.

"You're a jealous brat—that's what you are. I've done nothing but support you, to the point where I even came to work for you. And the moment I got even the tiniest bit of attention, you lost your mind. If you were secure, if you weren't dripping in self-doubt, then you would have realized I was never trying to hurt your career or compete with you. But you saw me—someone who loves you more than anything—as an enemy and turned this into a contest. That doesn't only make you a fool; it makes you pathetic." I released the pole, pushing my back against the wooden banister.

"You reached out to clear your conscience, not for any other reason, but you have a long way to go before you gain my forgiveness. I hope you think about what you've done and the way you've acted, and I hope for once in your life, you realize this is all on you. You need to take responsibility, and do the right thing." I paused, waiting for her to say something.

Anything.

But there was only silence.

"I have to go," I said. "Good-bye, Daisy."

I set down my phone and looked out into the dark water, trying to find my breath again, my head filled with thoughts I could barely process.

My sister.

My fucking sister.

She hadn't pulled the trigger, but she'd fed him the bullets.

In my mind, that made her just as guilty.

My phone lit up, and my attention was drawn to the screen, where a series of texts came in from Daisy. I wasn't sure why, but I opened them.

They were screenshots, showing the conversation between her and the guy—exactly the way she had described. The texts were timestamped. I was sure if I looked up when the alert had gone out, the timeline would jive, showing that he had in fact warned her after the news was already released.

That didn't make me feel any better.

I turned around and headed back into the bedroom, seeing the light was on from the hallway. Dominick was sitting up in bed once I walked in, staring at me like he was hunting an animal.

"The balcony is open, baby."

My eyes flitted to the French doors, realizing he was right.

"Then, I'm sure you already heard." I tossed my phone onto the mattress. "Look at her texts."

He held my cell in his hands, reading the messages from Daisy. "I'm going to fucking bury that guy."

"And her?"

He ground his teeth together. "Kendall ..."

THIRTY-FOUR

DOMINICK

"You don't have to sit in on today's meeting if you don't want to," I said to Kendall while we ate lunch outside on the deck.

Forty-eight hours had passed since I'd stormed into Ted's office, and our video chat was scheduled to begin in fifteen minutes. Kendall needed to reenter the world at her own pace. I didn't want her to feel any pressure to face those mother-fuckers.

"It's okay," she said. "I want to be there."

"You're sure?"

She nodded and took a bite of her fruit salad before setting down her fork. "I already know who's responsible. Nothing they can say will come as a shock."

Daisy, that fucking cunt.

She'd been on my short list when I was coming up with people who could be at fault. I wanted to be wrong about her. I wanted to give her the benefit of the doubt. But every goddamn time, she'd proven that she was a self-centered piece of shit, and this episode had taken the fucking crown.

As far as the studio was concerned, this was on the asshole who worked in the editing room. They didn't even know about Daisy's involvement.

But in my eyes, she was far from innocent.

I would leave it up to Kendall on how she wanted to handle her sister. If she wanted me to destroy what was remaining of Daisy's career, I would. With a fucking smile on my face.

If Kendall wanted me to do nothing, letting Daisy rot in her narcissism, I'd oblige but not before I gave that cunt a piece of my mind.

"You do know that the studio is going to put their own spin on what happened," I said. "They don't want a lawsuit or for anyone to poke around in their business, so they're going to make you an offer and hope this goes away."

She rolled her eyes. "I figured."

I took a drink of my iced tea. "The moment you're ready to strike a deal, I'll have my team draw up the paperwork."

She traced her fork around the plate, her eyes on the food she hadn't touched. "I still don't know what I want to do."

"You don't have to decide on the settlement right now, but as far as shooting goes, you will have to come up with a plan fairly soon. They're going to want you to report to set within a day, two at the most."

"I know." She sighed. "And I'm sure my new followers are waiting for a response instead of the silence I've been giving them."

I reached across the table, setting my hand on hers. "In the media world, silence causes fire to spread. We want to put out those fires and speculation before anything else burns."

Her eyes finally connected to mine. "I just don't know what to say."

"Don't worry, baby; we'll figure it out." I checked my

watch. "But we should head inside; the meeting is going to start in a few minutes."

She followed me into the home office, where multiple monitors were set up on the large desk. I pulled another chair around, so we could sit beside each other, and I logged in to the network.

I held the mouse over the Connect button. "Are you ready?"

"I think so." She slowly inhaled. "Yes."

When the video turned on, I saw a boardroom, the same men as our prior meeting sitting around it, Shane there as well.

"Dominick, Miss Roy, thank you for joining us," Ted said.

He then made the introductions, so Kendall knew the names of his team.

Details that made no goddamn difference because the result was still the same.

They had fucked up.

And now, they were going to pay.

"We would first like to offer our sincerest apologies," Ted continued. "We understand that you must feel extremely violated. Privacy and trust are things we hold in the highest regard, and we never want our talent to be put in a situation like yours."

"No, Ted, the situation is one *you* put her in," I clarified.

I understood there were certain things he needed to say, but I wasn't going to tolerate a single word of bullshit. Someone was going to take ownership of this, and since Ted was the CEO, it was going to be him.

"Normally, we like to conduct thorough investigations, spending several weeks interviewing staff and going over feeds and footage to pinpoint the exact nature of the circumstances," Ted said. "Unfortunately, in this case, we weren't given the amount of time we would have liked, so we don't have all the information yet."

"But you have enough," I told him.

There was silence as Ted looked at his attorney and a few of the employees sitting around his section of the table. "We were able to draw a conclusion as to what had occurred and how the still shots had been leaked."

I took a quick peek at Kendall, her back so stiff, her face trying to conceal her emotion.

With the camera only aimed on our faces, I reached across the chair and linked our fingers. Her palm was sweaty, and there was a tremor in her hand as she squeezed back.

"There are only three people who have access to the footage we're currently filming and our archives. After process of elimination, we've been able to identify that it was Mark Hall, a senior editor on our staff. We don't know why he released those pictures—he's not revealing his reasoning—but he did take responsibility."

I wondered if Daisy had paid him off to ensure he would never give up her name.

Mark couldn't be that much of a fucking moron to think this couldn't be traced back to him, or maybe Daisy's pussy was so good that he didn't care.

Something had certainly gone down.

It pissed me off that I would probably never get the answer to that.

"I assume he's no longer working for your studio," I said.

"We don't tolerate that kind of behavior," Ted replied. "Mark violated several moral codes and company-wide rules, so yes, he was terminated." He folded his hands on the table, almost looking relieved that the hard part was over. "Personally, I'm appalled by his actions. I'm ashamed this happened at our

studio, with one of our high-ranking employees, and at a prop-
erty we provided for Miss Roy to live in."

Mark was a fucking asshole, and he would never work in
this industry again.

I would make sure of that.

But now, it was time for the studio to make this right.

"Let's talk about the cameras," I started. "Why were they
on when your contract clearly stated they wouldn't be?"

Ted looked at the attorney, who replied, "We can't respond
to that."

"They weren't supposed to be on," Shane said. "And we
don't know why they were, but I can tell you that this was a
terrible mishap, and I assure you, it won't ever happen again."

"Assure me?" I laughed. "What good does that do when the
damage has already been done? You're speaking about the
future when we haven't even resolved the past."

"You can't honestly believe that firing Mr. Hall and apologizing to my client are enough," I said. "One of your employees
released naked photographs of my client and myself. There are
long-lasting effects to that damage. Contracts she's going to lose
now. A reputation that she's going to have to build again from
scratch. So, tell me, gentlemen, what are you going to do for
Kendall Roy?"

A few seconds of quietness passed before Ted said, "We're
happy to offer the settlement that we have prepared and will be
emailing to you the moment this meeting is adjourned. We
would like you to review the offer with Miss Roy and have her
sign it at her earliest convenience, so this is all behind us." He
glanced at the attorney, who nodded at him. "In the meantime,
Miss Roy will need to report to filming tomorrow—"

"You can stop yourself right there, Ted. My client is under
no obligation to return to filming. It has become very clear to
me that Happy Lite isn't a safe environment for her or any of

her costars. Let me remind you, you haven't just violated her trust and reputation; you've violated the terms of her contract as well. Whether my client returns to your set, that's still up in the air. We will review the settlement, and I'll let you know if it even comes close to meeting her expectations. I'll also let you know her anticipated return date—if that's what she decides."

There was silence.

Because every motherfucker around that table knew I was right.

"Do you have anything else to say?" I inquired. "Any other apologies you'd like to offer while we're still on the line?"

Shane took a couple of minutes to say a few words to Kendall, but I didn't listen—none of what he was saying was important.

What I thought about were ways I could milk the settlement because money wasn't what Kendall was after. She needed to be coddled, for the world to know this wasn't her fault and she was not the girl the Celebrity Alert had portrayed her as.

"Dominick," Ted said once Shane finished, "we'll be anticipating your correspondence. Thank you both for taking the time to speak with us."

Kendall thanked him, and I disconnected the call.

"How do you feel?" I asked as I turned to her.

She shrugged, shaking her head. "I honestly don't know. They took responsibility—that's all I can really ask for, I guess."

"No, baby, you can ask for a hell of a lot more than that."

"But they've already done more than my sister has."

Her tone fucking broke me, and I lifted her out of her chair and set her on my lap. I put my hand on the back of her head, staring into those gorgeous, big light-blue eyes. "Talk to me."

"I'm just angry." She paused. "And I'm so upset. I'll never understand her motives or how someone could hurt me the way

261

Mark did." Her voice softened. "I just need some time to get over this."

I brushed my hand across her cheek. "They're going to send over the settlement. We'll review it today, we'll sleep on it, and I'll respond tomorrow. Does that sound all right?"

She nodded, slowly falling against my chest.

As I rubbed her back, holding her as close as I could get her, an idea began to brew.

I couldn't make this completely disappear, but my plan could take away some of her pain.

THIRTY-FIVE

KENDALL

Since we'd arrived in Bimini, nights were the hardest. Dominick would be asleep next to me, the French doors wide open, the sheer white curtains beside them flowing high in the air like wings, the sounds of the ocean filling the room. It was the optimal scenery for rest.

But I couldn't.

There was far too much on my mind.

Too many unanswered thoughts.

Too much anxiety about my future.

Was it possible for life to resume the way it had been before? Could I return to shooting, putting myself back in the spotlight when the world had seen so much of my body?

Was that even what I wanted?

The taste of fame wasn't what I'd expected. Aside from money, it had brought nothing good. I didn't like the expectations, the lack of privacy. Things I hadn't even realized were important to me now that they were gone.

Dominick had said he could get me out of my contract. I certainly liked the sound of that, but then what would I do?

Would I return to graphic design at an advertising agency? Would I make stationery and greeting cards for some mom-and-pop printing press? And when the clients requested meetings with the designer, would they remember my bare ass? The way I had looked when I was mounting my boyfriend? Or when I was on my knees, giving him head? Or the smeared pink lips from the actor I'd supposedly fucked in a public restroom?

They would think I was the biggest slut ever.

With these thoughts running on a continuous loop, sleep was even further away than before. I needed something to distract my brain, so I tiptoed out of bed and grabbed my phone, quickly bringing it back beneath the covers.

I knew better than to check Instagram, but my finger automatically pressed the app, and I typed Daisy's name into the search bar.

She was a poster, constantly providing fresh content, wanting to always stay relevant to her fans.

But there was nothing new on her page. No posts for a few days, no stories.

Maybe Daisy and her assistant were too busy, which could have been the case, or maybe she was actually feeling some sort of emotion from what had happened between us, drowning in a sea of thoughts, like me.

I typed Mark Hall's name into the search, clicking his profile once it appeared. He didn't have many followers, and his photos were mostly of his dog, some of his family, and a few in the editing room of the studio, showing him hard at work.

There wasn't a single one of Daisy.

His most recent post was a quote that he'd shared yesterday.

YOUR ACTIONS DON'T DEFINE YOU.

MOMENTS HAPPEN. SOME EARN YOU TROPHIES; OTHERS
EARN YOU PARKING TICKETS.
HOW YOU HANDLE TOMORROW IS WHAT COUNTS.
BY THEN, I'LL BE A BETTER VERSION OF ME.
BECAUSE I'M NOT PROUD OF THE MAN I WAS.

This was a guy who had been so willing to hurt me. I just wanted a peek into his life, to see the things that were important to him. I didn't expect to find remorse. Even though he hadn't apologized to me, it looked like he was sorry.

It also looked like he was in pain.

He'd lost a girl he liked.

A job that probably meant everything to him.

And now, he was left with only memories of both.

"You should be sleeping," Dominick whispered as he rolled toward me.

I appreciated that he'd pulled me out of this brain cloud, and I exited out of the app and set my phone on the nightstand. "I can't."

His hair was ruffled, his cheeks dark from him being so lax about shaving since we'd arrived on the island. I enjoyed the scratchiness every time he kissed me, knowing once we flew back to LA, he would shave it off and return to suits and aftershave rather than the swim trunks and suntan lotion he'd been living in.

I ran my fingers across his face while he gripped my hips.

"*Mmm*," I moaned from his touch, the way his lips were nuzzling into my neck. "I know one way you can get me to relax."

He moved me beneath him, like I weighed no more than a pillow, and slipped my tank top off, kissing me the second I was naked. My legs parted, and I instantly felt the probing of his tip, my wetness greeting him.

"Fuck me," he growled. "Your cunt is dripping."

The roughness of his face kept me in the moment.

"And it's tight ... goddamn it."

My head sank into the pillow as he slid in deeper, sucking my nipple into his mouth.

"I've been thinking about this all day." He moved to the other side, licking the peak back and forth. "How hard I was going to fuck you."

"I can't believe you waited this long to have me."

"I was going to wake you in the middle of the night, surprising you with my mouth." He smiled as he looked up at me. "But if you're not sleeping, I can't do that."

"I need this." I swallowed while he buried the rest of himself inside me. "I need you."

He held the back of my head and thrust forward. "Then, I won't make you wait for more."

The arch of his hips sent a burst through me, a second wave as he reared back and repeated the same motion.

As the air came in through my lips, the emotions that had been keeping me awake released, my chest loosening, the strain in my stomach letting go.

"Fuck yes." He plunged all the way in. "You have the tightest pussy." His lips were on top of mine. "You pulse and clench every time I'm inside you."

I could feel it. The fullness. Almost like he was hitting the end of me each time.

"A pussy molded just for me."

He reached down, slowly brushing the top of my clit. He didn't use a pattern; he gave me nothing to get used to. He just knew how to build my body around him.

I could barely breathe.

I couldn't even control the fluttering of my eyes.

He was owning me.

And I was lost in the sucking of my nipples, in the rubbing and friction between my legs.

Swirls of bliss dominated my stomach, my thighs turning numb, my back lifting off the bed.

No amount of bristles could keep me present.

"Yes," he hissed. "I can feel you coming."

There was a surge in my clit, an explosion of tingles that moved up my body, first shooting through my abdomen, causing a scream to ripple through my mouth and, "Dominick," following. Once the air was out of my lungs, a mix of sensitivity and shuddering came next, a flood of both gliding through me.

He didn't pause.

He definitely didn't still.

He continued to caress my clit, his cock diving into my wetness, his power not letting up at all.

"Fuck," I huffed, trying to inhale as a second round blew through me, unable to stop moaning from the intensity. "Oh God."

He calmed for just a moment but only to reposition us, sitting on the end of the bed, where I found myself on his lap, facing away from him with my feet on the ground.

And directly in front of us was a mirror.

The moonlight gave off enough of a glow to show our bodies.

The placement of his hands.

The way I was spread over him.

The tip of his cock aimed at my center.

And I observed myself slowly lowering over his crown.

Oh God.

"I want you to watch yourself ride me." The heat from his lips scorched my skin as he kissed the back of my neck. "You're going to see how much you fucking love my cock."

With his eyes boring through mine, I had nothing to hold

on to, aside from my knees. No shoulders to stab, no face to kiss.

"Fuck," I gasped as I went all the way down, the sensuality completely taking over me.

His fingers suddenly moved to my lips. "Don't speak. I want your body to do all the talking." He pinched my nipple, and when I went to make a sound, he squeezed harder. "No, not even a moan."

I relished in how far he reached inside of me, the thickness, the length of him. Since I couldn't tell him how good he felt, I bounced over his shaft.

And again.

My head fell back, which he straightened as he said, "No, I want you to watch." He lifted one of my hands, placing my own finger on my clit. "And I want you to rub yourself."

"Oh—" I cut myself off, trembling instead as the feeling spread through me.

"Touch yourself for me, baby, while you fuck me."

His voice wasn't just doing the talking; his eyes were commanding, telling me what he wanted.

And this mirror showed every one of his orders.

I rose over him, the glow of light revealing every inch that had been inside me, a pad of my finger skimming that sensitive spot at the top.

My hips bucked as though I were releasing a scream.

"Fuck yes. That's it." His nails acted like teeth around my nipple. "Make yourself come again." He gripped my hair in a ponytail, pulling my head back until our eyes met. "I want you to see what you look like when you shudder over my cock."

As he released my locks, my head faced forward, my eyes back on us.

He cupped both breasts as I lifted higher before thrusting him back in, my finger moving faster.

Circling.

Flicking.

Working that sensitivity.

"You're so sexy when you fuck me." He surrounded my earlobe. "Look at your legs"—he touched my thighs—"and your fucking hips"—he moved up to clench those—"and this bad, bad pussy, taking in all of my dick."

It was so hard to hold in my breath, to keep my sounds silent.

But where his eyes were so loud, so was my body, relentlessly plunging him in and out of me.

His mouth shifted just below my ear. "Your orgasm is about to be mine."

Maybe it was the way he demanded one from me.

Maybe it was the sharp, incessant friction across my clit, adding to the delicious fullness of his cock.

Maybe it was the way we looked, locked together, my body grinding over his.

But it was there again.

That build.

"Now, watch yourself come."

I gripped the bed, keeping myself lowered, and rotated around his dick while he devoured me with his gaze.

The quaking instantly ignited in my stomach, tugging at that bliss, heightening it.

My body was no longer mine; it was as though there were a string inside that controlled the sparks and flutters and ripples and he was yanking on it with all his strength.

"Show me, Kendall. Show me how fucking good it feels."

I couldn't shout.

I couldn't moan.

All I could do was circle around him, losing myself.

His teeth grazed the back of my shoulder. "Yes, baby." His nipping was the pain that I needed. "Fuck that cock."

Spasms completely shattered my body, and when I couldn't move a second more, he took over, clenching an arm around my stomach, pounding his dick into me.

"Mine." He aligned our fingers, guiding them across my clit. "All fucking mine."

His dominance floated through me, every feeling possessed by him, and I held on, watching as the orgasm rocked through me.

I sank my fingers into his thighs, melting from his penetration, keeping my screams in, feeling them echo through my body until there was only stillness left.

His eyelids narrowed, his lips feral as he said, "Now, we're going to do that again." He pressed his lips against my throat. "This time, I want to hear every sound."

I looked over my shoulder, seeing his defined chest, a thin layer of sweat glistening across his skin. "Oh God, I want more."

Before I had even finished speaking, I was moving again, and this time, he was lifting me into the air. He carried me across the room, pressing my back against the adjacent wall, the view of the ocean in front of me. My legs clung to his waist, my arms on his shoulders, and I held on while he pummeled into me.

"Take my cock, baby." He nipped my bottom lip, fucking me harder, deeper. "Take it like you want to fucking come again."

I didn't dare say this, but I thought he'd drained my body of pleasure, making it impossible to reach that a third time. But when he buried himself inside me, it continued to feel better. And as he positioned me higher on his cock, the top of him rubbing against my clit, that build instantly returned.

I quivered, my nails finding his skin. "Don't stop."

"Yes, baby," he roared against my lips. "You've earned yourself this ..."

I expected him to move faster, use more power, but that wasn't what happened.

His hand lowered, and he was suddenly teasing that forbidden spot, dragging some of my wetness there and tracing around the hole.

The taunting didn't last.

Because soon, he was up to his knuckle, and I was moaning even louder than before.

"I knew you'd like that."

With my back smashing into the paint and texture, I lifted my hips, meeting him, pushing him in and out of me.

"Jesus fucking Christ, Kendall." He gave me his entire finger, twisting his wrist. "If you keep this up, I might have to finger-fuck your ass every time."

I wouldn't stop him.

The feeling was one I couldn't get enough of. The combination a fullness that I'd never thought I'd enjoy, but one that was so satisfying.

"You just got wetter."

He was rotating, driving into me, that friction returning like it had never left.

"You're going to make me come again."

A grin moved across those handsome lips right before he chewed on one of mine, releasing it to say, "And you thought I couldn't give you a third one."

"Come with me."

"And stop this feeling?" He added another finger, earning himself a moan. "This tightness? This fucking dripping wetness?" He stopped speaking to growl. "Not a chance."

I cupped his face to hold on, loving the shadow and the way it felt against my lips. "Please, Dominick," I breathed. "Please."

He aimed upward, the rough hairs scraping my clit, causing

a burst of tingles to fly through me.

"Is that what you want?"

"Yes."

"For me to fill you with my cum?"

"Oh God, yes."

"Then, fucking tell me." His teeth gnawed on my neck. "Tell me how badly you want me to fucking come."

I moved my hands to his neck and pressed my shoulders into the wall, using both to lift myself up and rock over his dick. "Baby!" The sensations were building, especially as he increased his speed, giving me every beautiful inch of his perfect cock. "I need you—all of you." As the feeling intensified, my nails dug into him, my heels pushed into his ass, as I craved more of those fierce, hard strokes. "Dominick," I begged. "Give it to me."

My orgasm was within reach. I couldn't hold it off any longer, not with what he was doing to my ass, my clit, my whole body.

"Your cunt is squeezing me." His head leaned back, exposing his throat, that sexy Adam's apple that bobbed with each breath. "You feel so fucking good."

"*Ahhh!*" As I shattered, the feelings bursting through me, I bucked against his dick.

It only took a few more pumps before I felt the change in him. His jabs turned sharper, his grunts filling my ears.

"Oh fuck." His mouth was finally on mine again. "You want my cum, don't you?"

"Yes."

"You want me to blow my load in that sweet fucking pussy?"

I shivered as the orgasm closed in around me, pulling me into that lost land. "Yes, Dominick." I sucked in more air. "Yes!"

"You're even milking my fucking finger."

The tone of his voice told me he was there, rearing up. "Kendall ..." His cock got even harder. "Take it, baby. Take my fucking cum."

Shudders were collapsing through me, and I could feel the same was happening in him, but I still kept up the fast, hard pumps.

And so did he.

"Goddamn it," he cried out.

Pulses were flowing through my navel and up my chest, eventually stilling, and that was when I released his neck and hugged him against me. He was still slamming into me, his force only now starting to die.

His lips slowly pecked mine until he was motionless.

"I think I took half the paint off the wall," I joked, searching for my breath.

He laughed, a sound so yummy that I had to kiss him. There was a sweetness on his skin and a saltiness from the sweat.

"I know how you like it ... and I didn't hold back."

"I didn't want you to."

He moved us over to the bed, sitting on the edge, holding me just as tightly. The moon let off enough light that I could see his face, knowing his eyes were on mine.

"Kendall," he whispered, our noses brushing, our air mixing, "I love you." His hands moved to my face, holding me with a strength that filled me with so much emotion.

This feeling was different than the orgasms I'd just had, this caused my heart to hammer away in my chest. "Oh God."

I hadn't been searching for him. He certainly hadn't been looking for me. And he'd made me work so hard to bring us to this place. But we were here, and I never appreciated anything more.

"Dominick, I love you."

THIRTY-SIX

DOMINICK

"If you brought me in here to yell at me, then save your breath," Daisy said from the other side of the conference room table, her stare bouncing from Brett's to mine.

Kendall and I had returned from Bimini last night after the studio approved the counteroffer I'd made on their settlement. Now that we were back, I had loads of work to catch up on.

Handling Daisy was at the top of my list.

A meeting Kendall had no idea was taking place.

"There won't be any yelling," I said, reminding her it worked both ways. "We asked you to come in because we have a deal for you." I decided to cut right to the chase. The less time I spent with this cunt, the better. "But you know how these things work. I do something for you; you do something for me."

Her eyes narrowed, and she took a drink of her coffee, glaring at the lid once she set it down, as though the contents disappointed her. "You really think you know me, don't you, Dominick?"

I laughed.

I couldn't help myself.

There was so much bullshit sitting across from me that I could fucking smell it.

I ground my teeth together. "We both know there's only one reason you're here, Daisy."

"What do you want?" Her eyes left me to move to Brett, her arms crossing over her chest. "And if it's to offer me a role on *Glitzy Girls*, I'm not interested."

The studio hadn't released the news yet that Kendall was resigning from the show, but I wasn't shocked to hear that Daisy knew. When it came to Daisy's sister, there seemed to be no secrets.

But before I got down to business, I had to see if there was anything living, breathing inside that chest of hers or if it was just pure fucking evil. "Do you have any remorse at all?"

She was quiet for several moments, taking a few deep breaths. "It's a shame what happened."

"But it's not your fault," I said.

"Like I told Kendall, I didn't seek this man out. I didn't put a plug in his ear. I didn't tell him to release those photos—I didn't even know there were inappropriate photos. I simply told him how upset I was with my sister, and he took matters into his own hands."

As she sighed, I processed what she had said. There was a hell of a lot more than just photos in that editing room, there was actual footage of us fucking, but it didn't sound like Daisy knew that. Maybe there was some truth to her story.

"Do I wish it happened?" She shook her head. "No, I don't. But if you must know, I'm happy she's leaving television. Not because of the reason you think—although, yes, I'm happy to no longer share the screen with her." She twisted her coffee over the table as though it were the stem of a wineglass. "She's just not as tough as me; she doesn't have thick skin. The rejection and criticism are obviously too much for her, and over

time, it will only get worse. Believe it or not, I don't want that
for her."

This was the first time I had ever heard any empathy or
humanity from her.

Finally, I was getting somewhere.

"Why don't you tell her that?"

Her hand paused, her lips opening, no words coming out.

"I understand vulnerability is hard for you, Daisy." I shifted
tones and positions, playing on a new angle. "It's hard for most
people, but she's your sister, and she cares about you more than
anything."

Her eyes bored through me. "I didn't come here for a
therapy session."

I leaned on the table, getting as close to her as I ever would.
"I just want to make sure you hear me."

"Loud and clear."

I pushed a folder toward her, and she opened it, reading the
details I'd outlined.

"But Balmy Hard Seltzer fired me weeks ago." She closed
the folder. "Is this some sort of joke?"

Brett and I had gone out on a goddamn limb to secure this
contract for Daisy. Since they had offered the role to Kendall
but she was no longer taking any endorsements, we had gone
back to the company to negotiate a deal on Daisy's behalf.

One that involved many promises.

"Here's the situation," I said to her. "Balmy Hard Seltzer is
willing to work with you again under a few conditions."

"What?"

"You go onto the set, and you do what they say. You keep
your lips shut, and you don't mouth off or give their staff any
shit. I'm talking a full attitude adjustment. They're not going to
tolerate any nonsense. They're not going to give you a second
chance, so you have one shot to get this right."

She opened the folder again, reading the contents. "This offer is higher than what they were paying me before."

"I know."

And it had taken a fucking miracle to get that amount.

A contract that had been one of the accolades of my career, considering they hadn't even wanted to hear me mention Daisy's name when I first got them on the phone.

She glanced up at me. "What's the stipulation?"

"I want you to do the right thing."

Her brows rose. "As in?"

It pained me how fucking self-centered she was.

"Let me spell this out for you ..." I moved the second folder to the side of me and clenched my hands together, the anger in my body causing them to twitch. "There are people in your life who would do anything for you, love you unconditionally, who would never in a million fucking years hurt you. Kendall is one of those people." I paused, letting some of the emotion calm before I fucking exploded.

"I have two brothers; both are lawyers. Was I pissed when they enrolled in law school, worried they were going to take away my clients? Hell no. I was thrilled that I would get to share this experience with them, that I would have a team I could trust because there's no one I can count on more than family. But you didn't look at Kendall that way. You looked at her like she was a goddamn vulture. I don't understand it. I can't wrap my head around the fact that you saw her as competition and not someone you could share this ride with. Someone who could make you even more money because the media loves to see siblings together." I exhaled, rubbing my fingers together.

"But instead, you shit on her, you hurt her, you jeopardized her career, and you changed the way the world now views her." I swallowed, letting that sink in. "And when she needed you the most, where were you? You weren't blowing up her phone or stopping by her apartment to be there to catch her fucking tears. But had roles been reversed, we know she would have been there for you."

"What do you want from me, Dominick?" she asked after a long pause. "An apology? For me to get on my knees and beg for forgiveness?"

I nodded toward the door, letting her know this meeting was over. "I'm not going to force you; I'm not going to hold this contract over your head. As someone who went out of his way to get this contract back for you—and at twenty-five percent higher than before—I'm just asking you to do the right fucking thing."

She pulled the folder into her grasp and stood from the table. "Is there anything else?" She looked at Brett and then back to me.

"You have twenty-four hours to let us know if you want to proceed with that contract," Brett told her.

"Does that mean you're representing the deal?"

His jaw flexed as he stared at her. "My name is on it."

"What about going forward?" She pointed at both of us. "Will the two of you be representing me now?"

I knew Brett's feelings on this.

He knew mine.

But I had a motive, and sometimes, we had to take one for the goddamn team to get what we wanted in the long run.

"Let's see how this contract goes and the way you behave on the shoot. If Dominick and I are happy with the way you act and you do what we've asked, then we'll consider exploring other deals together."

She smiled as she walked out the door.

The moment it was shut, Brett turned toward me and said, "Man, she's fucking poison." He ran his hands through his hair. "Are you happy with the way that went?"

I crossed my foot over my knee. "I got in her head. I just don't know what she's going to do about it."

"She wants us on her team."

"And that'll be the motivating factor, not Kendall, which is just fucking sad."

He shook his head. "I don't know that I can work with her, Dominick."

"We're going to be the reason that bitch turns her shit around. You know if she had the right attitude and confidence, we could triple her income. Consider it a new mission."

"You owe me, and you owe me for you settling down with Kendall—don't think I've forgotten about our bet. When you least expect it, I'm going to come collecting."

I laughed and reached for the phone on the table, dialing the number for Brett's assistant. "Send him in," I told her.

I hung up, and within a few seconds, the door was opening again. A smiling face with glossy pink lips walked in, taking a seat in the same chair Daisy had been in.

"Daddy Dominick," Charlize said, getting comfortable. "What in the heavens have you called me in here for?"

"Daddy Dominick." Brett chuckled. "Christ."

This was the meeting I had been looking forward to the most.

One that Kendall knew about and had everything to do with.

I took the folder that I'd moved to my side and pushed it toward Charlize. "We have an offer we'd like to make you."

"An offer, huh?" He eyed up Brett before he opened the folder, reading the contract I'd placed inside. "This can't be true," he said, looking up at us. "You have to be tugging my leather collar."

"We're not tugging anything, Charlize."

Brett shook his head. "Nope. Definitely not."

"But ..." He glanced down again. "How is this even possible?"

"Kendall isn't returning to the show," I told him.

"I kinda figured," he replied. "But still, oof."

"Since you've already appeared in multiple hours of footage and her costars really enjoy you, we think you would be the perfect fit to take her place."

"Let me get this straight." He glanced at the contract again. "You want me to take Kendall's spot on *Glitzy Girls*?"

"That's right," Brett said. "And they're going to pay you a quarter of a million dollars for the role." He cleared his throat. "We know the pronoun in the show's title isn't correct. If you do accept the offer, the producers are willing to work with you to make it right."

"We also know you're a makeup artist," I added. "We're not asking you to give that up. You just have to report to filming and follow the rules, most of which you already know since you've filmed with Kendall."

Brett gave Kendall's best friend a smile. "What do you say, Charlize?"

He held the folder against his chest, wrapping his arms around it, swaying his shoulders. "I say, hell fucking yes."

THIRTY-SEVEN

KENDALL

W hen I'd returned to my apartment to box up my
things, the cameras had been removed. Charlize and I
could move around my place and say whatever we wanted, and
I didn't have to worry about any of it being aired. It had taken
us several hours to pack everything up, the closet our one last
destination, and we slumped onto the couch to take a break.

"It was a good ride," I exhaled, resting my head on his
shoulder.

He patted my face. "You're going to be so much happier
now."

"And you?"

"Girlfriend, you know this is going to explode my business.
Losing gigs to other makeup artists will be a thing of the P-
A-S-T."

When I'd discussed this idea with Dominick and Brett,
there was no one more deserving or perfect for the role than
Charlize. I knew he'd handle the fame much better than me
and what this would do for him professionally.

I lifted my chin to look at him. "That makes me the happiest bestie in the entire world."

"Heart you, woman." His arm wrapped around me, his foot tapping one of the boxes that sat on the coffee table. "So, all this stuff is going into storage?"

"Yep, minus my clothes and cosmetics—those are going to Dominick's."

"Moving in with Daddy. That makes me the happiest bestie."

"Now, I just need to find a job."

"I can't imagine you have to find something immediately. The show paid you the rest of your contract, right?"

I nodded, but the truth was, the show had paid me a lot more than just that. Since they were at fault for what had happened, Dominick had made sure I was financially taken care of. Even though I'd told him I didn't want a huge settlement, I'd still gotten one.

That didn't mean I was going to sit on my ass all day.

It just meant I could pay off my student and car loans and the credit card debt I'd accumulated since I'd graduated, leaving a rather large cushion in my savings account so I could hopefully retire one day. In the meantime, I needed a job and benefits and to find my purpose again.

"You know me; I don't sit still very well," I said. "And it's not like I can return to the job I had before this reality show nightmare."

"Ugh." He twirled a piece of my hair around his finger. "Any word from Sparkle Toes?"

"Not since our conversation in Bimini."

"Have your parents gotten involved?"

"Oh, yes." I sighed. "Once I told them about the source of the pics, they lost their shit. They hadn't wanted to get in the middle before, but they're not holding back now. They've told her a hundred different ways how wrong she is and how pissed they are and that they're ashamed and disappointed. It's ugly, Charlize. Like wicked ugly." I pulled the throw pillow into my arms and hugged it against my chest. "I'm just so happy this show is behind me. I was not at all prepared for how nuts my life was going to get."

"Hey, a lot of good shit happened." He dropped that tiny section of hair and started on a new one. "I found you, you found Dominick, and we found out we're the only two people on the planet that Delilah hasn't tried to fuck."

I laughed. "You don't start filming *Glitzy & Fabulous* until tomorrow. Delilah has several more weeks to try and work her magic on you."

"The new name is *sooo* me, isn't it?" He wrote a check mark in the air, a move that only he could make look incredibly sassy. "And, good Lord, I hope I don't need to remind Delilah that this tree isn't ever going to meet her forest."

"Charlize, we both know she's got no forest down there." I snorted and lifted my bottle of water off the table, taking a drink. "Seriously though, can you imagine if I had stayed on and tried to weather that media storm on camera? Episode after episode showing how I was handling my ass being revealed to everyone and their mother?" I offered him a sip. "I'm so grateful Dominick got me out of that contract."

"Another reason we—yes, me too—are smitten with him." He put the cap back on and set the bottle down. "So, now what, honey? Are you polishing up your résumé? Are you and Dominick going to travel? Are you going to start walking the dogs in his building? For the record, aside from makeup, that's my other dream job."

I glanced toward the large, uncovered window, searching for that answer in the sunlight. "I wish I knew, but I have no idea." My phone chimed, a ringtone that belonged to

Dominick. "One sec. That's Dom." I got up, searching for my cell among the boxes and chaos, finding it in the kitchen.

I smiled as I read the screen.

Dominick: I can't stop thinking about you.
Me: You just saw me this morning, silly.
Dominick: Come by my office when you're done packing.
Me: It won't be for a few more hours.
Dominick: I don't care when it is, just make it happen.
Me: See you soon, baby.

"Yo, Miss Googly Eyes," Charlize said from the other side of the room. "I'm going to pee, and then let's finish up your bedroom. I'm ready to attack that beautiful, big closet of yours."

I grinned at my friend. "Then, lunch is on me."

"You're unemployed, girlfriend, and you just scored me a monstrous payday. Lunch is on me—for the rest of our lives."

"Not even a chance." I gave him a stern look, letting him know there was no negotiation. "But you need to find us a place that's far from the paparazzi's radar. I'm sure they're looking for a shot of me—they haven't gotten one since the pics were released—and I just can't handle that attention right now."

"Are you going to make a statement soon?"

I nodded. "Dominick wants me to wait for the right time. He said within the next few days after the studio airs my resignation."

"Makes sense." He put his hands on his hips. "Let me think. *Hmm* ... I know the perfect spot. There's this hole-in-the-wall diner that I went to once in West Hollywood. Best tater tots I've ever had."

"Sold."

He fluttered his fingers at me and headed for the bathroom, and I held up my phone, loading the camera on the screen. I had on a baseball hat with a long braid hanging over one side of my chest, tons of hair that had fallen loose around my face, and not a drop of makeup on.

This was the look Dominick liked the best.

I puckered my lips to blow him a kiss and snapped a selfie. Satisfied with the photo, I attached it to a text and sent it to him.

Dominick: Damn it, I'm one lucky son of a bitch. You are so fucking hot, Kendall. I need that mouth. Now.
Me: You'll have it very soon.
Dominick: I also need you.
Me: Good thing that my lips and I are a package deal. ;)
Dominick: I should punish you for making me wait.
Me: Yes ... please.

"All right, girl, let's get this done," Charlize said from the hallway, halfway between the living room and my bedroom.

I slid the phone into my back pocket and followed him into the closet. I scanned the upper and lower racks that were the whole length of the rectangular-shaped room. Lots of the clothes and shoes and accessories were things I'd brought when I moved in, and the rest were things the show had provided.

I lifted a sparkly, backless gold dress into my hands. "I offered to return all the outfits they gave me, and Shane said I could keep them."

"Finally, homeboy said something worth listening to."

"Except where am I going to wear all this stuff?" I set the dress in a box and took a flaming-hot red jumpsuit off the rack. "Clubbing is no longer my full-time profession."

He walked over to the far wall, where a blazer was hanging on one of the hooks, and he held it in front of him. "Hair up, big hoops in your ears, and only pasties underneath this jacket.

Button both buttons, so the tatas stay hidden and just your cleavage shows. Leather pants on the bottom and stilettos." His stare left the jacket and moved over to me. "If you don't wear that exact outfit to our next dinner date, I'm divorcing you."

It did sound like the perfect ensemble.

But getting out of the house without Dominick tearing off all my clothes and spreading me over the kitchen counter would be a miracle.

"How about you come over and style me for dinner?" That would certainly be one way to keep myself from getting ravaged. "And I'll edit your photos for social media."

"Honey, for that deal, I'll do your hair and makeup too."

"Done."

He pulled a stack of jeans off a shelf. "I'm dreaming about the custom closet you're going to have at Prince Charming's house."

"His is impressive and quite full." I loaded a handful of yoga pants into a box. "So, I'm sure I'll take over one of the guest rooms."

"Which he'll pimp out for you, I'm sure."

"I doubt it."

"Seriously?" He eyed me down as I knelt in front of a pile of tank tops. "The man is wildly in love with you. He invited you to move in, and he's going to give you somewhere to hang your clothes that's not just a lonely little rack in a guest room."

I shrugged. "And if he doesn't, I'll keep my stuff in boxes, and I'll make it work."

"Jesus ... I know why that man loves you." He came closer, his hands cupping my cheeks. "I swear, every time we hang out, you prove that point further and further." He pulled me against him. "They just don't make them like you anymore."

I squeezed back. "Or you."

The sound of Dominick's ringtone came from my back

pocket, and I released him to grab the phone. "Hey," I said, holding it against my face. "Weirdly, we were just talking about you."

"You're at the apartment?"

I stared at Charlize's glowing face as I said, "Yes. Why?"

"Go turn on your TV, channel forty-two. Baby, hurry."

Holding the phone to my ear, I rushed over to the night-stand and picked up the remote, turning on the flat screen that hung on the wall. I pressed the buttons, channel forty-two appearing on the screen.

I recognized the logo for the popular network, two of their famous newscasters talking at the desk.

"What am I watching?" I asked Dominick, Charlize standing next to me.

"You'll see," Dominick replied.

"Before we answer your burning questions on why Selena Gomez and Bella Hadid are rumored to be after the same man, we have a little bit of a newsbreak interruption," Penelope said, one of the anchors of the celebrity news channel.

"That's right," Niko said, her coanchor. "We have to pause things for just a moment to welcome a guest on our show." The camera widened, showing Ted taking a seat between them. "For those of you watching who aren't familiar, this is Ted Truscott, the CEO of Happy Lite, the studio that's producing the highly anticipated show *Glitzy & Fabulous*. Welcome, Ted. We're happy to have you here."

"Oh my God," I gasped.

"Keep watching," Dominick instructed.

"Thank you," Ted said. "I appreciate you letting me stop by."

The screen behind them suddenly showed my headshot, and I stopped breathing.

"This woman"—Ted pointed at the photo of me—"hardly

needs any introduction, as she's seen quite a wave of popularity since agreeing to be on our show, but if you aren't aware, this is Kendall Roy. Our poor Kendall has been involved in a bit of a media scandal lately when some private footage of her was released."

Charlize grabbed my hand, and Dominick said, "Trust me, this is about to get good."

"Since the scandal," Ted continued, "rumors have been swirling, and I've come here to set the record straight."

"I know we've certainly heard a bunch," Penelope mentioned, using her hand to count. "That the show is getting canceled before it even airs; that Kendall is being replaced with someone new; that her sister, Daisy Roy, is going to be the star of the show now. Ted, please clear up this gossip. Our viewers are dying for the truth."

"First, I want to state that Kendall had nothing to do with the release of the footage. The person who sent the shots to Celebrity Alert was, regrettably, a member of our staff."

Penelope almost choked.

Niko scowled at Ted.

"As the CEO, I'm horrified that this took place, that an employee would disrespect Kendall, our studio, and our trust in such a disgusting, disrespectful way."

Emotion was surging in my chest, my entire body shaking as I listened.

"And I would like to personally apologize to Kendall," Ted went on. "What took place is unacceptable, and it's not what we represent as a company. We're adding extreme safety and security measures, and we can only hope our actions will ensure a situation like this never happens again."

"Holy fucking shit," Charlize said.

"Ted," Penelope started, "let me make sure I heard you correctly. You're saying someone employed by your company went behind Kendall's back and submitted naked photos of her, intentionally hurting her this way?"

"I'm afraid so, Penelope," Ted replied. "Believe me, I wish that weren't the case, but I can assure you, that individual is no longer employed by us. We don't tolerate any kind of malicious behavior. We want every one of our actors and actresses, reality stars, and employees to feel comfortable on our sets. We never want to jeopardize the trust we've established, and that's exactly what happened with Kendall. We're at fault, and we take full responsibility."

I could feel my lips open, my hand holding the phone to my face, my eyes practically popping out of their sockets.

But the rest of this felt like a dream.

"How disappointing to hear," Penelope said. "Has anyone on your team spoken to Kendall? How is she doing? I know our producers have reached out to her representatives numerous times, but we've gotten no response. She hasn't posted on social media; she hasn't been seen around town. We've been worried, Ted, and now that I hear this, I'm extremely concerned."

Charlize looked at me, his eyes so wide, his head shaking. "I'm literally dying right now."

"She's doing the best she can, given the circumstances," Ted answered. "It pains me that this happened to such a sweet girl. I don't know if either of you have had the pleasure of meeting Kendall, but everyone who crosses her path only has the most wonderful things to say about her." He glanced at my photo. "Everyone loves her—her costars, my staff, all of production. They call her a ray of sunlight." He frowned as he added, "That's one of the reasons it hurts me to say that Kendall won't be appearing on our show."

"Dude ..." Charlize said. "This is fucking bananas."

"We were afraid that rumor might be true," Niko said. "I

know I'm sad to hear this, Ted. Penelope and I were really looking forward to seeing her in front of the camera."

"I'm positive everyone feels the same way," Ted agreed. "But Kendall's dealt with enough in her short time of filming, and we know that girl is going to do some amazing things in this world."

"Are you going to share with us who's been cast for the role?" Penelope asked.

"We're going to save that information and keep today all about Kendall," Ted replied. "The first episode of *Glitzy & Fabulous* will be airing in a few months, but in the meantime, we want to make sure the viewers give Kendall some time to heal."

Charlize shook my hand in the air, like it was a gavel.

"As a woman who values her privacy, my heart breaks for her," Penelope said. "I can't imagine how she must be feeling. I know I certainly wouldn't want any of my private moments to be released without my knowledge or approval."

"I have to agree," Niko said. "If I were in her situation, I know I wouldn't want to be on the show anymore either."

"There must be something we can do," Penelope offered.

"I think the best thing would be to show her some support," Ted suggested.

"Excellent idea, Ted." Penelope took out her phone, and the camera zoomed in to show her clicking the Follow button on my Instagram account. "I'm going to show her some love right now." She began to type and stopped, looking at the camera to say, "In fact, why don't all of our viewers take out their phones and show that girl some much-needed support?"

"Headed there right now," Niko said, his phone also in his hands.

Charlize's grip tightened, my stomach doing the same thing.

Penelope eventually set her phone down and said, "Ted, thank you for stopping by the studio and giving us the cold, hard truth behind these rumors. We know it's not easy to take responsibility for something like this."

"Thank you again for having me," Ted said, and the show switched to a commercial break.

I pulled the phone away from my face, the screen now exploding with notifications.

"To all things holy," Charlize said, showing me my Instagram account, which was doubling in followers every time he refreshed. "The comments under your photos are blowing up, girlfriend. Everyone is telling you how much they love you. They're red-hearting every damn thing on your page."

"I ..." My voice faded as I tried to process what had just happened.

Dominick hadn't told me the final details of the settlement, aside from the amount they were giving me. He'd asked me to trust him, and I'd signed my name across the bottom of the agreement.

This was what I hadn't seen.

I was positive of that fact because there was no way the CEO of a studio would have gone on national TV to apologize to me, making sure everyone knew who was at fault, without Dominick having something to do with it.

My lawyer had negotiated the best possible deal.

But my boyfriend had known this would make me feel better than any dollar deposited into my bank account.

"Dominick," I whispered, placing the phone back against my ear.

"How do you feel, baby?"

I cleared my throat, moving some of the emotion away so I could speak. "I honestly don't think I have words right now."

"Making you speechless is exactly what I wanted."

Tears were stinging my eyes.

My lips wouldn't stop quivering.

My breath was long gone, my chest far too tight to take a breath. "You made it right." I swallowed, my spit so thick. "You made it better."

"I told you I would."

Charlize's hand was on my shoulder, the biggest smile on his face as he showed me the comment Kylie Jenner had just left, sending me her love.

"Dominick ..." A tear dripped, hitting my lip. "I love you."

"I love you more," he replied, a growl then erupting as he said, "Now, get over to my office. I have something planned for that mouth."

EPILOGUE

DOMINICK

My girl never stopped smiling. Even during the darkest moments when she was hurting more than she was letting on, I could still find a grin on her lips. She was tough. Far tougher than her sister, who wouldn't have survived a second of that media shitstorm.

Since Kendall had been released from the studio, from shooting every day, and from sharing her life with the whole goddamn world, her personality was really shining. She wasn't weighed down by all these false narratives being spread about her, her tears were at bay, and she was no longer trying to hide from the public eye.

She was even posting again on social media, sharing her art and quotes about life—things that were important to her.

I could never take away the scandalous photos—they would live online forever. But I could make the situation better, and that was what I'd done.

And I was making sure she enjoyed every moment of that emotional freedom.

Once I wrapped up a few important meetings and was able

to clear my schedule, I planned a surprise trip. The morning of, I told her to pack a suitcase for a warm, sunny climate. That was the only hint I gave her, and a few hours later, we boarded my company's private jet. I even made sure all the monitors inside the plane were covered, so she couldn't see the destination or the route.

The moment the plane landed, I moved her over to the stairs, where two women were waiting for us at the bottom, leis in their hands.

"Aloha," they sang.

Kendall turned toward me, her lips in that grin that I loved so fucking much. "Hawaii? Are you serious?" She threw her arms around my neck, making me the happiest motherfucker. "Tell me this is a dream."

"We're here for two weeks, baby, and we're going to island hop." I leaned back, my thumb tugging at her lips. "You're going to be dreaming later when you see the sunset from Kailua Beach." I pressed my lips to hers, tasting the heat from her mouth and the tropical scent on her skin that smelled so much like the breeze. My hands dipped to her ass, gently slapping it. "Go get your lei, so I can see you in that bikini I brought you."

"A bikini, huh?"

I'd known about this trip for over a week, so I'd had time to prepare.

And this one was a thong that only I'd get to appreciate since I'd rented us a private house on Oahu.

Kendall descended the stairs, and I followed. A flower necklace was placed over her head and mine, welcoming us, and then we got into the SUV that was parked next to the jet. While we waited for our bags, I pulled her toward the middle of the backseat, wrapping my arm around her, and the driver loaded our things into the back and drove us toward the road.

Kendall watched the scenery through the window, making

little noises as we passed beautiful views. But my eyes were on her, appreciating the sight in front of me even more, one that couldn't stop beaming.

"Goddamn it, you're gorgeous."

Her eyes slowly moved to mine. "It's like you're seeing me for the first time."

"Sometimes, it feels like that's the case."

She shook her head. "I wish you knew how that made me feel." She found my hand, squeezing it. "The love that you fill me with." A redness moved across her cheeks. "This intense, deep passion."

I pulled her even closer, needing a taste of her lips, to feel them against mine.

But one kiss wasn't enough.

It never was.

When it came to Kendall, I always wanted more.

Needed more.

Desired more.

"You make it"—she panted, licking across her mouth—"so hard to breathe."

"Wait until I get you alone."

I gave her neck a quick kiss and positioned her back toward the window, so she could take in the last bits of Honolulu before we arrived at the house.

The place I had rented was directly on the beach, its own secluded section, where we could do anything we wanted in the ocean and every room inside had windows that faced it.

Within a few minutes' drive, we were parked in front of the two-story glass structure, and I clasped her hand and led her up the stairs, unlocking the door with a code.

"My God." She stood frozen in the entryway. "This is magical."

I pecked her cheek and took her into the kitchen, where the

chef poured us two glasses of champagne. Once the drinks were in our hands, I immediately brought her out onto the massive patio.

"You're insane." She clinked her bubbly against mine. "I mean, we could have just stayed in a hotel, but that's not good enough for my boyfriend. He rents us this palace that's straight out of a Hawaiian postcard." She glanced toward the horizon, where there was endless blue.

"Why do simple when I can give you something this beautiful?" I moved in behind her, holding her flat stomach and narrow waist, my lips close to her ear. "And I know you prefer the simpler way, but you know how much I like to spoil you."

"Like my brand-new closet."

"Baby, that's only the start."

My phone vibrated in my pocket, and I took it out, checking the screen to see a text from my assistant.

One I'd been waiting for since we'd boarded the plane in LA.

Once I read her message, I put the phone away and said, "We're here for four nights, and then we're off to Maui. I don't plan on letting you wear anything more than a bathing suit." I nibbled on her earlobe. "I hope that isn't a problem."

"All this sun and salt and sand sounds heavenly, so I see no problem in that."

I kissed down to her collarbone, the thought of her in a bikini far better than what she was describing.

She turned around, throwing her arms around my neck. "Is it time that I go change into one?"

"*Mmm* ... I like how you think."

I led her into the master bedroom, where our bags were waiting for us, and opened my suitcase, finding the bikini I'd brought for her and the swim trunks I was going to put on. As I unbuttoned my jeans, I watched her strip out of her clothes.

The sun was coming in through the tall bedroom windows, leaving shadows across her body that resembled zebra stripes.

Standing at the end of the bed, my jeans halfway down, my cock already so fucking hard, I couldn't take my eyes off her. "Jesus," I groaned as she slipped off her bra. "Look at you."

Since she didn't wear panties, she had nothing left to take off.

She glanced down her naked body, unaware of her beauty, talent, the way she made people feel just by being with her.

How she'd made this untamed bachelor crave to wake up next to her every fucking morning.

Whether it was to fold my arms across her, holding her against my body, to wrap her legs around my face, eating her delicious pussy, or to rest in the spot next to her, watching her sleep.

I just wanted her there.

With me.

Forever.

"You're crazy." She looked at me again, smiling. "This is still the same body as it was this morning when you saw me getting dressed."

"Something's different." I quickly put on my swim trunks, my stare then slowly dipping down her body, all the way to her toes and back up. "I love you more now than I did this morning."

She walked over to me, gripping my face. "Who knew underneath all those growls and profanity was the most incredibly sweet man?"

"It's our secret." I winked at her, kissing her fingertips. "I have something else for you."

"You mean ... there's more?"

I cupped her ass as I said, "My grandparents are in an assisted living facility in Malibu." Her eyes narrowed, and I could tell she had no idea where this was going. "I spoke to them a few weeks ago, and my grandmother had to let me go because she was going downstairs for a crafting class." I tightened my hold on her. "It got me thinking, and I called the owner of the facility—he's a client of Ford's, and he owns eight of the same kind of facilities within a sixty-mile radius."

"Dominick ..."

"He's looking to hire a director who can coordinate art and activities across all of his locations. The position would be based from home, but you would travel to each place, making sure the programs are all running smoothly, interacting with the residents, ensuring they're all happy."

Tears were filling her eyes, her hands on my shoulders digging in harder with each breath.

"His wife has been doing this job, but she's pregnant with their third baby, and she just can't do it anymore."

"I don't"—she swallowed—"even know what to say."

I kissed her, tasting the tears on her lips. "This isn't a reality show or an endorsement or a billboard on Melrose. This is you, Kendall, and I know how happy it will make you." I moved my hands up to her face. "All you have to do is say yes, and you'll meet the owner as soon as we get back."

"Yes. Oh God, yes." She kissed me. "Thank you."

"I'm not done yet." I paused. "There's one more thing you need to see. Go open your Instagram app and pull up your sister's account."

Her brows rose. "Daisy's? But why?"

"Go."

She found her purse and pulled out her cell, backing up to take a seat on the bed. "Oh my," she whispered, her hand going over her mouth.

I sat next to her, knowing what I was about to see since my assistant had alerted me that Daisy had posted.

The video had gone live about fifteen minutes ago. *Kendall* was the caption, followed by an emoji of twin girls.

Kendall hit Play, and Daisy appeared in front of her camera phone, wearing little makeup, her eyes even slightly puffy.

"I just wanted to come on here and say that some people are blessed enough in life to have someone they can always count on, someone they can share their life with, someone who will answer their calls, no matter what time of day or night it is. I had that someone in my life, and I'll admit, I didn't always appreciate that fact. I didn't always see my sister the way I should have, nor did I always make the right decisions when it came to her."

As she took a breath, she glanced down, taking a few seconds before she made eye contact again.

"Kendall, I'm sorry. I'm really, truly sorry. It's taken some time, but I realize the only way to grow is to be able to see your faults, recognize them, and try harder. Be better. And that's the promise I'm making. The promise we should all be making to ourselves." She took another breath. "I love you, Kendall."

The video ended, and Kendall gradually lowered her phone, looking at me. "Did you have anything to do with this?"

"I told her to do the right thing. I certainly didn't know she was going to post online and make a whole spectacle out of it, but that's Daisy, so it shouldn't surprise me." I grazed her chin. "For what it's worth, she sounds sincere."

"She is." She glanced at her phone, pulling up her texts, and the first one listed a message from Daisy. "I guess there's more."

Daisy: I called about an hour ago, and my call went straight to voice mail, so I'm trying this way instead. I know we have lots of things to work out and discuss and that you're frustrated and angry—I can't blame you. After a chat with Mom and Dad and

*Dominick and a very interesting run-in with Charlize, I've
realized how wrong I've been. Long overdue, I know, but I'm
hoping you'll at least talk to me about it.*
*Me: I just landed in Hawaii, and I'll be here for the next two
weeks.*
Daisy: Maybe we can have lunch when you get back?
*Me: Daisy, I need some time. I'm still processing what you did
and how you hurt me so easily. I appreciate you taking the first
step. I'll let you know when I get back to LA.*
Daisy: That's all I can ask for right now. Have a good trip.
*Daisy: And just know, you have two men in your corner who
love you very much.*

She tossed the phone on the bed, her arms resuming their position around my neck. "Please don't tell me you have anything else up your sleeve. My heart literally can't take any more right now."

I lifted her, straddling her naked body over my lap. "I don't have anything in my sleeves, but there's something extremely hard in these shorts and one thing on my mind ..."

"My ass."

"It's mine." I held her wrists behind her back, kissing down her neck and up her jaw until I reached her lips. "And when I'm done, your cunt is next."

*Interested in reading the next two books in the Dalton Brothers
Series ...*
The Billionaire—Jenner's Book
The Single Dad—Ford's Book
Or check out Signed, which stars Brett Young

ACKNOWLEDGMENTS

Nina Grinstead, every time I reach The End, so many monumental things have happened for us, and this one is certainly no exception. There are a million things on the horizon for us, and the tears are already in my eyes. I'm so proud of you, us, and what we've already achieved. We're in this together until the very end—and I'm talking about walkers, not words. *Love you* doesn't even come close to cutting it. Team B forever.

Jovana Shirley, we've worked on so many books together, and the way you treat my words still amazes me each time. What you've taught me, what you've pushed me to reach and achieve, and how my craft has grown because of you are things I'll never take for granted. I'm forever grateful for you. Like I say at the end of every book, I wouldn't want to do this with anyone but you. Love you so hard.

Hang Le, my unicorn, you are just incredible in every way.

Judy Zweifel, as always, thank you for being so wonderful to work with and for taking such good care of my words. <3

Chanpreet Singh, thanks for always holding me together and for helping me in every way. Adore you, lady. XO

Kaitie Reister, I love you, girl. Thanks for being you.

Nikki Terrill, my soul sister. Every tear, vent, dinner, virtual hug, life chaos, workout, you've been there through it all. I could never do this without you, and I would never want to. Love you hard.

Sarah Symonds, another one down, my friend. Thank you for always being there for my words—and me—and for all your love and support. I wouldn't want to do this without you. Ever.

Ratula Roy, like I always say, being inside your head is the best feeling and blessing I could ever have. You always have my back, my heart, and my love. Forever, baby. Love you.

Dawn Fuhrman and Patricia Reichardt, thank you for being such a massive part of this process. I said this last time, and I'll say it again—no one has ears like you two. Heart you both.

Kimmi Street, my sister from another mister. There's no way to describe us; there's just something special when it comes to our unbreakable bond. Nothing and no one will ever change that. I love you more than love.

Extra-special love goes to Valentine PR, Kelley Beckham, Kayti McGee, Chris Fletcher, Tracey Waggaman, Sally Ilan, Elizabeth Kelley, Jennifer Porpora, Pat Mann, and my group of Sarasota girls, whom I love more than anything. I'm so grateful for all of you.

Mom and Dad, thanks for your unwavering belief in me and your constant encouragement. It means more than you'll ever know.

Brian, my words could never dent the love I feel for you. Trust me when I say, I love you more.

My Midnighters, you are such a supportive, loving, motivating group. Thanks for being such an inspiration, for holding my hand when I need it, and for always begging for more words. I love you all.

To all the bloggers who read, review, share, post, tweet, Instagram—Thank you, thank you, thank you will never be enough. You do so much for our writing community, and we're so appreciative.

To my readers—I cherish each and every one of you. I'm so grateful for all the love you show my books, for taking the time to reach out to me, and for your passion and enthusiasm. I love, love, love you.

MARNI'S MIDNIGHTERS

Getting to know my readers is one of my favorite parts about being an author. In Marni's Midnighters, my private Facebook group, I post covers before they're revealed to the public and excerpts of the projects I'm currently working on, and team members qualify for exclusive giveaways. To join Marni's Midnighters, click HERE.

ABOUT THE AUTHOR

USA Today best-selling author Marni Mann knew she was going to be a writer since middle school. While other girls her age were daydreaming about teenage pop stars, Marni was fantasizing about penning her first novel. She crafts sexy, titillating stories that weave together her love of darkness, mystery, passion, and human emotions. A New Englander at heart, she now lives in Sarasota, Florida, with her husband and their yellow Lab. When she's not nose deep in her laptop, working on her next novel, she's scouring for chocolate, sipping wine, traveling, or devouring fabulous books.

Want to get in touch? Visit Marni at ...
www.marnismann.com
MarniMannBooks@gmail.com

ALSO BY MARNI MANN

STAND-ALONE NOVELS

Even If It Hurts (Contemporary Romance)

Before You (Contemporary Romance)

The Assistant (Psychological Thriller)

The Unblocked Collection (Erotic Romance)

Wild Aces (Erotic Romance)

THE DALTON BROTHERS SERIES—EROTIC ROMANCE

The Lawyer

The Billionaire

The Single Dad

THE AGENCY SERIES—EROTIC ROMANCE

Signed

Endorsed

Contracted

Negotiated

MOMENTS IN BOSTON SERIES—CONTEMPORARY ROMANCE

When Ashes Fall

When We Met

When Darkness Ends

THE PRISONED SERIES—DARK EROTIC THRILLER

Prisoned

Animal

Monster

THE SHADOWS DUET—EROTIC ROMANCE

Seductive Shadows

Seductive Secrecy

THE BAR HARBOR DUET—NEW ADULT

Pulled Beneath

Pulled Within

THE MEMOIR SERIES—DARK MAINSTREAM FICTION

Memoirs Aren't Fairytales

Scars from a Memoir

NOVELS COWRITTEN WITH GIA RILEY

Lover (Erotic Romance)

Drowning (Contemporary Romance)

THE BILLIONAIRE

DALTON BROTHERS SERIES: BOOK TWO

The Billionaire is coming March 1, 2022, Jenner's sexy, swoony, forbidden romance ...

If you would like to pre-order The Billionaire, *click* HERE.

THE SINGLE DAD

DALTON BROTHERS SERIES: BOOK THREE

The Single Dad is coming June 28, 2022, Ford's sexy, steamy, single dad romance ...

If you would like to pre-order The Single Dad, *click* HERE.

SNEAK PEEK OF SIGNED

Did you enjoy Brett Young from The Lawyer?
Then, check out, Signed, *which is live now!*

James

"Nothing says single like black Versace," Eve, my best friend, said from behind me as I stood in front of the mirror. "It's like the dress was made just for you."

I turned to check out the whole outfit, starting at the bottom where the fabric lay several inches above my knees, rising to hug my ass, molding across my sides, and finishing around my breasts. It was so tight; it pushed them high and gave me plenty of cleavage.

I smiled as I glanced at her reflection. "That's because it was."

"I thought your stylist dropped it off this morning?"

I shook my head. "That was Tom Ford. Versace sent this a few months ago for my eighteenth birthday."

Before choosing to wear this one, I'd tried on the Tom Ford and several others. They weren't right for tonight.

This one was.

Eve started fixing the back of my hair, and a sly grin came over her face.

"Spill it," I said.

"Abel who?" She laughs. "Seriously, once everyone sees you in this dress, they'll forget you two even dated."

The trouble was, I hadn't forgotten.

I'd met Abel on the set of my first sitcom when I was only thirteen. We were the same age, casted to be siblings, and we'd kept those roles until the series finale five years later. Our relationship had started almost immediately and ended six months ago when I caught him in our bed with Sophia Sully.

I turned toward her. "He's on location, right?"

We shared friends. Favorite bars. A house that I no longer wanted.

I would die if he and Sophia were there tonight since the only reason I was going out was to make it look like I was completely over him and had moved on.

"Let me check." Eve slipped her phone out of the top of her dress and opened a social media app. She held her cell in front of me, and the screen showed a picture that had been taken a few hours ago of Abel riding a fake bull. "He's at some bar in Nashville. We're safe."

I took a few steps closer to the glass, so I could get a better look at myself. There was loose powder under my eyes that my makeup artist had missed. I caught it with my fingers and then smoothed out the chunks of curls to frame them around my face.

I'd been filming in Toronto for the last four months, and this was my first night back. While I'd been away, Abel and Sophia had made their relationship public. He'd moved her into the house we'd purchased together. They'd bought a puppy and named it Country, as though they needed to be reminded of the kind of music Sophia sang.

Because the LA crowd had barely seen me since the breakup, I was going to be hit with questions, and the paparazzi would be snapping my picture as soon as I got to the bar. So, I had to get it all right—the answers everyone wanted to hear, the dress, and most importantly, the smile. The same smile that the whole world loved. The one that earned me leading roles. The one that acted like a mask, so no one could tell I was hurting.

I could do this.

"Fuck Abel," I whispered.

"Yeah, fuck Abel," she repeated. She grabbed my clutch off the bathroom counter and looped her arm through mine. "Now, let's go find you a rebound."

"I tried that once, don't you remember? I'm all set."

Since ending things with Abel, I'd been with only one guy, and it was three months ago. I'd flown home from filming in Toronto to move out of the house I shared with Abel. Sophia had watched me the whole time I was there and again at the party I'd seen them at later that night. The guy was someone I had just met, and he was supposed to make me feel like I had moved on. I had gone with him to a hotel in Malibu, and after the next morning, we never spoke again.

"Then, let's go get wasted," Eve said.

"I can do that."

She pulled me through the house and out the door, knowing I'd never feel fully ready to face this and dragging me was probably the only way she'd get me there. Once we got outside, the SUV was waiting in my driveway.

"Where to, Miss Ryne?" the driver asked as we settled and put on our seat belts.

"Chateau Marmont," I told him.

317

As we made our way to West Hollywood, Eve filled me in on the gossip I'd missed while I was away, things that hadn't made the celebrity news sites. None of the people she spoke about were good friends even though most of their numbers were saved in my phone. Not one of them had checked on me after the breakup, although they'd texted me tonight to ask if I was going out.

They wanted to be seen with me.

That was the way Hollywood worked, and I'd been playing this game since I was a kid. Except, when I had been with Abel, there wasn't this pressure to go out and be seen in order to stay relevant. The public had loved our relationship, and that was enough to keep the paparazzi on our asses. But, without him, the media wanted to see what the single version of me looked like.

I was about to give them that visual.

The driver pulled up in front, and the backseat door was immediately opened. A hand was extended to help me out, and I waited for Eve, looping her arm through mine as she reached me.

We walked toward the entrance, and hundreds of cameras flashed in our direction.

Questions were being thrown at me.

"How are you feeling after the breakup?"

"What's the next movie you'll be starring in?"

And, "Should your fans stop listening to country music?"

The smile was glued across my lips as I glanced at both sides of the crowd, giving them a final wave before we disappeared inside the dark bar. The darkness was one of the reasons I enjoyed coming here. The red and gold back lighting didn't just make it dim and sexy, but it also hid runny makeup and accidental nip slips—something certainly possible with a dress cut this low. And, as if those rich colors didn't already set the most seductive vibe, the heavy wood furnishings and the smell of leather brought it right over the top.

"Drink," I said to Eve as I took in the room.

She brought me straight to the bar where the bartender greeted us with, "Good to have you back, James."

If you were anyone in this town, you were called by your first name and you were never asked for an ID. I always tried my hardest to remember my favorites. Tony was one.

The smile still hadn't left my face. "Two cosmos, Tony. Charge them to my account, please."

"You got it," he answered.

"Everyone is here," Eve said, facing the opposite direction as me, so she could wave at the people passing.

There was a mirror behind the bar, and that was what I used to scan the room. I saw a group of regulars standing in the middle, who we'd chat with once we had our drinks. A few Hollywood old-timers were sitting on barstools around the high-tops. With the amount of celebrities here, this place was practically an audition, and I was sure they were scouting. Leaning around the front of the bar was a musician, a few LA hockey players, and *him*—a man who was four people over, whose eyes locked with mine.

Eyes that made my lips part.

Eyes that made my chest feel tight and anxious.

He was deliciously handsome—from his messy, gelled hair to his square jaw and the dark scruff that covered it.

I didn't know his name.

I had no idea who he was.

But he had to be someone if he'd gotten in here.

Asking would give me a reason to look away, to take a break from those eyes that were holding me captive.

Since my attraction to him was already so obvious by the

way I was staring, I turned toward Eve and whispered, "Who is he?"

She glanced in both directions. "Who's who?"

"The hottie at the bar four people down from me. All dark everything—suit, tie. You'll know him when you see him."

A few seconds passed, and she said, "I have no idea whom you're talking about."

"Oh my God," I sighed, glancing back at the mirror. "He's the one—" I cut myself off when I realized he was no longer standing there. I looked across the bar, over the group in the middle, and on the side near the restrooms.

He was gone.

"Two cosmos," Tony said, setting them in front of us. "Can I get you girls anything else?"

"No, thank you," I said, grabbing my drink and holding it up in front of me. "Let's toast." I quickly gazed over my shoulder to see if the guy had come back. He hadn't. "To tonight, being single, being back together after two months apart, and being best bitches."

"To not remembering anything in the morning." She hit her glass against mine. "Oh, and to Abel, fuck you."

I laughed, and we each took our first sip.

Cosmo number one went down so quickly, and so did the second. After round three, I completely lost track, and I was sure our toasts had started to repeat. I knew it was time to switch to water when I was coming out of the restroom, and my heel got caught in the carpet. As I tried to take a step, my foot came out of my shoe, and I tripped.

Someone's hands gripped my waist from behind and caught me before I hit the ground.

"Thank you," I panted, using their fingers to steady myself.

Once I was sure everything was in place—the bottom of my

dress was down, and the top was covering my breasts—I turned to see whom the hands belonged to.

My breath hitched when I saw his face. "It's you," I said.

I knew that made no sense to him, but it made perfect sense to me.

It was the guy who had been standing at the bar.

Whose eyes had held me hostage.

Who had made me feel anxious.

Who was making my chest tight again.

He laughed, and the movement showed me a smile that caused a tingle between my legs. A grin that would make him the most famous person in here if the world saw him on the big screen. That was how I knew he was either just starting out or wasn't in the field at all.

"Most people call me Brett."

Even though I'd slipped my heel back on, he was still about four inches taller than me and looked even sexier now that I was so close to him. The lines in his forehead and the crinkles just to the sides of his eyes told me he was in his late twenties or early thirties—certainly a lot older than me. All that meant was, he had experience, and that was the biggest turn-on.

"I'm James."

He said nothing and made no attempt to move.

"I saw you at the bar, and then you were gone."

"And?"

That voice.

If sex had a sound, it was Brett's tone.

"Is someone expecting you to return, or am I about to get jumped by some jealous girlfriend or..."

"Or what?"

I started to speak and stumbled over my words.

How can I tell this man with the beautiful eyes that I don't want him to walk away because I can't get enough of the way he looks at me and the warmth I feel from his stare?

"Or maybe I could hear more of your voice," I said.

He licked across the inside of his bottom lip, and when he exhaled, I tasted the whiskey on his breath and smelled the cologne from his skin. It was a mix of spice and sandalwood, and it made every pore in my body open up and want to suck him in.

"All you want is my voice?"

I broke our contact again, almost dizzy from the intensity, and took a step back to lean against the wall behind me. Brett followed. His arm went up in the air, his hand pressing on the space above my head. He didn't touch me. He didn't have to. Having him huddled over me, caging me in, did so much to my body that I couldn't breathe.

If you would like to keep reading, click HERE *to purchase Signed.*

Made in United States
North Haven, CT
20 July 2022

21593157R00200